BREAKNECK VELOCITY

Sandor kicked into Pell Star jump range with velocity that had the incoming-range buoy screaming its automated indignation at him, advising whatever lunatic had just come within its scan that he was travelling too fast and headed dead-on for trafficked zones.

Dump! it warned him, dopplered and restructured by his com. Its systems were hurling machine to machine warnings at *Lucy's* autoalert, which *Lucy* was primed to obey. She was kicking in the vanes in hard spurts, which shifted him in and out of realspace in bursts of flaring nausea. There were red lights everywhere until he hit the appropriate button and confirmed the dump order *Lucy* was obeying.

MERCHANTER'S LUCK

C. J. Cherryh

DAW Books, Inc.
Donald A. Wollheim, Publisher
1633 Broadway, New York, N.Y. 10019

FIRST PRINTING, JULY 1982

7   8   9   10   11   12

PRINTED IN THE U.S.A.

I

Their names were Sandor and Allison . . . Kreja and Reilly respectively. Reilly meant something in the offices and bars of Viking Station: it meant the merchanters of the great ship *Dublin Again*, based at Fargone, respectable haulers on a loop that included all the circle of Union stars, Mariner and Russell's, Esperance and Paradise, Wyatt's and Cyteen, Fargone and Voyager and back to Viking. It was a Name among merchanters, and a power to be considered, wherever it went.

Kreja meant nothing at Viking, having flourished only at distant Pan-paris and Esperance in its day: at Mariner, under an alias, it meant a bad debt, and the same at Russell's. The Kreja ship was currently named *Lucy*, and she was supposedly based at Wyatt's, which was as far away as possible and almost farther away than reasonable for such a small and aged freighter, claiming to run margin cargo for a Wyatt's combine. Customs always searched her, though she called here regularly. Small, star-capable ships on which the crew was not related by blood, on which in fact there were only two haggard men, and one not the same as at last docking . . . such ships were not comfortably received at station docks, and received careful scrutiny.

Lucy was a freighter by statement, a long-hauler which ran smallish consignments independent of its combine's close direction, since the combine had no offices on Viking. She was a passenger carrier when anyone would trust her—no one did, though the display boards carried her offer. She took merchanter transfers if she could get them.

That was how Sandor Kreja lost his crew at Viking, because the crew, one old and limping sot who was paying work for his passage, found his own ship in port and headed for it without a by-your-leave. The old man had only signed as far as Viking; he had been left behind at Voyager for a stay in hospital, and he was simply interested in catching his own ship again and rejoining his family: that was the deal.

It made Sandor nervous, that departure, as all such departures did. The old man had been more curious than most, had nosed about contrary to orders, had been into everything—lied, with epic distortion, about where his *Daisy* had been, lied about deals they had made and what they had done in the wars and what he had done in dockside sleepovers, entertaining as it was. His departure left Sandor solo on *Lucy*, which he had been before and had no wish to try more often than he had to, running a freighter blind tired. But more, the old man left him with a nagging worry that he might have turned up something, and that his considerable talent for storytelling might spread tales in stationside bars that *Lucy* had peculiarities. Viking had tightened up since *Lucy*'s last docking: warships had pulled in and rumors surmised pirate trouble. They were nervous times; and a little talk in the wrong places could get back to station offices. It might, Sandor thought, be time to move on.

But he had conned his way onto the loading schedule, which meant they were going to fill his tanks and he was going to get cargo if he could only subdue his nervousness and keep from rousing suspicions this trip round. Forged papers labeled him and *Lucy* as Wyatt's Star Combine, which had a minor interest-bearing account at Voyager and Viking, outside its territories, a fund meant for emergency use if ever one of its ships should have to divert over from regular WSC ports. It was his seventh call here on the same faked papers—in fact he foresaw the time when the stamp sheets in the book would be filled and station would have to renew his papers with the real thing, a threshold he had crossed before, and which made life for a time much more secure . . . until some needed repair ran him over his margin and the questions got sharp and closer.

He was not a pirate: *Lucy* was too small for piracy and her smallish armament was a joke. He was, in his own reckoning, not even completely a thief, because he skimmed enough to keep him going, but nothing on a large scale. He delivered his cargoes where they belonged and let the money right back into WSC accounts. He made a very little profit, to be sure, and that little profit could be tipped right into the loss column if *Lucy* got stalled at dock without cargo, if *Lucy* needed some major repair. It was the reason why no combine would accept her honest application. She was small and carried small cargoes, across the too-large distances the bigger ships could cross much more quickly. She had gone into the red now and again at Viking, losses that would have broken an independent, without the forged papers to draw credit on. But all a big company like WSC would notice when the accounts cycled round at year's end was that the main fund had neither increased nor decreased. As long as *Lucy* paid back what she took out by year's end, the excess could stay in her illicit working account, to cushion her future ups and downs of profit. WSC spread over light-years and timelag. Alarms only rang down the system at audit time . . . and Sandor had no desire at all to go beyond small pilferage, no ambition to reach for profits that might get him caught. He was twenty-seven and impossibly rich, in terms of being sole remaining heir to a star-freighter, however small, which had been a legitimate trader once, before the Company War created pirates, and pirates stopped and looted her, and left her a stripped shell mostly filled with dead. Now *Lucy* survived as best she could, on her owner's ingenuity, under a multitude of names and numbers and a succession of faked papers. Now selling out was impossible: his scams would catch up with him and eat away even the thirty of silver he would get for his ship. Worse, he would have to sit on station and watch her come and go in the hands of some local combine—or see her junked, because she was a hundred and fifty years old, and her parts might be more valuable than her service.

He kept her going. She was his, in a way no stationer-run combine could understand. He had been born on her, had grown up on her, had no idea what the universe would be like without the ship around him and he never meant to find out. The day he lost *Lucy* (and it could happen any day, with one of the station officers running up with attachment warrants from somewhere, or with some sharp-eyed dockmaster or customs agent taking a notion to run a test on his forged papers) on that day he figured they would have to kill him; but they would take him in whole if they could, because station law was relentlessly humane and Union took as dim a view of shootings on dockside as they did of pilferage. They would put him in the tank and alter his mind so that he could be happy scrubbing floors and drawing a stationside living, a model Union citizen.

Stations scared him spitless.

And that talkative old man who had gone back to his ship scared him.

But he had it figured out a long time ago that the worst thing he could do for himself was to look scared, and the quickest way to rouse suspicions was to act defensive or to stay holed up in *Lucy's* safety during dockings, when any normal merchanter would use the chance to go out bar-hopping dockside, up the long curve of taverns and sleepovers on the docks.

He was smooth-faced and good-looking in a gaunt blond way that could be a stationer accountant or banker bar-hopping—except that the gauntness was hunger and the eyes showed it, so that he laughed a great deal when he was scouting the bars, to look as if he were well-credited, and sometimes to get drinks on someone else. And this time—this time, because his life depended on it . . . he aimed for more than a free drink or a meal on some other combine's credit. He needed a crewman, someone, *anyone* with the right touch of minor larceny who could be conned and cozened aboard and trusted not to talk in the wrong quarters. This was flatly dangerous. Merchanter ships were family, all of the same Name, born on a ship to die on that ship. Beached merchanters were beached only for a single run, like the old man he had gotten from hospital; or if they were beached permanently, it was because their own ships' families had thrown them out, or because they had voluntarily quit their families, unable to live with them. Some of the latter were quarrelsome and some were criminal; he was one man and he had to sleep sometimes . . . which was why he had to have help on the ship at all. He scanned the corners of the bars he traveled on the long green-zone dock of Viking, trying not to see the soldiers and the police who were more frequent everywhere than usual, and looking constantly for someone else as hungry as he was, knowing that they would be disguising their plight as he disguised it, and knowing that if he picked the wrong one, with a shade too much larceny in mind, that partner would simply cut his throat some watch in some lonely part of the between, and take *Lucy* over for whatever purposes he had in mind.

It was the first day of this hunt on the docks, playing the part of honest merchanter captain and nursing a handful of chits he had gotten on that faked combine account, that he first saw Allison Reilly.

The story was there to be read: the shamrock and stars on her silver coveralls sleeve, the patches of worlds visited, that compassed all known space, the lithe tall body with its back to him at the bar and a flood of hair like a puff of space-itself in the dim neon light.

In his alcohol-fumed eyes that sweep of hip and long, leaning limbs put him poignantly in mind of sleepovers and that other scanted need of his existence—a scam much harder than visa forging and far more dangerous. In fact, his life had been womanless, except for one very drunk insystem merchanter one night on Mariner when he was living high and secure, which was how Mariner knew his name and laid in wait for him. And another insystemer before that, who he had hoped would partner him for good: she had lost him Esperance when it went bad. He was solitary, because the only women for merchanters were other merchanters, who inevitably had relatives; and merchanters in general were a danger to his existence far more serious than stations posed. Stations sat fixed about their stars and rarely shared records on petty crime for the same reasons the big combines rarely bothered with distant and minor accounts. But get on the bad side of some merchanter family for any cause, and they would spread the word and hunt him from star to star, spread warnings about him to every station and every world humans touched, so that he would die; or so that some station would catch him finally and bend his mind, which was the same to him. There were no more women; he had sworn off such approaches.

But he dreamed, being twenty-seven and alone for almost all his days, in the long, long night. And at that silver-coveralled vision in front of him, he forgot the tatter-elbowed old man he had been trying to stalk, him with the vacant spot in the patches on his sleeve, and forgot the short-hauler kid who was another and safer prospect. He stared at that sleek back, and saw that fall of hair like a night in which stars could burn—and saw at the same time that arm resting on the bar, patched with the Reilly shamrock, which burned green in the green neon glare from the over-the-bar lighting, advising him that among merchanters this was one of the foremost rank, a princess, a Name and a patch which was credit wherever it liked, that walked wide and did as it pleased. Nothing like

Lucy had a prayer against *Dublin Again*, that great and modern wonder which meant clean corridors and clean coveralls and credit piled in station accounts from Cyteen to Pell. They were Dubliners with her, cousins or brothers, big, dark-haired men of varying ages. He saw them in a fog beyond her, talking to her; and her arm lifted the glass and her hair swung with the spark of the changing neon like red stars . . . she was turning on her elbow to set the glass down, a second swirl of starry night.

Ah, he pleaded to God fuzzily, not wanting to see her face, because perhaps she was not beautiful at all, and he could look away in time and make that beautiful back and cloud of hair into his own drink-fogged dream to keep him company on the long watches—as long as she had no face. But he was too paralyzed to move, and in that same long motion she turned all the way around, shook back the living night from her face that was all blue now in the changing neon lights.

He was caught then, because he forgot to laugh and forgot everything else he was doing in that bar, stared with his mouth open and his eyes showing what they showed when he was not laughing—he knew so, because she suddenly looked nettled. She stood straight from the bar, which movement drew his eyes to the A. REILLY stitched over the blue-lit silver of a breast, while she was looking him over and sizing him up for the threadbare brown coveralls he wore and the undistinguished (and lying) E. STEVENS his pocket bore, and the gaudy nymph with *Lucy* ribbonned on his sleeve . . . the nymph was a standard item in shops which sold such things. It decorated any number of ships and sleeves, naked and girdled with stars and badly embroidered with the ribbon blank, to be stitched in with any ship's name. Insystem haulers used such things. Miners did. He did, because it was what he could afford.

She stared a good long moment, and turned then and searched her pocket . . . her crewmates had gone elsewhere, and she paused to glance at one who was himself making slow stalk of a woman of another crew off in the dim corner. She tossed a chit down on the water-circled counter and walked for the door alone, while Sandor stood there watching that retreating back and that cloud of space-itself enter the forever day of the open dock outside.

He called the bartender urgently and paid . . . no tip, at which the man scowled, but he was used to that. He hurried, trying not to seem in haste, thinking of the woman's cousins and not wanting to have *them* on his tail. His heart was pounding and his skin had that hot-cold flush that was part raw lust and part stark panic, because what he was doing was dangerous, with the docks as tense as they were, with police watching where they were never invited by merchanters.

He had dreamed something in the lonely years, which was—he could no longer remember whether the dream *was* different from what he had seen standing alive in front of him, because all those solitary fancies were murdered, done to cold pale death in that collision, because he had seen the one bright vision of his life. He was going to hurt forever—the more so if he could not find out in brighter light that her face had some redeeming flaws, if he could not have her herself murder the image and his hopes at once and give him back his common sense. You'll not have tried, kept hammering in his brain. You'll never know. Another, dimmer self kept telling him that he was drunk, and yet another self cursed him that he was going to lose everything he had. But the self that was in control only advised him that he was lost out here in the glare of dock lights, that she had gotten away into another bar or a shop somewhere close.

He looked about him, at the long upcurve of the dock which was curtained by section arches and peopled with hundreds of passersby, battered with music and bright lights and sounds of machinery. Tall metal skeletons of gantries ran skeins of umbilicals to the various lighted caverns that were ship-accesses across the dock, but she surely had not had time to reach one. He went right, instead, to the next bar up the row, looked about him in the doorway of the dim, alcohol-musked interior, which drew attention he never liked to have on him. He ducked out again and tried the next; and the third, which was fancier—the kind of place where resident stationers might come, or military officers, when they wanted a taste of the docks.

She was there . . . alone, half-perched on a barstool in the silver extravagance of the place, a waft of the merchanter life stationers would come to this dockside bar to see, a touch of something exotic and dangerous. And maybe a stationer was what she was looking for, some manicured banker, some corporation man or someone she could run a high scam on, for the kind of inside information the big ships got regularly and the likes of *Lucy* never would. Or maybe she wanted the kind

of fine liquor and world-grown luxury a local might treat her
to and some liked. He was daunted. He stood just inside the
doorway, finding himself in the kind of place he avoided,
where drinks were three times what they ought to be and he
was as far as he could possibly be from doing what he had
come to do—which was to find some crewman in as desperate straits as he was.

She saw him. He stared back at her in that polished, over-
priced place and felt like running.

And then, because he had never liked running and because
he was a degree soberer than he had been a moment ago and
insisted on suffering for his stupidity, he walked a little closer
with his hand in his pocket, feeling over the few chits he had
left and wishing they posted prices in this place.

She rested with her elbow on the bar, looking as if she belonged; and he had no cover left, not with her recognizing
him, a man with a no-Name patch on his sleeve and no way
to claim coincidence in being in this place. He had never felt
so naked in his life, not even in front of station police with
faked papers.

"Buy you a drink?" he asked, the depth of his originality.

She was—maybe—the middle range of twenty. She bar-
hopped alone with that shamrock on her sleeve, and she was
safe to do that: no one rolled a Dubliner in a sleepover and
planned to live. It might be her plan to get very drunk and to
take up with whomever she fancied, if she fancied anyone;
she might be hunting information, and she might be eager to
get rid of him, not to hamper her search with inconsequence.
She was dangerous, not alone to his pride and his dreams.

She motioned to the stool beside hers and he came and
eased onto it with a vast numbness in the middle of him and
a cold sweat on his palms. He looked up nervously at the
barkeeper who arrived and looked narrowly at him. "Your
choice," Sandor said to A. Reilly, and she lifted the glass she
had mostly finished. "Two," he managed to say then, and the
bartender went off.

Two of that, he was thinking, might be expensive. They
might be the most expensive drinks he had ever bought, if a
bad bar bill brought questions down on the rest of his currently shaky finances. He looked into A. Reilly's midnight
eyes with a genuine desperation, and the thought occurred to
him that being arrested would be only slightly worse than admitting to poverty in the Dubliner's presence.

"*Lucy*," she read his patch aloud, tilting her head to see the side of his arm. "Insystemer?"

"No," he said, a hot flush rising to his face. His indignation won him at least a momentary lift of her hand and deprecation of the question she had asked, because a jumpship was far and away a different class of operation from the insystem haulers and miners. In that sense at least, *Lucy* and *Dublin* were on the same scale.

"Where are you based, then?" she asked, either mercy-killing the silence or being sensibly cautious in her barside contacts. "Here?"

"Wyatt's," he said. The barkeeper returned with two drinks and hesitated, giving him the kind of look which said he would like to see a credit chit if it were him alone, but the barman slid a thoughtful eye over the shamrock patch and moved off in silence. Sandor took both glasses and pushed the one toward A. Reilly, who was on the last of her first.

"Thanks," she said. He limited his swallow to less than he wanted, hoping to make it last, and to slow her down, because they laid down more in tips in this place than he spent on meals.

And desperately he tried to think of some casual question to ask of her in return. He could not, because everyone knew where *Dublin* was based and asking more sounded like snoopery, from someone like himself.

"You in for long?" she asked.

"Three days." He pounced on the question with relief. "Going to fill the tanks and take on cargo. Going on to Fargone from here. I don't have a big ship, but she's *mine*, free and clear. I'm getting a little ahead these days. Trying to take on crew here."

"Oh." A small, flat oh. It was apprehension what class he was.

"I'm legitimate. I just had some bad luck up till now. You don't know of any honest longjumpers beached here, do you?"

She shook her head, still with that look in her eyes, wary of her uninvited drinking partner. Sometimes such uncrewed ships and such approaches by strangers in bars meant pirate spies; and even huge *Dublin* had *them* to fear. He saw it building, foresaw an appeal to authorities who would jump fast when a Dubliner yelled hazard. There were fleet officers drinking at a nearby table. Security was heavy out on the docks, with rumors of an operation against the pirates; but others said it had to do with Pell, or interzone disputes, or they were checking smuggling. He smiled desperately.

"Pirates," he said. "Long time back. . . . My family's all dead; and my hired crew ran on me and near robbed me blind, one time and the other. You know what you can hire off the docks. It's not safe. But I haven't got a choice."

"Oh," she said, but it was a better oh than the last, indeterminate. A frown edged with sympathy, and hazardous curiosity. "No, I don't know. Sometimes we get people wanting to sign on as temporaries, but we don't take them, and we haven't had any at Viking that I've heard of. Sorry. If station registry doesn't list them—"

"I wouldn't take locals," he said, and then tried the truth. "No, I would, if it got me out on schedule. Anyway, *Lucy's* mine, and I was out hunting prospects, not—"

"You rate *me* a prospect?"

She was laughing at him. That was at least better than suspicion. He grinned, swallowing his pride. "I couldn't persuade you, could I?"

She laughed outright and his heart beat the harder, because he knew what game she was playing at the moment. It was merchanters' oldest game of all but trade itself, and the fact that she joined the maneuvering in good humor brought him a sweating flush of hope. He took a second sip of the forgotten glass and she took a healthy drain on her second. "Lost your crew here?" she asked. "You can't have gotten in alone."

"Yes. Lost him here. He'd been in hospital; he hired on for passage, and caught his ship here, so that was it." He drank and watched in dismay as she waved at someone she knew, an inconspicuous wave at a dark-bearded man who drifted in from the doorway and lingered a moment beside them.

"All right?" that one asked.

"All right," she said. He was another Dubliner, older, grim. The shamrock and stars were plain on his sleeve, and he carried a collar stripe. Sandor sat still under that dark-eyed, unloving scrutiny, his face tautened in what was not quite a smile. The older man lingered, just long enough to warn; and walked on out the door.

Sandor stared after him, turned slightly in his seat to do so, still ruffled—turned back again with the feeling that A. Reilly would be amused at his discomfiture. She was.

She took the second drink down a third. Her cheeks were looking flushed. "What kind of hauling *is* your *Lucy*? General?"

"Very."

"You don't ask many questions."

"What does the A. stand for?"

"Allison. What's the E.?"

"Edward."

"Not Ed."

"Ed, if you like."

"Captain."

"And crew."

She seemed amused, finished the drink and tapped a long, peach-lacquered fingernail against the glass, making a gentle ringing. The barkeeper showed up. "I'll stay with the same," she said, and when he left, looked up with a tilt of her head at Sandor. "I mixed that and wine on Cyteen once and nearly missed my ship."

"They don't taste strong," he said, and with a sinking heart cast a glance at the bartender who was mixing up another small glass of expensive froth . . . and second one for him, which was a foul trick, and one they could pull in a place like this.

"Love them," she said when the bartender came back and set both down. She picked up hers and sipped. "A local delicacy, just on Viking and Pell. You come all the way from Wyatt's, do you? That's quite a distance for a smallish ship. What combine is that? I didn't hear you say."

"WSC." He was close to panic, what with the bill and the questions which were hitting into areas he wanted left alone. Misery churned in his stomach which the frothy drink did nothing to comfort. "I run margin, wherever there's room for a carrier. I'm close to independent. But *Dublin* fairly well runs her own combine, doesn't she? You go the whole circle. That's independent." He talked nonsense, to drag the question back to *Dublin*, back to her, staring into her eyes and suspecting that all this was at his expense, that some kind of high sign had just been passed between her and her bearded kinsman who had strayed through the door and out again. Possibly someone was waiting outside to start trouble. Or she was going to have her amusement as far as frustrated him and walk off, leaving him the bill. He was soberer after this one more drink than he had been when he came in here, excepting a certain numbness in his fingers, and while she looked no less beautiful, his desire was cooled by that sobriety, and by a certain wry amusement which persisted in her expression. He put on a good face, as he would do with a curious customs agent or a dockside dealer who meant to bluff his price down. He grinned and she smiled. "None of the chatter means anything to you," he said. "What questions am I supposed to ask?"

"You buy me a drink," she said, and set hers down, half-finished. "You don't buy anything else, of course, being wiser than some stationers I know, who don't know how far their money goes. Thank you, Stevens. I did enjoy it. Good luck to you, finding crew."

The bartender, operating on his own keen reflexes, was headed his way in a hurry, seeing who was leaving and who was being left to pay. Sandor saw that with his own tail-of-the-eye watch for trouble, felt in his pocket desperately and threw down what he had as Allison Reilly headed for the door and the lighted dock. He was off the stool and almost with her when the voice rang out: "*You*! You there, that's *short*."

Sandor stopped, frozen by that voice, when in another place he might have dodged out, when in ordinary sanity he would not be in that situation. The military officers had looked up from their drinking. Others had. He felt theatrically of his pocket. "I gave you a twenty, sir."

The bartender scowled and held out the palm with the chits. "Not a twenty. Demis and a ten."

Sandor assumed outrage, stalked back and looked, put on chagrin. "I do beg pardon, sir. I was shorted myself, then, next door, because I should have had a twenty. I think I'm a little drunk, sir; but I have credit. Can we arrange this?"

The bartender glowered; but there came a presence at Sandor's shoulder and: "Charge it to *Dublin*," Allison Reilly said. Sandor looked about into Allison Reilly's small smile and very plain stare: they were about of a size and it was a level glance indeed. "Want to step outside?" she asked.

He nodded, fright and temper and alcohol muddling into one adrenalin haze. He followed that slim coveralled figure with the midnight hair those few steps outside into the light, and the noise of the docks was sufficient to cool his head again. He had, he reckoned, been paid off well enough, scammed by an expert. He smiled ruefully at her when they stopped and she turned to face him. It was not what he was feeling at the moment, which was more a desire to break something, but good humor was obligatory on a man with empty pockets and a Dubliner's drinks in his belly. There were always her cousins, at least several hundred of them.

"Does that line work often?" she asked.

"I'll pay you the tab," he said, which he could not believe he was saying, but he reckoned that he could draw another twenty out of his margin account. He hated having been trapped and having been rescued. "I have it. I just don't walk the docks with much."

She stared at him as if weighing that. Or him. Or thinking of calling her cousins. "I take it that all of this was leading somewhere."

She did it to him again, set him completely off balance. "It might have," he said with the same wry humor. "But I'm headed back to my ship. You got all my change and I'm afraid *Lucy's* accommodations aren't what you're used to."

"Huh." She looked in her pocket and brought out a single fifty. "Bradford's. I know it. It's a class accommodation."

He blinked, overthrown again, trying to figure if she had believed him anywhere down the line, or what she saw in the likes of him. She might be setting him up for another and worse joke than the last; but he wanted her. *That* was there again worse than before, obscuring all caution and choking off all clever argument. Years of dreaming solitary dreams and looking to stay alive, barely alive, which was all it came to . . . and one night in a silver bar and a high-class sleepover. He had gotten hazardously drunk, he told himself, floating in an overload of senses; and so had she gotten drunk. She was deliberately picking someone like him who was a risk, because she was curious, or because she was bored, or because Bradford's was a *Dublin* hangout and one shout was going to bring more trouble down on him than he could deal with. His hand was still cold-sweating when they linked arms and walked in the direction she chose, and he wiped his palm on his pocket lining before he took her cool, dry hand in his.

They walked the dock, along which gantries pointed at the distant unseen core, towers aimed straight up beside them as they walked, and farther along aimed askew, so that they looked like the veined segments of some gigantic fruit, and the dock they walked unrolled like some gray spool of ribbon with a tinsel left-hand edge of neon-lit bars and restaurants and shop display windows. Viking dock had a set of smells all its own, part food and part liquor and part machinery and chemicals and the forbidding musky chill of open cargo locks; it had a set of sounds that was human noise and machinery working and music that wafted out of bars in combinations sometimes discordant and sometimes oddly fit. It was a giddy, sense-battering flow he had never given way to, not like this, not with a silver Dubliner woman arm in arm with him, step for step with him, weaving in and out among the crowds.

They reached Bradford's discreet front, with the smoked oval pressure windows and the gold lettering . . . walked in, checked in at the desk with a comp register presided over by a clerk who might have been a corporate receptionist. They stood on thick carpets, under fancy lighting, everything white and gold, where the foyer door shut out the gaudy noise of the docks. She paid, and got the room card, and grinned at him, took his arm and led the way down the thick-carpeted hall to a numbered doorway. She thrust the card into the slot and opened it.

It was a sleeper of the class of the bar they had just come from, a place he could never afford—all cream satin, with a conspicuous blue and cream bed and a cream tiled bath with a shower. For a moment he was put off by such luxury, which he had never so much as seen in his life. Then pride took hold of him, and he slipped his arm about Allison Reilly and pulled her close against him with a jerk which drew an instinctive resistance; he grinned when he did it, and she pushed back with a look that at once warned and chose to be amused.

He took account of that on the instant, that in fact his humor was a facade, which she had seen through constantly. It might not work so well—here, with a Dubliner's pride, on a Dubliner's money. He reckoned suddenly that he could make one bad enemy or—perhaps—save something to remember in the far long darks between stations. She scared him, that was the plain fact, because she had all the cards that mattered; and he could too easily believe that she was going to laugh, or talk about this to her cousins, and laugh in telling them how she had bought herself a night's amusement and had a joke at his expense. Worst of all, he was afraid he was going to freeze with her, because every time he was half persuaded it was real he had the nagging suspicion she knew what he was, and that meant police.

He steadied her face in his hand and tried kissing her, a tentative move, a courtesy between dock-met strangers. She leaned against him and answered in kind until the blood was hammering in his veins.

"Shouldn't we close the door?" she suggested then, a practicality which slammed him back to level again. He let her go and pushed the door switch, looked back again desperately, beginning to suspect that the whole situation was humorous, and that he deserved laughing at, even by himself. He was older than she was; but he was, he reckoned, far younger in such encounters. Naïve. Scared.

"I'm for a shower," Allison Reilly said cheerfully, and started shedding the silver coveralls. "You too?"

He started shedding his own, at once embarrassed because he was off balance in the casualness of her approach and because he still suspected humor in what with him was beginning to be shatteringly serious.

She laughed; she splashed him with soap and managed to laugh in the shower and tumbling in the bed with the blue sheets, but not at all moments. For a long, long while she was very serious indeed, and he was. They made love with total concentration, until they ended curled in each other's arms and utterly exhausted.

He woke. The lights were still on as they had been; and Allison stirred and murmured about her watch and *Dublin*, while he held onto her with a great and desperate melancholy and a question boiling in him that had been there half the night.

"Meet you again?" he asked.

"Sometime," she said, tracing a finger down his jaw. "I'm headed out this afternoon."

His heart plummeted. "Where next?"

A little frown creased her brow. "Pell," she said finally. "That's not on the boards, but you could find it in the offices. Going across the Line. Got a deal working there. Be back— maybe next year, local."

His heart sank farther. He lay there a moment, thinking about his papers, his cargo, his hopes. About an old man who might talk, and fortunes that had shaved the profit in his account to the bone. Year's end was coming. If he had to, he could lay over and skim nothing more until the new year, but it would rouse suspicion and it would run up a dock charge he might not work off. "What deal at Pell?" he asked. "Is that what's got the military stirred up?"

"You hear a lot of things on the docks," she said, cautious and frowning. "But what's that to you?"

"I'll see you at Pell."

"That's crazy. You said you were due at Fargone."

"I'll see you at Pell."

The frown deepened. She shifted in his arms, leaned on him, looking down into his face. "We're pulling out today. Just how fast *is* your *Lucy?* You think a marginer's going to run races with *Dublin?"*

"So you'll be shifting mass. I'm empty. I'll make it."

"Divert your ship? What's your combine going to say? Tell me that."

"I'll be there."

She was quiet a moment, then ducked her head and laughed softly, not believing him. "Got a few hours yet," she reminded him.

They used them.

And when she left, toward noon, he walked her out to the dockside near her own ship, and watched her walk away, a trim silver-coveralled figure, the way he had seen her first.

He was sober now, and ought to have recovered, ought to shrug and call it enough. He ought to take himself and his ideas back to realspace and find that insystemer kid who might have ambitions of learning jumpships. He had knowledge to sell, at least, to someone desperate enough to sign with him, although the last and only promising novice he had signed had gotten strung out on the during-jump trank and not come down again or known clearly what he was doing when he had dosed himself too deeply and died of it.

Try another kid, maybe, take another chance. He talked well; that was always his best skill, that he could talk his way into and out of anything. He ought to take up where he had left off last night, scouting the bars and promoting himself the help he needed. He had cargo coming, the tag ends of station commerce, if he only waited and if some larger ship failed to snatch it; and if a certain old man kept his gossip to his own ship.

But he watched her walk away to a place he could not

reach, and he had found nothing in all his life but *Lucy* herself that had wound herself that deeply into his gut.

Lucy against *Dublin Again*. There was that talk of new runs opening at Pell, the Hinder Stars being visited again, of trade with Sol, and while that rumor was almost annual, there was something like substance to it this time. The military was stirred up. Ships had gone that way. *Dublin* was going. Had a deal, she had said, and then shut up about it. The idea seized him, shook at him. He loved two things in his life that were not dead, and one of them was *Lucy* and the other was the dream of Allison Reilly.

Lucy was real, he told himself, and he could lose her; while Allison Reilly was too new to know, and far too manysided. The situation with his accounts was not yet hopeless; he had been tighter than this and still made the balance. He ought to stick to what he had and not gamble it all.

And go where, then, and do what? He could not leave *Dublin*'s track without thinking how lonely it was out there; and never dock at a station without hoping that somehow, somewhen, *Dublin* would cross his path. A year from now, local . . . and he might not be here. Might be—no knowing where. Or caught, before he was much older, caught and mindwashed, so that he would see *Dublin* come in and not remember or not feel, when they had stripped his *Lucy* down to parts and done much the same with him.

He stood there more obvious in his stillness than he ever liked to be, out in the middle of the dock, and then started for dockside offices with far more haste than he ever liked to use in his movements, and browbeat the dockmaster's agent with more eloquence than he had mustered in an eloquent career, urging a private message which had just been couriered in and the need to get moving at once to Voyager. "So just fill the tanks," he begged of them, with that desperation calculated to give the meanest docksider a momentary sense of power; and to let that docksider recall that supposedly he was Wyatt's Star Combine, which might, if balked, receive reports up the line, and take offense at delay. "Just that much. Give me dry goods, no freezer stuff if it takes too long. I'll boil water from the tanks. Just get those lines on and get me moving."

There was what he had half expected, a palm open on the counter, right in the open office. He sweated, recalling police, recalling that ominous line of military ships docked just outside these offices on blue dock, two carriers in port, no less, with troops, troops like Viking stationers, unnervingly alike in size and build and manner, the stamp of birth labs. But tape-trained or not, Union citizen or not, there was the occasional open hand. If it was not a police trap. And that was possible too.

He looked up into eyes quite disconnected from that open palm. "You arrange me bank clearance, will you?" Sandor asked. "I really need to speed things up a bit. You think you can do that?"

Clerical lips pursed. The man consulted comp, did some figuring. "Voyager, is it? You know your margin's down to five thousand? I'd figure two for contingencies, at least."

He shuddered. Two was exorbitant. Dipping to the bottom of his already low margin account, the next move went right through into WSC's main fund: it would surely do that with the current dock charges added on. There had been a chance of coming back here—had been—but this would bring the auditors running. He nodded blandly. "You help me with that, then, will you? I really need that draft."

The man turned and keyed a printout from a desk console. Comp spat out a form. He laid it on the counter. "Make it out to yourself. I can disburse here for convenience."

"I really appreciate this." He leaned against the counter and made out the form for seven, smiled painfully as he handed it back to the official, who counted him out the money from the office safe. . . . Union scrip, not station chits; bills, in five hundreds.

"Maybe," said the clerk, "I should walk with you down there and pass the word to the dock supervisor about your emergency. I think we can get you out of here shortly."

He kept smiling and waited for the clerk to get his coat, walked with him outside, into the busy office district of the docks. "When those lines are hooked up and when the food's headed in," he said, his hand on the bills in his pocket, "then I'll be full of gratitude. But I expect frozen goods for this, and without holding me up. You sting me like I was a big operation, you see that I get all the supplies I'm due for it."

"Don't push your luck, Captain."

"I'm sure you can do it. I have faith in you. If I get questioned on this, so do you. Think of that."

A silence while they walked. There were the warship accesses at their right, bright and cheerful as merchanter accesses, but uniformed troops came and went there, and security guards with guns stood at various of the offices on dockside. Birth-lab soldiers, alike to the point of eerieness. Perhaps stationers, many of them from like origins, found it all less strange. This man beside him now, this man was from the war years, might have been on Viking during the fall, maybe had memories, the same as a merchanter recalled the taking of his ship. Bloody years. They shared that much, he and the stationer. Dislike of the troops. A certain nervousness. A sense that a little cash in pocket was a good thing to have, when tensions ran high. There was a time they had evacuated stations, shifted populations about, when merchanters had run for the far Deep and stayed there for self-protection, while warships had decided politics. No one looked for such years again, but the reflexes were still there.

"Hard times," Sandor said finally, when they were on blue dock's margin and walking through the section arch to green. "Big ships take care of themselves, but small ships have worries. I really need those goods."

Continued silence. Finally: "You hear anything down the line?" the man asked.

"Nothing solid. Mazianni hitting ships—Hang, what can I do? I don't have the kind of margin I can take out and not haul for months like some others might do. I don't have it. Little ships like me, combine forgets about us when trouble hits on that scale. WSC is stationer-run, and they're going to say haul, come what may. And some of their big haulers are going to hide out while the likes of me gets caught in the middle. But who'll keep the stations going? Marginers and independents and the like. I'd really like those frozen goods."

"Cost you extra."

"No way. You stung me for the two. I do it again and I get closer and closer to a company audit, man. You think two thousand's nothing? In an account my size it's something."

"You think your combine's pulling you out of here?"

"Don't know what they're going to do."

"Running under-the-table courier, it sounds like they want you out of here."

"I don't know."

Silence again. "Bet they're not going to check that account too closely. Bet they'll be more than glad to get their ships herded in to safer zones if there's action around here. They're realists. They know their ships have got to protect themselves. In all senses. You know the gold market?"

His pulse sped. "I know I'm not licensed to transport."

"Times like these, value goes up. The less on a station, value goes up. A lot of merchanters like to carry a little in pocket."

"I can't do that kind of thing. WSC'd have my head."

"Get you, say, some oddments. Little stuff. You put fourteen more with that extra thousand, and I know a dealer can get you station standard price plus fifteen percent, good rate for a merchanter, same as the big ships get."

The station air hit his face with a sickly chill, touching perspiration. "You know you're talking about felony. That's not skimming. That's theft."

"How worried are you? If your combine pulls you out, if it gets hot, maybe it's going to cost you heavy. As long as you put it in again where you're going, you're covered, and you can pocket the increase it's made."

"Won't increase that much, going away from the trouble."

"Oh, it will. It always does. It's the smart thing. Always good on stations. Can't be traced. Buys you all kinds of things. And if there's any kind of trouble—it goes up."

He swallowed the knot in his throat. "Right. Well, you get me that check and I'll do it, but I don't handle it at any stage."

"It'll cost you another thousand on all that deal: my risk."

"If I'm first on the docking schedule and those goods get aboard while I'm filling."

"No problem."

He was loaded in two hours, signed, cleared, and belted in, undocking from Viking with a gentle puff of *Lucy*'s bow vents, which eased him back and back and tended to a little pitch. He let the accustomed pitch increase, which was a misaimed jet, but he knew *Lucy* and had never fixed it. The pitch always set her for an axis roll and a little aft venting sent her over and out still within her given lane, because she was small and could pull maneuvers like that, which were usually for the military ships. He never showed more flash than that in a station's vicinity. He had more potential attention than he wanted. He had committed felony theft, faked papers, faked IDs, had unlicensed cargo aboard, and it was time to change *Lucy*'s name again—if he had had the time.

He put on aft vid and saw *Dublin Again*, had gone right past her, that silver, beautiful ship all aglow with her own running lights and the station's floods, in station shadow, so that she shone like a jewel among the others. Not so far away, a Union dartship stood off from dock, dull-surfaced and ominous, with vanes conspicuously larger than any merchanter afforded. It watched, its frame bristling with armaments and receptors. Viking's sullen star swung behind it as he moved, silhouetting it in bleeding fire, and he lost sight of *Dublin* in the glare—shut vid down, listening to station central's ordinary voice giving him his clear heading for the outgoing jump range, for a supposed jump for Voyager Station.

II

It was no small job, to clear *Dublin Again* for undock.
Gathering and accounting for the crew was an undertaking in
itself: 1,082 lives were registered to *Dublin,* of which the vast
majority were scattered out over the docks on liberty, and
most of those had been gone for four days, in one and the
other sleepover around the vast torus of Viking, not alone on
green dock, but spread through every docking section but
blue and the industrial core. They knew their time and they
came in, to log their time at whatever job wanted doing, if
there was a job handy—to shove their ID tags into the slot
when they were ready for absolute and irrevocable boarding,
passing that green line on the airlock floor and walls, that let
them know they were logged on and would be left without
search or sympathy if they recrossed that line without leave
of the watch officer.

One hundred forty-six Dubliners were entitled to wear the
green stars of executive crew; of that number, 76 wore the
collar stripe of senior, seated crew, mainday and alterday.
Four wore the captain's circle, one for each of four duty
shifts; 24, at one level and the other, were entitled to sit the
chair in theory, or to take other bridge posts. And 16 were
retired from that slot, who had experience, if not the physical
ability; they advised, and sat in executive council. It took
seven working posts at com to run *Dublin* in some operations, at any one moment; eight posts at scan, with four
more at the op board that monitored cargo status. Twenty-
five techs and as many cargo specialists on a watch kept
things in order; and with all told, posted crew and backup
personnel, that was 446 who wore the insignia of working
crew; and 279 unposted, who trained and waited and worked
as they could. There were the retired: over 200 of them,
whose rejuv had given out and whose health faded, some of

whom still went out on dockside and some of whom took to
their quarters or to sickbay and expected to die when jump
stress put too great a burden on them. There were the children, nearly 200 under the age of twenty, 120 of whom had
duties and took liberty when *Dublin* docked, and 40 of those
on the same privilege as the crew, to sleepover where they
chose.

And at mainday 1550 hours, *Dublin*'s strayed sons and
daughters headed aboard like a silver-clad flood, past the hiss
and clank of loading canisters. Some of them had had a call
for 1400, and some for 1200, those in charge of cargo. All
the Reillys—they *were* all Reillys, all 1,082 of them, excepting Henny Magen and Liz Tyler, who were married aboard
from other ships (everyone forgot their alien names and
called them Reillys by habit, making no distinction)—all the
Reillys were headed in, out of the gaudy lighted bars and glit-
tering shops and sleepovers, carrying purchases and packages
and in many cases lingering for a demonstrative farewell to
some liberty's-love on the verge of *Dublin*'s clear-zone. No
customs checked them off the station: they came as they
liked, and Allison Reilly walked up the ramp and through the
yellow, chill gullet of the access tube to the lock, carrying
two bottles of Cyteen's best, a collection of microfiches, two
pair of socks, a deepstudy tape, and six tubes of hand
lotion—not a good place to shop, Viking, which was mostly
mining and shipbuilding: there was freight and duty on all of
it but the microfiches and the tape, but they were headed
Over the Line into Alliance territory, and most everyone was
buying *something*, in the thought that goods in that foreign
territory might be different, or harder come by, and there was
a general rush to pick up this and that item. She needed the
socks and she liked the particular brand of hand lotion.

Crossing the green line, she fished out her dog tags and
pulled them off one-handed as she reached the watch desk
just the other side of the lock, smiled wearily at her several
cousins of varying degree who sat that cheerless duty, and
stuck the key-tag into the portable comp unit while Danny
Reilly checked her off. It was Jamie and little Meg behind
her; she turned and nodded them a courtesy, they seventeen
and nineteen and herself a lofty twenty-five, that made her
ma'am to them, and them a merest nod from her. She took
her packages on to the checkin desk, stripped the packing

materials off and put the merchandise in the lidded bin a
cousin offered her, with a grease-penciled ALLISON II on the
end amid the smears of previous notes. Nearly a thousand
Dubliners returning with purchases, with most of their quarters inaccessible during dock and only an hour remaining before departure: it was impossible, otherwise, to handle that
much personal cargo; and it had to be weighed and reckoned
against individual mass allotment. There would be a scramble
after first jump, while they were lazing their way across the
first nullpoint on their way to Pell, everyone going to the car-
gomaster to collect their purchases. There was something psy-
chological about it, like birthday packages, that everyone
liked to have something waiting for that sort-out, be it only a
bag of candy. And when a body went over-mass, well, one
could weigh it out again, too, and trade off, or consume the
consumables, or pay the mass charge with overtime and sell
off one's overmass at the next port liberty, along dockside, or
(at some stations with liberal customs) in merchanters' ba-
zaars, themselves a heady excitement of barter and docksid-
ing stationers looking for exotica. A bin waited for packing
materials; she stripped it all down, closed the lid and watched
her purchases go down the chute to cargo, walked on, burdenless. When *Dublin* had collected all the packing and the
debris, down to the last moment before the cargo hatch was
sealed, out would pop a waste canister, everything from paper to reusable nylon, and station recycling would seize it and
carry it off to be sorted, sifted, and used again. *Dublin* shifted
nothing through jump but what was useful; station threw
nothing away that had to be freighted in, not even worn-out
clothing.

"Are we still on schedule?" she asked the cousin nearest.

"Last I heard," the woman said. "The bell goes in about
forty-five minutes."

"Huh." She threw an involuntary glance at the desk clock
and walked on through, burdenless, putting her dog tags to
rights again, dodging past cousins with last-minute business in
cargo, mostly maintenance who were taking wastage to the
chute, and now and again someone with a personal bit of debris to jettison, a nuisance that should have been run through
comp before now, but there was always someone trying to
break through the line of incomers with something outgoing.

There was at least a reasonable quiet about the traffic

toward the lift . . . a few others her seniors, a few her junior, with some of the other unposteds . . . people in a hurry in uncommonly narrow spaces, because the great cylinder that was *Dublin*'s body still sat in docking lock, and no one in dockside boots could take any corridors but the number ones. The rest remained dark, up the upcurve of the intersecting halls, waiting the undock and start of rotation which would restore access to the whole circumference of the ship.

The pale green of outer corridors became Op Zone white, the dock smells which wafted in from the lock gave way to bitingly crisp air, tiles and corridors and lighting panels in pristine pallor that would show any smudge or streak—notoriously clean, because Dubliners in their youth spent hour on aching hour keeping the corridors that way. The lift, in the white zone, had a handful of cousins waiting for it; Allison nodded to the others and waited too—a glance and a hello to Deirdre, of her own year, another of her unit; got of a *Cato* man on Esperance liberty, so it ran. Deirdre had that knit-browed absentia of a four-day binge, a tendency to wince at noise. Allison folded her own arms and disdained to lean against the wall, being unposted exec, and not general crew, but her knees ached and her feet ached from walking, while she thought with longing of her own soft bunk, in her quarters topside.

"Good night?" someone asked. She blinked placidly at another unposted who had been with her in Tiger's last night.

"Yes," she said, thinking about it for a moment, drew in a breath and favored Curran with a thoughtful glance. "What happened to yourself?"

Curran grinned. That was all. The lift arrived, and seniors went on first; there was room for the three of them, herself and Deirdre and Curran, and a jam of others after that. The lift whisked them up to second level, and they lost the juniors, who were bound for their own territory; it stopped again on main, and they let the seniors off first, then followed through the corridor into the main lounge, into the din of laughter and conversation in a room as big as most station bars, curve-floored and with the float-based furniture now tilted out of trim with the ship's geometries. Posted crew and seniors gathered in the lounge beyond, and Allison wove her way through the center standing area to the archway, looked inside to find her mother, Megan, who was posted scan 24.

"I'm back," she hand-signed past the noise, the gathering in
the two lounges. Megan saw her and walked over, across the
white line into the unposted lounge to talk to her. "I worried," Megan said.

"Huh. I'm not about to miss the bell. Have a good stay?"

"Got some new tapes."

"Nothing else?"

Her mother grinned and went sober again, irrepressibly
reached out and straightened her collar. "The number ones
are still in conference. We think we're going to get undocked
on schedule. The military's talking to the Old Man now."

"No question about clearance, is there?" She straightened
her collar herself, minor irritance. "I thought that was settled."

"Something about some papers on the cargo. Trans-Line
protocols. Viking stationmaster is insisting we re-enter Union
space via Viking; we make no promises, and the military's
backing us on it. The bell's going on schedule, I'm betting."

"I don't see it's Viking's prerogative."

"Balance of trade, they say. They'll raise a fuss all the way
to Council."

She frowned—glanced about as a heavy hand came down
on her shoulder; it was her mother's half-brother Geoff,
dark-bearded, brows knit. "Allie," her uncle said, "you mind
how you go on the docks."

"He was safe," Allison said.

"Huh," Geoff said, and looked past her at Megan. "Mind
this one, Meg. Did that fellow ask questions, Allie? Did you
answer any?"

"He wasn't curious and no, nothing he couldn't get by
asking anywhere. I asked the questions, Geoff, sir, and I was
soberer than he was."

"Stay to Names you know," Megan said. "Nowadays particularly."

"Ma'am," Allison said under her breath. "Sir." Drew
breath and ducked past with a pat on the shoulder as her
half-sister Connie showed up to report in, relieving her of
more discussion. There was no great closeness between herself and Connie, who was pregnant and occupied in that,
whose study was archives and statistics. "Lo, Connie," and
"Hello, Allie," was all that passed between them. Curran was
closer, Geoff was, or Dierdre, but Megan loved freckled Connie, so that was well enough with Allison who moderately

liked her, at the distance of their separate lives. "Hello," she said to Eilis, who made a touch at her as she passed through the crowd; and "Ma'am" to her grandmother Allison, who on rejuv was silver-haired, sterile, and looked no more than forty (she was sixty-two). And there was greatgrand Mina, scan 2, who also looked forty, and was twice that—seated crew, Mina, who was back in unposted territory talking to Ma'am herself, who was sitting down on one of the benches—Ma'am with a capital M, that was Colleen, whose rejuv was fading and who had gone dry and thin and wrinkled, but who still got about in the lounges during maneuvers despite brittle bones and stiffening joints. Ma'am was the point at which she was related to Curran and Deirdre both. Ma'am was retired com 1, and kept the perks she had had in that post, but evidently chose not to be in council at the moment. Ma'am and Mina deserved courtesy on boarding, and Allison worked her way across the room and the noise and paid it, which Mina answered with a preoccupied nod, but Ma'am grabbed her hands, kissed her on the cheek as if she had been one of the toddlers, and let her go again, talking past her to Mina nonstop in a low tone that involved the military and the rights of merchanters. Allison lingered half a breath, learned nothing, strayed away again, past other hellos and the delicate tottering of a two-year-old loose in the press.

She found a bench and sat down, lost in the forest of standing bodies, glanced across the tops of red contoured furniture which wrapped itself up the curve of the room: some of the unposteds had stretched out sideways on the benches with their eyes shielded. Too much celebration, too late. The inevitable bands of knee-high youngsters yelled and darted as high on the floor curve as they could, occasionally taking a spill and risking being collared by one of their elders if their antics knocked into someone. Someone's baby was squalling, probably Dia's; it always did, hating the noise. The older children squealed: it was their time to burn off all the energy, and it was part of their courage, the racing and the play and the I-dare-you approach to undock that made a game of the maneuvers *Dublin* went through. It gave them nerve for the jump that was coming, which merchanter babies went through even unborn. These were the under fives, the youngsters loose among them. The sixes through sixteens were up in the topside of the cylinder, where they spent most of their

dockside time (and all of it for the six-through-nines) in a
topsy-turvy ceiling-downside nursery, where a padded
crawlthrough made *G* reorientation only another rowdy, tumbling game. Every Dubliner remembered, with somewhat of
nostalgia, how much better that was than this adult jam-up in
the downside lounge.

They gained no numbers in a generation: the matrilineal
descent of merchanters generated new Dubliners of sleepover
encounters with more concern for too few children than too
many: another was always welcome, and if one wanted half
a dozen, and another wanted none, that was well enough: it
all balanced out from one generation to the next: Ma'am and
Mina and Allison Senior came down, among others, to
Megan and Geoff. Geoff had no line on *Dublin*, being male;
but Megan had her and Connie, which balanced out; and
Connie was already taking the line down another generation.
Only rejuv kept five and sometimes six generations living at
once: like Ma'am, who was pushing a hundred fifty and had
faded only in the last decade, Ma'am, who had been Com 1
so long her voice was *Dublin's* in the minds of everyone. It
still made shockwaves, thin as it had gotten, when Ma'am
made it snap and handed out an order; and there was still the
retired Old Man, who had been the Old Man for most of Allison's life, and seldom got about now, snugged in his cabin
that was downmost during dock, attended by someone always
during jump, listening to tapes for his entertainment and
sleeping more and more.

Allison herself . . . was Helm 21, which was status among
the unposteds, Third Helm's number one of the alterday shift.
What do you want to be? Megan had asked her as early as
she could remember the question. When a Dubliner was taking his first study tapes he got the Question, and started
learning principles before awkward fingers could hold a pen
or scrawl his letters, tapestudy from *Dublin's* ample library.
So what do you want to be? Megan had asked, and she had
wanted to be bridge crew, where lights flashed and people sat
in chairs and did important things, and where the screens
showed the stars and the stations. What do you want to be?
The question came quarterly after that, and it went through a
range of choices, until at ten: I want to be the Old Man, she
had said, before she had hardly gone out on a station dock or
seen anything in the universe but the inside of *Dublin's* com-

partments and corridors. The king of the universe was the Old Man who sat in the chair and captained *Dublin*, the Number One mainday captain, who ruled it all.

Be reasonable, Megan had told her then, taking her in the circle of her arm, setting her on the edge of the bed in her quarters and trying to talk sense into her. Only one gets to be the Old Man; and you know how many try the course and fail? Maybe one in four survives the grade to get into the line; and one in fifty gets to Helm 24, up where you're even going to sit a chair on watch; and after that, age is against you, because the sitting captains are too young. You go ask in library, Allie, how long the sitting captains are going to live, and then you do the math and figure out how long the number two chairs are going to live after taking their posts behind them, and how long it takes for Helm 24 to work up to posted crew.

Can't I try? she had asked. And: yes, you can try, Megan had said. I'm only telling you how it is.

Maybe there'll be an accident, she had thought to herself, with a ten-year-old's ruthless ambition: an accident to wipe out everyone in Second Helm.

You study everything, Megan had said, when she had complained about learning galley maintenance; the Helm course fits you for everything. So if you fail, you drop into whatever other track you're passing. You think Helm's just sitting in that chair: it's trade and routings; law; navigation and scan and com and armaments; it's jack and jill of all trades, Allie, ma'am, and doing all the scut before you hand it out, and you can always *quit*, Allie, ma'am.

No, ma'am, she had said, and swallowed all they gave her, reckoning to be stubbornest the longest, and to make it all the way, because there was a craziness in her, that once launched, she had a kind of inertia that refused to be hauled down. She was Helm 21, and when Val retired as she was likely to, Helm 6 and on the fading edge of rejuv, she would be Helm 20, and one more Dubliner got a post as Helm 24. She walked wide among the unposteds, being Helm. It had its perks. But Lallie, over there, Maintenance 196, was Second Maintenance second shift alterday at barely twenty-one, posted main crew before her hair grayed, while Helm 21 had little chance indeed, with a possible forty years until another seated Helm decided to give it up and retire. She would be on rejuv before the list got her past Helm 20, would still be lording it over the unposteds, silver-haired and still not able to cross the line into the posteds lounge, still waiting, still working the number two bridge to stay current.

She shut her eyes, leaned back, seeing blue dock again, and soldiers in their black uniforms. They talked about opening up Sol trade, shut down since the war; about opening the mothballed stations of the Hinder Stars. They talked new routes and profits to be made—putting their hand into Alliance territory, creating a loop that would link the Union stars to the Pell-based Alliance. Trade and politics.

So much she knew, sitting in on *Dublin* executive councils, which was all of Helm and only sitting crew of other tracks. She knew all the debate, whether *Dublin* should take the chance, whether they should just sit out the building and wait for the accomplished fact; but *Dublin* had always stood with one foot on either side of a crisis, always poised herself ready to move to best advantage, and the Merchanter's Alliance, once an association of merchanter captains who disputed Union, now held the station at Pell's Star for a capital, declared itself a sovereign government, passed laws, in short . . . looked like a power worth having a foot inside. A clean record with Union; a clean record with the Alliance thus far, since *Dublin* had operated far out of the troubled zones during the war—she could get herself a Pell account opened and if that new trade really was opening up there, then *Dublin* could get herself dual papers. Union Council was in favor of it, wanted moderates like themselves in the Alliance, good safe Unionside haulers who would vote against Pell-side interests as the thing got bigger. Union talked about building merchant ships and turning them over to good safe Unionsiders like *Dublin* to increase their numbers—which talk quickened Allison's pulse. A new ship to outfit would strip away all the Second Helm of *Dublin*, and get her posted on the spot. She had lived that thought for a year.

But more and more it looked like a lot of talk and a maintenance of the status quo. Rapprochement was still the operative word in Union: Alliance and Union snuggling closer together after their past differences. Recontacting Sol, after the long silence, in an organized way. Clearing the pirates out. All merchanters having equal chance at the new ships that might be built.

Hopes rose and fell. At the moment they were fallen, and she took wild chances on dockside. Geoff was right. Stupidity. But it had helped, with the soldiers crawling all over station that close to crossing the Line into foreign space. So she scattered a bit of her saved credit on a fellow who could use a good drink and a good sleepover. In a wild impulse of charity it might have been good to have scattered a bit more on him: he looked as if he could have used it . . . but touchy-proud. He would not have taken it. Or would have, being hungry, and hated her for it. There had been no delicate way. He fell behind her in her mind, as Viking did, as all stations did after they sealed the hatch. If she thought persistently of anyone, it was Charlie Bodart of *Silverbell*, green-eyed, easygoing Charlie, Com 12 of his ship, who crossed her path maybe several times a loop, *Silverbell* and *Dublin* running one behind the other.

But not now. Not to Pell, across the Line. Good-bye to *Silverbell* and all that was familiar—at least for the subjective year. And it might be a long time before they got back on Charlie's schedule—if ever.

A body hit the cushion beside her, heavy and male. She opened her eyes and turned her head in the din of voices. Curran.

"What," Curran said, "hung over? You've got a face on you."

"Not much sleep."

"I'll tell you about not much sleep."

"I'll bet you will." She looked from him to the clock, and the bell was late. "I got along. I got those fiches too. And a couple of bottles."

"We'll have those killed before we get to Pell."

"We'll have to kill them at dock if they don't get the soldierlads organized and get us out of here."

"I think they've got it straightened away," Curran said. Helm 22, Curran, right behind her in the sequence. Darkhaired, like enough for a brother; and close to that. "I heard that from Ma'am."

"I hope." She folded her arms, gathered up her cheerfulness. "I had an offer, I want you to know. My friend last night was looking for crew. Number one and only on his own ship, he said. Offered me a Helm 2 chair, he did. At least that's what I think he was offering."

Curran chuckled. It was worth a laugh, a marginer making offers to *Dublin*. And not so deep a laugh, because it touched hopes too sensitive, that they both shared.

"Cousin Allie." That shrill piping was aged four, and barrelled into her unbraced lap, to be picked up and bounced. Allison caught her breath, hauled Tish up on her leg, bounced her once dutifully and passed her with a toss over to Curran, who hugged the imp and rolled her off his lap onto the empty cushion beside him. "Going to *go*," Tish said, having, at four, gotten the routine down pat. "Going to walk all round *Dublin*."

"Pretty soon," Curran said.

"Live up *there*," Tish said, jabbing a fat finger ceilingward. "My baby up *there*."

"Next time you remember to bring your baby down," Allison said. "You bring her with you the next time we dock."

There had been no end of the wail over the forgotten doll at the start of their liberty. Middle zones of the ship went inaccessible during dock; and young Will III had offered to eel through the emergency accesses after it, but no, it was a lark for Will, but a good way to take a fall, and Tish learned to keep track of things. Everyone learned. Early.

"Go," Tish crowed, anxious. Prolonged dock was no fun for the littlest, in cramped spaces and adult noise.

"Bye," Allison said, and Tish slid down and worked her way through adult legs to bedevil some of her other several hundred cousins, while Allison shut her eyes and wished the noise would stop. Her wishes were narrow at the moment, centered on her own comfortable, clean-smelling bed.

Then the bell rang, the Cinderella stroke that ended liberty and liberties, and the children were shushed and taken in arms. Conversations died. People remembered hangovers and feet and knees that ached from walking unaccustomed distances on the docks, recalled debts run up that would have to be worked off oddjobbing. "I lied," someone said louder than other voices, the old joke, admitting that after-the-bell accounts were always less colorful. There was laughter, not at the old joke, but because it was old and comfortable and everyone knew it. They drifted for the cushions, and there was a general snapping and clicking of belts, a gentle murmur, a last fretting of children. Allison bestirred herself to pull her belt out of the housings and to clip it as Eilis settled into the seat next to hers and did the same.

Bacchanale was done. The Old Man was back in the chair again, and the posted crew, having put down their authority for the stay on station, took it up again.

Dublin prepared to get underway.

III

Lucy was never silent in her operation. She had her fan noises and her pings and her pops and crashes as some compressor cycled in or a pump went on or off. Her seating creaked and her rotation rumbled and grumbled around the core . . . a rotating ring with a long null *G* center and belly that was her holds, a stubby set of generation vanes stretched out on top and ventral sides: that was the shape of her. She moved along under insystem propulsion, doing her no-cargo best, toward the Viking jump range, outbound, on the assigned lane a small ship had to use.

Sandor reached and put the interior lights on, and *Lucy's* surroundings acquired some cheer and new dimensions. Rightward, the corridor to the cabins glared with what had once been white tiles—bare conduits painted white like the walls; and to the left another corridor horizoned up the curve, lined with cabinets and parts storage. Aft of the bridge and beyond the shallowest of arches, another space showed, reflected in the idle screens of vacant stations, bunks in brown, worn plastic, twelve of them, that could be set manually for the pitch at dock. Their commonroom, that had been. Their indock sleeping area, living quarters, wardroom—whatever the need of the moment. He set *Lucy's* autopilot, unbelted and eased himself out of the cushion: that was enough to get himself a stiff fine if station caught him at it, moving through the vicinity of a station with no one at controls.

He found the pulser unit in under the counter storage, taped it to his wrist and handed himself across the bridge, fighting the spiral drift along to the right-hand corridor, a controlled stagger with right foot on the tiled footing curve and left on the deck. He got the pharmaceuticals he wanted and brought them back to his place on the bridge, another stagger down the footings and swing along the hand grips. Then he knelt down in the pit and used tape and braces to

38

rig her as she had been rigged before, taped the drugs he would need for jump to the side of the armrest where he could get at them; taped down some of the safety controls— also illegal; he set up the rig for the sanitation kit, because he would need that too, much as he dreaded it.

A second trip, rightward, this time, past sealed cabins, into the narrow confines of the galley and galley storage. He filled water bottles, and took an armful of them back to the bridge, jammed them into the brace he had long ago rigged near the command console . . . scared, if he let himself think about it. He swallowed such feelings, bobbed his head up now and again to check scan, down again to open up the underdeck storage where he had shoved some of the dried goods, not to have to suit up for the chill of the holds to hunt for them. He knelt there counting the packets out, taped them where he could get at them from the chair. His braced limbs shook from the strain of *G*. He dropped a packet and lunged after it, taped it where it belonged.

The lane still showed clear. He crawled up and held onto the back of the cushion, staring at the instruments, finally edged his way back to one of the brown plastic bunks at the aft bulkhead, to give his back a little relief from the strain. His eyes stung with fatigue. He rested his hands beside him, arms pulled askew by the spiral stress of acceleration, leaned his head against the bulkhead, not really comfortable, but it was a change from the long-held position in the cushion, and he could get the com or the controls from here if he had to.

There were compartments all about the ring, private quarters. Diametrically opposite the bridge was the loft, where the children had been . . . he never went around the ring that far. This was home, this small space, these bunks aft of the bridge, plastic mattresses patched with tape and deteriorating with age. One had been his when he was ten, that over there, nearest the partition spinward; and there had been Papa Lou's, which he never sat on; and one his mother's; he had had brothers and sisters and cousins once, and there had been three children under six, cousins too. But Papa Lou had vented them and old Ma'am too, when their boarders turned ugly and it was clear what they were going to do. They had had *Lucy*'s armament, but that had been helpless against a carrier and its riderships; they had had only two handguns on the ship . . . and the boarders who had ambushed them in the nullpoint had said they were not touching crew, only cargo. It had been *Lucy*'s clear choice then, open the hatch or be blown entirely. But they lied, the Mazianni, pirates even then, in the years when they had called themselves the Company Fleet and fought for Pell and Earth. They respected nothing and counted life nothing, and into such hands Papa Lou had surrendered them . . . not understanding.

He himself had not understood. He had not imagined. He had looked at the armored, faceless invaders with a kind of awe, a child's respect of such power. He had—for that first few moments they had been aboard—wanted to be one of them, wanted to carry weapons and to wear such sleek, frightening armor—one brief, ugly temptation, until he had seen Papa Lou afraid, and begun to suspect that something evil had come, something far less beautiful inside the armor, that had gotten into the ship's heart. He always felt guilt when he recalled that . . . that he had admired, that he had wanted to frighten others and not be frightened—he reasoned with himself that it was only the glitter that had drawn him, and that any child would have reacted the same, in the confusion, in the shaking of reliable references, in ignorance, if not in innocence. But he always felt unclean.

Most of it had happened here, on the bridge, in the commonroom and the corridor, in this widest part of the ship where they had gathered everyone but the children, and where the boarders started showing what they meant to do. But Papa Lou had gotten to the command chair and voided the part of the ship where the children and the oldest had taken refuge, before they shot him; and most of them had died, shot down in the commonroom and on the bridge; and some of them had been taken away for slower treatment.

But three of them, himself and old Mitri and cousin Ross, had lain there in the blood and the confusion because they were half dead—himself aged ten and standing with crew because he had slipped around the curve and gotten to his mother's side. They had not died, they three, which was Ross's doing, because Ross was mad-stubborn to live, and because after they had been left adrift, Ross had dragged himself from beside the bunk where he had fallen on him and Mitri, and gotten the med kit that was spilled all over where the pirates had rifled it for drugs. That was where his mother had been lying shot through the head: he recalled that all too vividly. She had gotten one of the boarders at the last, because they had given the women the two guns—they needed

them most, Papa Lou had said—and when Papa Lou vented
the children his mother had shot one of the boarders before
they shot her, got an armored man right in the faceplate and
killed him, and they dragged him off with them when they
left the ship, probably because they wanted the armor back.
But Aunt Jame had died before she could get a clear shot at
any of them.

Here they had fallen, here, here, here, twelve bodies, and
more in the corridor rightward, and himself and Mitri and
Ross.

Those were his memories at times like this, fatigued and
mind-numbed, or cooking a solitary meal in the galley, or
walking past vacant cabins, sights that washed out all the
happier past, everything that had been good, behind one red-
running image. Everywhere he walked and sat and slept,
someone had died. They had scrubbed away all the blood and
made the plastic benches and the tiles and the plating clean
again; and they had vented their dead at that lonely nullpoint, undisturbed once the pirate had gone its way—sent
them out in space where they probably still drifted, frozen
solid and lost in infinity, about the cinder of an almost-star. It
was a clean, decent disposal, after the ugliness that had gone
before. In his mind they still existed in that limbo, never de-
cayed, never changed . . . they went on traveling, no suit between them and space, all the starry sights they had loved
passing continually in front of their open, frozen eyes—a
company of travelers that would stay more or less together,
wherever they were going. All of them. Only Ma'am and the
babies had gone ahead, and the others would never overtake
them.

Mitri had died out on the hull one of the times they had
had to change *Lucy*'s name, when they had run the scam on
Pan-paris, and it had gone sour—a stupid accident that had
happened because the Mazianni had stripped them of equipment they needed. Ross had spent four hours and risked his
life getting Mitri back because they had thought there was
hope; but Mitri had been dead from the first few moments,
the pressure in the suit having gone and blood having gotten
into the filters, so Ross just called to say so and stripped the
suit and let Mitri go, another of *Lucy*'s drifters, but all alone
this time. And he, twelve, had sat alone in the ship shivering,
sick with fear that something would happen to Ross, that he
would not get back, that he would die, getting Mitri in.

Leave him, he had yelled at Ross, his own cowardice, before he had even known that Mitri was dead; he remembered that; and remembered the lonely sound of Ross crying into the mike when he knew. He had thrown up from fright after Ross had come in safe. Another lonely nullpoint, those points of mass between the burning stars that jumpships used to steer by; and he could not have gotten *Lucy* out of there, could not have handled the jump on his own, if he had lost Ross then. He had cried, after that, and Mitri had haunted him, a shape that tumbled through his dreams, the only one of *Lucy*'s ghosts that reproached him.

Ross had died on Wyatt's, dealing with people who tried to cheat him. The stationers, beyond doubt, had cremated him, so one of them was forever missing from the tally of drifters in the deep. In a way, that troubled him most of all, that he had had to leave Ross in the hands of strangers, to be destroyed down to his elements . . . but he had had only the quick chance to break *Lucy* away, to get her out before they attached her, and he kept her. He had been seventeen then, and knew the contacts and the ports and how to talk to customs agents.

He slept in Ross's old bunk, in this one, because it was as close as he could come to what he had left of family, and this one bed seemed warmer than the rest, not so unhappily haunted as the rest. Ross had always been closer than his own mind to him, and because he had not cast out Ross's body with his own hands, it was less sometimes like Ross was dead than that he had gone invisible after the mishap at Wyatt's, and still existed aboard, in the programs comp held—so, so meticulously Ross had recorded all that he knew, programed every operation, left instructions for every eventuality . . . in case, Ross had said, simply in case. The recorded alarms spoke in Ross's tones; the time signals did; and the instruction. It was company, of sorts. It filled the silences.

He tried not to talk to the voice more than need be, seldom spoke at all while he was on the ship, because he reckoned that the day he started talking back and forth with comp, he was in deep trouble.

Only this time he sat with his eyes fixed on the screens on the bridge, with his shoulder braced against the acceleration, and a vast lethargy settled over him in the company of his ghosts. Ross, he thought, Ross . . . I might love her; because Ross was the closest thing he had ever had to a father, a personal father, and he had to try out the thought on someone, just to see if it sounded reasonable.

It did not. There were story-tapes, a few aged tapes Ross had conned on Pan-paris when they were young and full of chances. He listened to them over and over and conjured women in his mind, but he knew truth from fancy and refused to let fancy take a grip on him. It had to do with living . . . and solitude; and there were slippages he could not afford. He had been drunk, that was all; was sober now, and simply tired.

He had been crazy into the bargain, to have paid what he had paid to get clear of station. And he was outbound, accelerating, committed. . . . He was headed for a real place out there, was about to violate lane instructions, headed out to new territory with forged papers. It was a real place, and a real meeting, where a dream could get badly bent.

Where it could end. Forever.

(Ross . . . I'm scared.)

No noise but the fans and the turning of the core, that everpresent white sound in which the rest of the silence was overwhelming. Little human sounds like breathing, like the dropping of a stylus, the pushing of a button, were whited out, swallowed, made null.

(Ross . . . this may be the last trip. I'm sorry. I'm tired. . . .)

That was the crux of it. The certainty settled into his bones. The last trip, the last time—because he had run out of civilized stations Unionside. Even Pell, across the Line—they had called at once, when it was himself and Ross and Mitri together; and *Lucy* had been *Rose*. They owed money there too, as everywhere. *Lucy* was out of havens; and he was out of answers, tired of fear, tired of starving and sleeping the way he had slept on the way into Viking, marginally afraid that the old man he had hired might rob him or get past the comp lock or—it was always possible—kill him in his sleep. And once, just once to see what others had, what life was like outside that terror, with the fancy bars and the fancy sleepovers and a woman with something other than larceny in mind—

He had never had a place to go before, never had a destination. He had lived in this narrow compartment most of his life and only planned what he would do to avoid the traps behind him. Pell, Allison Reilly said; and deals; and it agreed with the rumors, that there were routes opening, hope—hope for marginers like him.

It was a joke of course, the best joke of a humorous career. A surprise for Allison Reilly—she would turn and stare open-mouthed when he tapped her on the shoulder in some crowded Pell Station bar. He knew what *Lucy* could do, and what he could do that great, modern ship of hers would never try—

Stupid, she would say. That was so. But she would always think about it, that a little ship had run jump for jump against *Dublin Again*. And that was something of a mark to make in his life, if nothing else. There was, in a sense, more of *Lucy* left than there was of him . . . because there was no end to the traveling and no end to the demands she made on him. He had given all he had to keep her going; and now he wanted something out of her, for his pride. He had no Name left; *Lucy* had none. So he did this crazy thing—in its place.

He shut his eyes, yielded to that *G* that pressed him uncomfortably against the bulkhead, drowsing while he could. The pulser was taped to his wrist so that the first beep from the out-range buoy would bring him out of it. Station would have his head on a plate if they knew; but it was all the chance he had to go into jump with a little rest.

The pulser stung his wrist, brought him out of it when it only felt as if he had fallen asleep for a second. He lurched in blind fright for the controls and sat down and realized it was only the initial contact of the jump range buoy, and engine shutdown, on schedule.

Number one for jump, it told him; and advised him that there was another ship behind. A chill went up his back when he reckoned its bulk and its speed and the time. That was *Dublin*, outbound, overtaking him much more slowly, he suspected, than it could, because of their order of departure—because *Lucy*, ordinarily low priority, was close enough to the mark now that *Dublin* was compelled to hang back off her tail. The automated buoy was going to give them clearance one on the tail of the other because the buoy's information, transmitted from station central, indicated they were not going out in the same direction.

And that was wrong.

He checked his calculations, rechecked and triple-checked, lining everything up for an operation far more ticklish than calculating around the aberrations of *Lucy*'s docking jets. Nullpoints moved, being more than planet-sized mass, in the complicated motions of stars. Comp had to allow for that. No one sane would head into jump alone, with a comp that had no backup, with trank and food and water taped to the board: he told himself so, making his prep, darting glances back to comp and scan, listening to the buoy beeping steadily, watching them track right down the line. He put the trank into his arm. It was time for that . . . to dull the senses which were about to be abused. Not one jump to face . . . but three; and if he missed on one of them, he reckoned, he would never know it.

There was speculation as to what it was to be strung out in the between, and speculation about what the human mind might start doing once the drugs wore off and there was no way back. There were tales of ships which wafted in and out of jump like ghosts with eerie wails on the receiving com, damned souls that never came down and never made port and never died, in time that never ended . . . but those were drunken fancies, the kind of legends which wandered station docksides when crews were topping one another with pints and horror tales, deliberately frightening stationers and insystem spacers, who believed every word of such things.

He did not, above all, want to think of them now. He had little enough time to do anything hereafter but keep *Lucy* tracking and keep his wits about him if things went wrong. If he made the smallest error in calculation he could spend a great deal of time at the first nullpoint getting himself sorted out, and he could lose *Dublin*. The transit, empty as he was, would use up a month or more subjective time; and *Dublin* would shave that . . . would laze her way across the space of each nullpoint, maybe several days, maybe a week resting up, and head out again. *Lucy* did not have such leisure. He had no plans to dump all velocity where he was going, could not do that and hope to outpace *Dublin*'s deeper stitches into the between.

The trank was taking hold. He thought of *Dublin* behind him, and the hazard of it. He reached for the com, punched it in, narrow-focused the transmission, a matter between himself and that sleek huge merchanter that came on his tail. "*Dublin Again*, this is US 48-335 Y *Lucy*, number one for jump. Advise you the buoy is in error. I'm bound for Pell.

Repeat, buoy information is in error; I'm bound for Pell:
don't crowd my departure."

Lucy's cold eye located the appropriate reference star,
bracketed it, and he saw that. The terror he ought to feel
eased into a bland, tranked consciousness in which death itself might be a sensation mildly entertaining. He started the
jump sequence, pushed the button which activated the generation vanes while the buoy squalled protest about his track—
felt it start, the sudden, irreversible surety that bizarre things
were happening to matter and to him, that things were racing
faster and faster. . . .

. . . conscious again and still tranked, hyper and sedated
at once, a peculiar coincidence of mental states, in which he
was aware of alarms ringing and *Lucy* doing her mechanical
best to tell him she was carrying dangerous residual velocity.
The power it took to dump had to be measured against the
power it took to acquire—

No dice throws. Calculate. Move the arm, punch the buttons. Dump the speed down to margin or lose the ship on the
next—

Wesson's Point: present location, Wesson's Point, in the
appropriate jump range. Entry, proceeding toward dark
mass: plot bypass curve down to margin; remember the ac-
quire/dump balance—

"*Sandy.*" That was Ross's comp's voice. "*Sandy, wake up.
Get the comp.*"

There were other voices, that sang to him through the hum
of dissolution.

Dead, Sandor. All dead.

Sandy, wake up. Time to wake up.

Vent!

. . . acceptable stress. Set to auto and trank out for time
of passage; set cushion and pulser; two hours two minutes
crossing the nullpoint, set, *mark.*

Dead, Sandor. All dead.

He came out of sleep with the pulser stinging his wrist and
with an ache all the way to his heels, unbelted and leaned
over the left side of the cushion to dryheave for a moment,
collapsed over that armrest weighing far more than he
thought he should and caring far less about survival than he
should, because he had gone into this too tired, with his de-

fenses too depressed, and the trank was not wearing off. He ought to be attending to controls. He had to get something to eat and drink, because he was going again in half an hour, and that was too little time.

He reached down and got one of the foil packets, managed with palsied fingers to get it open, and got the ripped corner to his lips—chewed food which had no taste but salt and copper—felt after the water and sucked mouthfuls of that, dropped the empty foil and the empty bottle, felt the food lying inert in his stomach, unwanted. He got the other shot home, beginning to trank out again . . . forced his eyes to focus on the boards, while *Lucy* shot her way along at a hairbreadth margin from disaster. Sometimes there was other junk ringing a nullpoint, a dark platelet of rocks and ice and maybe, maybe lost spacers who used the deep dark of this place for a tomb. . . .

He held his eyes open, alternately trying to throw up and trying to cope with the flow of data which comp itself had to sort and dump in a special mode because it came so fast . . . still blind, ripping along at a velocity that would fling even a smallish planet into his path before the computer could deal with it. *Lucy* headed for the other side of the nullpoint's gravity well with manic haste, but in that close pass they had gotten bent as light was bent, and the calculations had to take that into account. He sat there ignoring the scan-blindness into which they were rushing, trying to tell by the fluttering passage of data whether the numbers converged, reality with his calculations, trying to learn if there was error in position, and how that was going to translate in jump.

And screaming in the back of his mind was the fact that he was playing tag with a very large ship which could play games with distances which *Lucy* barely made, in a time differential he could not calculate, and that on some quirk of malign fate he could still run into them, if they just happened to coincide out here. *Dublin* was either here now or out ahead of him, because his lead was going to erode and change to lag somewhere in the transit. Ships missed each other because space was wide and coincidences were statistically more than rare; but not when two ships were playing leapfrog in the same nullpoints. . . .

Second jump . . . statistically better this time . . . a vast point, three large masses in juxtaposition, a kink in the be-

tween that hauled ships in and slung them along in a complicated warping. . . . Dump it now, dump the speed
down. . . .

"Wake up, Sandy."

And his own voice, prerecorded: "The referent now is
Pell's Star. Push the track reset, Sandy. The track
reset. . . ."

He located the appropriate button, stared entranced at the
screen . . . no rest possible here. The velocity was still extreme. His tongue was swollen in his mouth. He took another
of the water bottles and drank, hurting. Food occurred to
him; the thought revolted him; he reached nonetheless and located the packet, ate, because it was necessary to do.

He was crazy, that was what—he swallowed in mechanical,
untasting gulps, unable to remember what buttons he had
pushed, trusting his own recorded voice giving him the sequences as comp needed them, trusting to that star he saw
bracketed ahead of him, if that was not itself a trick of a
mind which had come loose in time. He recalled *Dublin*; if
Allison Reilly knew remotely what he was doing this moment
she would curse him for the risk to her ship. He ought to
dump more of the velocity he had, right now, because he was
scared. Tripoint was deadly dangerous, with no margin for
high-speed errors. . . .

But *Lucy* was moving with the sureness of a woman with
her mind made up, and he was caught in that horrible impe-
tus and the solid power of her, because a long time ago she
had hollowed him out and taken all there was of him. He
moved in a continual blur of slow motion, while the universe
passed at much faster rates. There was debris in this place.
He was passing to zenith of the complicated accretion disc
. . . so he hoped. If he had miscalculated, he died, in an im-
pact that would make a minor, unnoticed light.

He dumped down: the recorded voice told him to. He
obeyed. The data coming in sorted itself into more manic
strings of numbers. He punched in when the voice told him,
froze a segment, matched up—found a correspondence with
his plotted course. He grinned to himself, still scared witless,
human component in a near *C* projectile, and stared at the
screens with trank-dulled eyes.

He kicked into Pell jump range with velocity that had the
incoming-range buoy screaming its automated indignation at

him, advising whatever lunatic had just come within its scan that he was traveling too fast and headed dead-on for trafficked zones.

Dump! it warned him, dopplered and restructured by his com. Its systems were hurling machine-to-machine warnings at *Lucy*'s autoalert, which *Lucy* was primed to obey. She was kicking in the vanes in hard spurts, which shifted him in and out of realspace in bursts of flaring nausea. There were red lights everywhere until he hit the appropriate button and confirmed the dump order *Lucy* was obeying.

IV

The velocity fell away: some time yet before the scan image had time to be relayed by the buoy to Pell central, advising them that a ship was incoming, and double that time before central's message could come back to *Lucy*. Sandor extricated himself from his nest with small, numb movements, offended by the reek of his own body. His mouth tasted of copper and bile. His hands were stiff and refused coordinated movement. He rolled out of the cushion in the pit and hit the deck on his knees in a skittering of empty water bottles and foil papers sliding under his hand. "Wake up, Sandy," comp was telling him. He reached the keyboard still kneeling, hooked an arm over it and managed to code in the one zero one that stopped it, about the most that his numbed brain was capable of doing in straight sequence.

Wake up. Not that much time left before they would want answers out of him, before his absence from controls would be noticed. He had the pulser still on his wrist. He levered himself up by his arms on the counter, looked at the blurring lights and the keys, trying to recall the sequence that would put it on watch. Autopilot was still engaged: *Lucy* was following lane instructions from the buoy. That was all right.

He located the other control, while his stomach spasmed and his vision grayed, got the code in—no acceleration now. He could not have stood with any stress hauling at him. He groped for the edge of the counter at his right and worked his way up out of the pit, walked blind along the counter until he blinked clear on the lighted white of the corridor that led to maintenance storage, and the cubbyhole of a shower in the maintenance section. He peeled everything off that he was wearing, shoved it in the chute and hoped never to see it again, felt his way into the cabinet and leaned there while the jets blasted off filth and dead skin and shed hair. Soap. He lathered; found his razor in its accustomed place and shaved

50

by feel, with his eyes shut and the water coursing over him.
He felt alive again, at least marginally. He never wanted to
leave the warmth and the cleanliness . . . could have collapsed
to the floor of the cabinet and curled up and slept in the
warm water.

No. Out again. There was not that much time. He shut the
water off, staggered out into the chill air and gathered clothes
from the locker there. He half-dried, pulled the coveralls on
and wiped his wet hair back from his eyes. The pulser, water-
proof, had not alerted him: *Lucy* was still all right. He went
out into the corridor with an armload of towels and disinfectant and went back to clean up the pit, smothering the queas-
iness in his stomach.

He disposed of all the untidiness, another trip back to storage and disposal, then came back and fell into the cushion
that stank now of disinfectant . . . shut his eyes, wilted into
the contours, fighting sleep with a careful periodic fluttering
of his eyelids.

They already had his ID, lying though that was. It was automatic in *Lucy*'s computer squeal, never ceasing. He had the
station scan image from the buoy, estimates of the positions
of all the ships in Pell System, large and small—and when he
brought his mind to focus on that, on the uncommon number
of them, a disturbance wended its way through his consciousness, a tiny ticking alarm at the scope of what he was seeing.
Ships in numbers more than expectation. Traffic patterns,
lanes in great complexity, shuttle routes for approach to the
world of Downbelow, to moons and mining interests. A collection of merchanters, who got together to set rates and to
threaten Union with strikes; who served Union ports and disdained the combines. . . . That was all it had been. But it
had grown, expanded beyond his recollections. Sol trade—
sounded half fanciful, until now.

Harder to run a scam here, if they were short and over-
crowded. Or it might even be easier, if station offices were
too busy to run checks, if they were getting such an influx on
the strength of these rumors that a ship with questionable papers could lose itself in the dataflow . . . no, it was just a
matter of rethinking the approach and the tactics. . . .

"This is Pell central," a sudden voice reached him, and the
pulser stung him mercilessly, confusing him for the instant
which to reach for first. He shut the pulser down, keyed in
the mike, leaning forward. "You have come in at velocity

above limit. Consult regulations regarding Pell operational restrictions, section 2, number 22. This is live transmission. Further instruction assumes you have brought your speed within tolerance and keep to lane. If otherwise, patrol will be moving on intercept and your time is limited to make appropriate response. Query why this approach? Identify immediately . . . We are now picking up your initial dump, *Lucy*. Please confirm ID and make all appropriate response."

It was all ancient chatter, from the moment of station's reception of his entry, the running monologue of lightbound com that assumed he would have begun talkback much, much earlier.

"We don't pick up voice, *Lucy*. Query why silence."

He reached lethargically for the com and punched in, frightened in this pricklishness on station's part. "This is Stevens' *Lucy* inbound on 4579 your zenith on buoy assigned lane. I confirm your contact, Pell central. Had a little com trouble." This was a transparent lie, standard for any ship illicitly out of contact. "Please acknowledge reception." In his ear, Pell was still talking, constant flow now, telling him what it perceived so that he would know where he was on the timeline. "Appreciate your distress, Pell central. This is Stevens talking, of Stevens' *Lucy*, merchanter of Wyatt's Star Combine, US 48-335 Y. Had a scare on entry, minor malfunction, put me out of contact a moment. I'm all right now. Had a backup engaged, no further difficulty. Please give approach and docking instructions. I'm solo on this run and wanting a sleepover, Pell central. I appreciate your assistance. Over."

Communication from Pell ran on, an overlapping jabber now, as the com board gave up trying to compress it and created two flows that would drive a sane man mad. He slumped in the seat which embraced him and held his aching bones, unforgiving even in its softest places. He blinked from time to time, kept his eyes open, to make sure the lines on the approach graph matched. He listened for key words out of the com flow, but Pell seemed convinced now that he was honest—still possible, another, dimmer voice insisted in his head, that some patrol ship could pop up out of nowhere, meaning business.

Station op, in the long hours, began to send him questions and instructions. He was on the verge of hallucinating. Once station queried him sharply, and he woke in a sweat, eyes scanning the instruments wildly, trying to find out where he was, how close—and too close, entering the zone of traffic.

"You all right, *Lucy?*" the voice was asking him. "*Lucy*, what's going on out there?"

"All right," he murmured. "I'm here. Receiving you clear. Say again, Pell central?"

Getting in was nightmare. It was like trying to line up a jump blind drunk. He stared slackjawed at the screens and did the hairbreadth lineup maneuvers on visual alone, which no larger ship could have dared try, but he was far too fuzzed to use comp and read it out, only to take its automated warnings, which never came. He was proud of himself with a manic satisfaction as he made the final touch, like the same drunk successfully walking a straight line: only one beep out of comp in the whole process, and *Lucy* nestled into the lockto dead center.

He was so satisfied he just sat there. Dockside com came on and told him to open his docking ports, and his hands were shaking so violently he had trouble getting the caps off the switches.

"This is Pell customs and dock security," another voice came through. "Have your papers ready for inspection."

He reached for com. "Pell customs, this is Stevens of *Lucy*. We've come in without cargo due to a scheduling foulup at Viking. You're welcome to check my holds. I'm Wyatt's Star Combine. I'm carrying just ship-consumption goods. Papers are ready." He tried to gather his nerves to face official questions, suddenly recalled the gold stored in a drop panel in the aftmost hold, and his stomach turned over. He reached and opened the docking access in answer to a blinking light and a repeated request from dock crews on the shielded-line channel, and his ears popped from the slight pressure change as the hatch opened. "Sorry, Pell dock control. Didn't mean to miss that adjustment. I'm a little tired."

A pause. "*Lucy*, this is Pell Dock Authority. Are you all right aboard? Do you need medical assistance?"

"Negative, Pell Dock Authority."

"Query why solo?"

He was too muddled to think. "Just limped in, Pell Dock." The fear was back, a knot clenched in the vicinity of his stomach. "This is a hired-crew ship. My last crew met relatives on Viking and ran out on me. I had no choice but to take her out myself; and I couldn't get cargo. I limped in all right, but I'm pretty tired."

There was a long silence. It frightened him as all thoughtful reactions did, and sent a charge of adrenalin through him. "Congratulations, then, *Lucy*. Lucky you got here at all. Any special assistance needed?"

"No, ma'am. Just want a sleepover. Except—is Reilly's *Dublin* at dock? Got a friend I want to find."

"That's affirmative on *Dublin*, *Lucy*. Been in dock two days. Any message?"

"No, I'll find her."

A silence. "Right, *Lucy*. We'll want to talk to you about dock charges, but we can do the paperwork tomorrow if you're willing to leave your ship under Pell Security seal."

"Yes, ma'am. But I need to come by your exchange and arrange credit."

A pause. "That was WSC, *Lucy*?"

"Wyatt's Star, yes, ma'am. A twenty, that's all. Just a drink, a sandwich, and a place to sleep. Want to open an account for WSC at Pell. Transfer of three thousand Union scrip. I can cover it."

Another pause. "No difficulty, *Lucy*. You just leave her open all the way and we'll put our own security on it while customs checks her. What's your Alliance ID?"

Apprehension flooded through him, rapid sort in a tired brain. "Don't have that, Pell Dock. I'm fresh from Unionside."

"Unionside number, then."

"686-543-560-S."

"686-543-560-S. Got you clear, then, *Lucy*, on temporary. Personal name?"

"Stevens. Edward Stevens, owner and captain."

"Luck to you, Stevens, and a pleasant stay."

"Thank you, ma'am." He reached a trembling hand for the board, broke contact and shut down everything, put a lock on comp and on the log; and already in the back of his mind he was calculating, about the gold, about turning that with a little dockside trade, a little deal off the manifest, very quiet, putting the profit into account, making it look right. There were ways. Dealers who would fake a bill. It might be good here. Might be the place he had hoped to find. And *Dublin*. . . .

She was here.

He hauled himself out of the cushion and walked back to the access lift at the side of the lounge, opened the hatch below and got a waft of mortally cold air. He got a jacket from the locker, shrugged it on and patted his coveralls pocket to be sure he had the papers, then committed himself and took the lift down into the accessway, got out facing the short dingy corridor to the lock, and the yellow lighted gullet of the station access tube at the end. He shivered convulsively, zipped his jacket, and walked down and through the tube into the noise of the dock and the thumping of the machinery that was busy blowing out *Lucy*'s small systems.

Customs was there. Police were. A noisy horde of stationers beyond the customs barrier, a crowd, a riot. He stopped in the middle of the access ramp with the customs agents walking toward him—neat men in brown suits with foreign insignia. His expression betrayed shock an instant before he realized it and tried to ignore it all as he fumbled his papers out of his pocket. "I talked with the dockmaster's office," he said, offering them. His heart beat double time as it did at such moments, while the crowd kept up the noise and commotion beyond the barricade. The senior officer looked over the forged papers and stamped them with a seal. "Your office is supposed to put my ship under seal," Sandor went on, trying not to look at the police who waited beyond, trying not to harass the agents at their duty. "Got no cargo this trip. They fouled me up at Viking. I'm bone tired and needing sleep. No crew, no passengers, no arms, no drugs except ship's use pharmaceuticals. I'm headed for the exchange office right now to get some cash."

"Carrying money?"

"Three thousand Union scrip aboard. Not on me. They promised me I could do the exchange papers later. After sleep."

"Items of value on your person?"

"None. Going to a sleepover. Going to get a station card."

"We'll locate you on the card when we want you." The man looked up at him. It was the same face customs folk gave him everywhere, hardly welcoming. Sandor gave it back his best, earnest stare. The man handed the false papers back and Sandor stuffed them into his inside breast pocket, started down the ramp.

The police moved in. "Captain Stevens," one said.

He stopped, his heart jumping against his ribs.

"You'll want to pick up a regulations sheet at the office," the officer said. "Our procedures are a little different here than Unionside. —Did they give you trouble clearing Viking, then?"

He stared, simply blank.

"Lt. Perez," the officer identified himself. "Alliance Security operations. Was it an understandable scheduling error? Or otherwise?"

He shook his head, confused in the crowd noise that echoed in the distant overhead. The question made no sense from a dockside policeman. From Customs. From whatever they were. "I don't know," he said. "I don't know. I'm a marginer. It happens sometimes. Somebody didn't have their papers straight. Or some bigger ship snatched it. I don't know."

The policeman nodded, once and slowly. It looked like dismissal. Sandor turned, hastened on through the barrier and toward the milling crowd, afraid, trying not to walk like a liberty-long drunk and trying to figure out why they chose his section of the dock to gather and what it all was.

"Hey, Captain," someone yelled as he met the crowd, "why did you do it?"

He looked that way, saw no one in particular, cast about again as he pushed his way through. Panic surged in him, wanting out, away from this place. Hands touched him; a camera bobbed over the shoulders of the crowd and he stared into the lens in one dim-witted moment of fright before ducking away from it.

"What route?" someone asked him. "You find some new nullpoint, Captain?"

He shook his head. "Nothing like that. I just came through Wesson's and Tripoint." He kept walking, terrified at the stationers who had come to stare at him. Someone thrust a mike in his face.

"You know the whole station's been following your com for five hours, Captain? Did you know that?"

"No." He stared helplessly, realizing—his face . . . his face recorded, made public, with *Lucy*'s name and number. "I'm tired," he said, but the microphone persisted, thrust toward him.

"You're Captain Edward Stevens, right? From Wyatt's Star? What's the tie with *Dublin*? *She,* you said. Personal?"

"Right." A small voice, a tremulous voice. His knees were shaking. "Excuse me."

"How long have you been out?" The mike followed him, persistent. "You have any special trouble running solo, Captain?"

"A month or so. I don't know. I haven't comped it yet. No. I don't know."

"You're meeting someone of Reilly's *Dublin,* you said."

"I didn't say. It's personal." He hesitated, searched desperately for a way of escape that would get him to the offices. Blue dock. That was where he had to go. Stations were universal in that arrangement, if not in their interiors. He was on green. It could not be far. He tried to recall the docks from years ago—he had been eleven—with Ross and Mitri by him—

"What's her name, Captain? Is there more to it?"

"Excuse me, please. I'm tired. I just want to get to the bank. I didn't do anything."

"You cleared Viking to Pell in a month in a ship that size, solo? What kind of rig is she?"

"Excuse me. Please."

"You don't call what you did remarkable?"

"I call it stupid. Please."

He shoved his way through, with people surging all about him, his heart hammering in panic. People—people as far as he could see. And of a sudden. . . .

She was there. Allison Reilly was straight in front of him, wide-eyed as the rest of the crowd.

He shoved his way past the startled curious and at the last moment kept his hands off her—stood swaying on his feet and seeing the anger on her face.

"You're crazy," she said. "You're outright crazy,"

"I told you I'd see you here. I'm tired. Can we talk . . . when I get back from the bank?"

She took his elbow and guided him through the crowd. The microphone caught up with him again; the newswoman shouted questions he half heard and Allison Reilly ignored them, pulled him across the dock to the line of bars—toward a mass of quieter folk, a line of spacers. Fewer and fewer of the stationer crowd pursued them; and then none: the spacer line closed about them with sullen and forbidding stares turned toward the intruding stationers. He paid no attention then where she aimed him—headed through the dark doorway of a bar and fell into a chair at the nearest available table. He slumped down over his folded arms on the surface

in blessed quiet and tried to come out of it when someone
shook him by the shoulder.

Allison Reilly put a drink into his hand. He sipped at it
and gagged, because he had expected a stiff drink and got
fruit juice and sugar froth. But it was food. It helped, and he
looked up fuzzily into Allison's face while he drank. A ring
of other faces had gathered, male and female, spacers ringing
the table, silver-clad, white, green and gold and motley insystemers, just staring—all manner of patches, all the same
silent observation.

"Sandwich," someone said, and he looked left as a male
hand set a plate in front of him. He disposed of as much of it
as he could in several graceless bites, then stuffed the rest,
napkin-wrapped, into his jacket pocket, a survival habit and
one which suddenly embarrassed him in the face of all these
people who knew what the odds were and what kind of poverty would drive a man to push a ship like that. *Dublin* knew
what he had done. Someone on *Dublin* had talked, and they
knew he had done it straight through, stringing the jumps, the
only way the likes of *Lucy* could possibly have tailed *Dublin*.
They would arrest him soon; someone would talk it over with
some official in station central, and they would start running
checks and talking to merchanters all over this station, some
one of whom might have a memory jogged: his now-notori-
ous ship, his face, his voice carried all over station on open
vid. He could not deal quietly, take that fourteen thousand
gold off the ship, deal as he was accustomed to deal, quietly,
on the docks. Not now. He was dead scared. Allison Reilly
was there, and the look on her face was what he had wanted,
but he was up against the real cost of it now, and he found it
too much.

"Allison," he said, when she sat down in the other chair
and leaned on her arms looking at him, "I want to talk to
you. Somewhere else."

"Come on," she said. "You come with me."

He pushed the chair back and tried to get up . . . needed
her arm when he tried to walk, to keep his balance in station's too-heavy gravity. Some spacer muttered a ribald and
ancient joke, about a man just off a solo run, and it was true,
at least as far as the mind went, but the rest of him was
dead.

He walked, a miserable blur of lights and moving
bodies—the dock's wide echoing chill and light and then a

doorway, a confusion of bizarre wallpaper and a desk and a clerk—a sleepover, a carpeted hall in either direction from here. . . . He leaned on the counter with his head propped on his hand while Allison straightened out the details and the finances. Then she took his arm again and led him down a corridor.

"Keep them out of here," she yelled back at someone, who said all right and left; she carded a door open and put him through, into a sleepover room with a wide white bed.

He turned around then and tried to put his arms around her. She shoved him in the middle of his chest and he nearly fell down. "Idiot," she said to him, which was not the welcome he had hoped for, but what he reckoned now he deserved. He stood there paralyzed in his misery and his mental state until she pulled him over to the bed and pushed him down onto it. She started working at his clothes with rough, abrupt movements as if she were still furious. "Roll over," she hissed at him, and pulled at his shoulder and threw the covers over him.

And he fell asleep.

V

He woke, aware of bare smooth skin next to his own, of a warm arm about him, and turned, blinked in confusion. She was still here, in the room's artificial twilight. "Allison," he said hoarsely, hoarse because his voice like the rest of him was not in the best of form. He stroked her hair and woke her without really meaning to ruin her sleep.

"Huh," she said, looking up at him. "About time." But when he tried with her, there was nothing he could do. He lay there in wretched embarrassment and thinking that at this point she would probably get up and get dressed and walk out of his life forever, about the time he had just spent most of it.

"What could you expect?" she said, and patted his face and took his hand and carried it against her mouth, all of which so bewildered him that he simply lay there staring into her eyes and expecting her to follow that statement with something direly cutting.

She did not. "I'm sorry," he said finally. "I'm really sorry."

"There's tomorrow. A few more days. What are you going to do, Stevens? Is it worth the handful of days you bought with this stunt?"

He thought about it. For a moment he found it even hard to breathe. It really deserved laughing about, the whole situation, because there was something funny in it. He managed at least to shrug. "So, well, maybe. But I think I'm done after this, Reilly. I don't think I can do it again."

"You're absolutely out of your mind."

He found a grin possible, which at least kept up his image. "I don't make a habit of it."

"Why'd you do it?"

"Why not?"

She frowned. Scowled. She shook her head after a moment, got up on her elbow, looking down at him, traced the old scar on his side, a gentle touch. "What are you going to tell your company?"

He lay there, stared at the ceiling with his head on his arms, considered the question and truth and lies, grinned finally and shrugged with what he hoped was monumental unconcern. "I don't know. I'll think of something good."

A fist landed on his ribs. "I'll bet you will. No cargo. No clearance. You jumped out of Viking on the wrong heading. What are they going to *do* to you, Stevens?"

"Actually," he said, "it's a minor problem." He shut his eyes, still with a smile painted on his face and a weariness sitting on his chest that seemed the accumulation of years. "I'll talk my way out of it, never fear." And after a moment: "Why don't we try it again, Reilly? I think it might work."

It did, oddly enough—and that, he thought, lying there with Allison Reilly tangled with him and content, was because he had started thinking again how to con his way through, and about saving his skin and *Lucy*'s, which got his blood moving again, however tired and sore he was. He was remarkably placid in contemplating his ruin, which he figured he could at least postpone until Allison Reilly had put out of Pell Station aboard *Dublin* some few days hence. And there was the gold: he had that. If by some miracle no one had known his face, he might get himself papers, get himself cargo—go back to Voyager without routing through Viking, a chancy set of jumps, then come in with appropriate stamps on his papers to satisfy Viking—if *Dublin* had not reported that message about his change of destination. . . .

He could find out. Allison might know. Would tell him. And maybe, the irrepressible thought occurred to him, he could claim some tie to *Dublin* for the benefit of Pell authorities, use that supposed connection for a reference, at least enough for dock charges. She might do it for him. He thought of that, lying there with her arms about him, in a bed she had paid for, that he might work one remarkable scam and get himself a stake charged to *Dublin*'s account, which would solve all his problems but Viking and, with the gold, get him a real set of papers.

He turned his head and looked at her, into eyes which suddenly opened, dark and deep and warm at the moment; and his gut knotted up at what he was thinking to do, which was to beg; or to cheat her; and neither was palatable. She hugged him close and he fell to kissing her, which was another pleasure he had discovered different with Allison Reilly.

It was hardly fair, he thought, that he himself had fallen into such hands as Allison's, who could con him in ways he had never visited on his most deserving victims. She was having herself a good time, not even maliciously, while he was paying all he had for it.

And it was finished if she knew, in all senses. She might not, even then, turn him in; but she would know . . . and hate him; and that was, at the moment, as bad as station police.

"Actually," he said during a lull, "actually I'll tell you the truth. I'm not in trouble. It's all covered, my shifting to Pell."

"Oh?" She stiffened, leaned back and looked at him. "How?"

"Because I've got an account to shift here. I'm a small enough operator the combine gives me quite a bit of leeway. All they ask is that I make a profit for them. They let me come and go where I can do that. Wyatt's can't be figuring down to the last degree where to have me break off an operation: that's my decision to make. You made Pell sound good. I heard the rumors. And you just tipped the balance."

"Huh." There was a sober look on her face. "Not me at all, was it?"

"I could have taken my time getting here. I wanted to see you. That part's so."

The sober look became a thinking look, a different, colder one. "Well, then, I guess you *will* get out of it all, won't you?"

"I will. No question."

"Huh," she said again. She rolled for the edge of the bed and he caught her wrist, stopping her.

"Where are you going?"

"Can't stay any longer. I have duty."

"What did I say?"

"You didn't say anything. I just have my watch coming up."

"It was something. What was it?"

Her face grew distressed. She jerked at his hand without success. "Let go."

"Not until you tell me what I said."

"If you put a mark on me, Stevens, you'll regret it. You want to think that through?"

"I'm trying to talk to you. I told you the truth."

"I don't think you know the truth from your backside. You didn't tell me the truth and I'll bet you didn't tell it to customs out there."

His heart slammed against his ribs, harder and harder. "So does *Dublin* tell the whole truth to customs? Don't ask me to believe that."

"Sure. I figure there are all kinds of reasons someone would give me one story and customs another; but maybe only one reason a ship would dog us the way you have, and I don't like the smell of it. You never have answered me straight, not once, and I gave you your chance. Now maybe you can break my arm and maybe you even figure you can kill me to shut me up, but, mister, I've got several hundred cousins who know who I'm with and where and you'll find yourself taking a slow voyage on *Dublin* if you don't let me out of here right quick."

"Is *that* why you stayed? To ask questions?"

"What do you expect?"

He stared at her with more pain than he had felt since Ross died, let go her arm so suddenly she almost rolled off her edge of the bed; and she sat there rubbing her wrist and glaring at him. He had no wish to be looked at. "Go on," he said. "I'm not stopping you."

"Don't tell me I've hurt your feelings."

"Impossible. Go on, get out of here and let me sleep."

"It's my room. *I* paid the bill."

That hurt. "I'll take care of it. I'll put the fifty in *Dublin's* account. And the fifty before that. Just take yourself off. No worry about the cash."

"It really looks like it. What are you doing, following us to get me to pay your bar bills? You going to hit me up for finance?"

"I don't charge," he said bitterly. His face burned. "Go on. Out."

She stood up, stalked over, collected her clothes from the chair and started pulling them on—paused, sealing up the silver coveralls, and looked back at him.

"Probably I'd better pay your rent for the week," she said. "I think you've got troubles, Stevens. I think your combine's going to have your head on a platter. You're not going to turn a profit on this."

"Don't bother yourself. I don't want your money and I don't want your help. I'll handle my combine."

"Oh, sure, you're going to explain how it all seemed a good idea at the time. This story's going to be told over and over again, bigger every time it hits another station. How you did it to see me again, how you did it for a bet, how you took out of Viking the wrong direction and triplejumped solo through Tripoint, that you're a Mazianni spotter or a Union spy with a hyped-up ship or an outright thief, and you know how much *Dublin* wants herself mixed into the story? The tale'll get back to Viking without our help. They'll hear it on Wyatt's real early; they'll hear it everywhere ships go . . . because they're all here, every ship, every family, every Name in the Merchanter's Alliance and then some. And Union military's coming in to call. It's going to spread. You understand that?"

He thought about that, with a chill feeling in his stomach. "So, well, then, it looks like I've got a bigger problem than you do, don't I? I'm sure *Dublin*'s going to survive it."

"Bastard."

"You came out on the dock, Reilly. That was your doing. I didn't arrange it."

"I've no doubt you'd have come to *Dublin* asking for me. You used our name over com. What more did it lack?"

"Out."

"You're flat broke, Stevens. Unless you're carrying something under the plates. And they'll look. You're going to get your ship attached. At the least."

"I've got funds."

"*What* have you got?"

"Maybe it's none of your business."

"You don't. Not worth this trip."

"None of your business."

"Huh."

He stared at her, unwilling to fight it out. Watched her walk to the door—and stop. She stood there. Looked back finally, dropping her hand from the door switch. "You tell me," she said, "really why you pulled this."

"Like you said."

"Which?"

"Take your pick. I'm not going to argue the point."

"No. You tell me, Stevens, how you're going to rig this. I really want to know."

He shrugged, sitting up, hooked his arm in the pillows and

propped himself against the headboard. "I told you already what I'm going to do. It's no problem."

"I think you're in bad trouble."

"Nothing I can't solve."

"So I'm flattered I made such an impression on you. But I'm not why you came. What made you?"

He tried a wry smile, reckoning he could hold it. "Well, it seemed reasonable at the time."

"I keep wanting to believe you. And I'm not getting any encouragement."

"I'm used to running solo," he said in a lingering silence. "It's no big deal. I've jumped her alone and I've twojumped. She's good, *Lucy* is. She kept up with your fancy *Dublin*, for sure. I'll tidy it up with WSC when I get back to Viking. I wouldn't mind seeing you, when."

She came back and sat down on the edge of the bed, leaned with her hand on his and looked into his face at too close an interval for comfortable pretenses. "Possibly," she said, "you can claim fatigue and they'll let you out of this. Maybe it was just being out there too long."

"Thanks. I hadn't thought of that one. I'll try it."

"I'd guess you'd better try something. You are in trouble. Aren't you?"

He said nothing.

"Stevens. If it is Stevens . . . How much truth have you told me? At any time?"

"Some."

"About what you are—how about that, for a start?"

He tried to shrug, which was not easy at close quarters. "I'm what I told you."

"You're broke, aren't you? And in a lot of trouble. I think maybe you thought I could finance you. I think maybe that's what this is all about, that you really did come chasing after me—because you've overrun your margin at Viking, haven't you; and maybe your company's going to be asking questions—and now you've got a combine ship where she doesn't belong."

"No."

"No?"

"I said no."

"You know, Stevens, I shouldn't ask this, but it does occur to me that you just may not be combine."

He stared at her, at a frown which was not anger, his hold

on his silence loosened for no good reason, but that she knew—he knew that she knew. She was headed back to her ship, to talk there, for certain.

"Not, are you?"

"No. I'm not. I'm—" His arm went out to stop her from bolting, but that shift had not been to get up, and he was left embarrassed. "Look, WSC never noticed me. I *made* them money. I never cost them a credit. . . ."

"Before now."

"I'll put it back."

"You *are* a pirate."

"*No.*"

"All right. So I wouldn't sit here if I thought that. So you skim. I'm not sure I want to know the details." She heaved a sigh and turned to sit sideways on the bed, slammed her fist into her knee. "Blast."

"What's that?"

"That's wishing I minded my own business. So I know. So I can't do anything about it. I'm not going to. You understand that? It's worth no money to you, whatever you planned to get."

Heat rose to his face. "No. I'll tell you the truth: it was getting tight there. Really tight. So you made me think of Pell, that's all. I figure maybe I've got a chance here."

"Just like that."

"Just like that. That's when I know to move. I feel the currents move and I go. It keeps me alive."

She stood up, thinking about the law: there was that kind of look on her face. Thinking about conscience, one way and the other. About police.

"I'll tell you," he said, and rolled over on his side, searching for his clothes. He located them on the floor and sat up, swung his feet out of bed to dress. "Reilly—I don't like it to go sour like this. I swear to you—any way you like—I know you're worried about it. I don't blame you. But that ship's *mine*. And that's the truth."

"I don't want to listen to this. I'm Helm, you hear me, and I keep my hands clean. We've got our Name, and I swear to you, mister, you crowd me and I'll protect it. I'm sorry for you. And I'll believe what you've told me in the hope that once a day you do tell the truth, and that I don't need to pass the word about you on the docks, but I don't think I want to hear any more about it than I have. And I don't think I'll be meeting you elsewhere. I don't think you'd better plan on that."

"You wait a minute. Just wait a minute." He pulled his clothes on, caught at disadvantage, zipped the plain coveralls and caught his breath and his dignity. "Listen—I'm sorry about that mess on the docks. It was crazy. I never—never intended that. I didn't expect them to be crazy here."

"Pell Operations is always on vid.—You didn't know that. You know how you sounded, coming in? Like a crazy man. Like someone crazy aiming a ship at the station; and then like somebody in trouble . . . it was on the news channel, and thousands of people were punching in on it. Misery, Stevens, it's Pell. Alliance captains are coming in here, big Names, flash ships . . . *Finity's End* and *Little Bear*, one after the other. *Winifred*. Pell folk *know* the Names. And some of these free souls don't take to regulations and some of them have privilege with a capital P. When something comes in like you came—they appreciate style, these Pell stationers. And being stationers they're just a little ignorant about what a stupid move you pulled and what dice you really shot out there at Tripoint. You've got a death wish, Stevens. Deep down somewhere, you're self-destructive; and you scare me. You're trouble. To me. To yourself. To a system full of ships and a station full of innocent people who had the good-heartedness to worry about you after they realized you weren't going to hit *them*. They think you did it on skill. On dockside they think something else. They think you're an ass, Stevens, and I'm embarrassed for you, but I got you in here because I was stuck with you after that scene on the docks; because you at least had the conscience to warn *Dublin* when you risked *our* lives at Viking, and my Old Man called me in on the carpet and looked me right in the eye and asked me what you were. When this liberty's over or before, I'm going to have to go on the carpet again and answer why I got *Dublin* involved with you. And I still don't know."

He stood and took it. It was the truth. It was all the things that had shivered down his backbone when he came in. "I've done the like before," he said in a quiet voice. "I told you that. Sometimes I've had to do it. I've had no choice. I came in high in the range. But I miscalculated myself, not the ship; too long on the dock at Viking, too little sleep, too little

food—I wasn't fit for it; that, I admit to. But the solo runs—
Lucy's not *Dublin*. I bend the regulations. That's how someone like me has to operate. You've got to sleep; you do it on
auto, wherever you are. You're redlighting and you've got to
see to it; and you run on auto. And you have to know that,
even on *Dublin*, you have to know that all those marginers
like me, we're running like that. It's not neat and failsafed. I
thought I could do it. And I did it on luck at the end, and I
should have let you pass me at Viking. I wanted out of there.
If I'd delayed my run when I had a clearance—there were
questions possible. And I went, that's all."

"And the interest in *Dublin*?"

He shrugged, arms folded.

"You make me nervous," she said.

"You. I wanted to see you."

She shook her head uneasily. "Most can wait for that privilege."

"Some don't have that much time."

"What's that supposed to mean?"

A second shrug, less and less comfortable. "I don't stay in
one place very long. And I'll be gone again. I'll stay low till
you go. I think that's about the best thing I can do under the
circumstances. When you pull out, I'll set about getting myself out of this. But no mention of *Dublin*. I promise that."

She stared at him sidelong, a good moment. "I'm not
posted. You understand—my getting involved here—can keep
me from being posted. Ever. It's not a lark, Stevens. It was."
She walked to the door, looked back. "I've got maybe ten
thousand I can lay my hands on. I can maybe keep you clean
here, if you take that and pay your dock charge and clear out
of Pell. Understand me, it's all I can get. I'll be another year
working off the last thousand of it. But I want you off *Dublin*'s record. I don't want you in trouble again until somewhere a long, long way off our trail."

He shook his head, his mouth gone dry. He hurt inside.

"Blast you, there's nothing more you can get."

"I don't want your money. I don't want your help. I'll take
out of here. I can pay the dock charges, and I'll take out."

"With *what*?"

"That three thousand. Maybe I can get a little cargo on the
side. I've got, well, maybe a little more than that."

"How much worth of cargo?"

"That's my business. You answer questions to strangers about *Dublin*'s holds? I'd think not."

She set her jaw. "I want you out of here."

"Tell your Old Man I'm going."

"I'll tell you you're taking the ten thousand. You're going out of Pell with some kind of a load, mine and yours together, that at least looks honest. And you forget the debt. Don't try to pay it. Don't talk about it. Or me. Or I go to station authorities."

"I understand you," he said very quietly. "I'd take your ten. And I'd promise to get it back to you, but I don't think you'd believe it. And it wouldn't be the truth. You're throwing it away, Reilly. I very much doubt I'm going to clear this dock at all."

"Someone here you know?"

"More than likely someone here that knows me. It's the publicity, Reilly. I'm usually a lot quieter."

"What," she asked in a lowered voice, "can they get you for? What's the worst?"

"Bad debts."

"Less than likely any merchanter would go to the police on that score. But something else—"

"I'm not one of the Names. They don't know what I might be. A pirate. They could think that. But I'll tell you the whole truth this time. I've got two thousand cash I'm not declaring. For dockside deals. —And fourteen thousand worth of WSC money in gold under the plates. That's why I ran out of Viking like my tail was afire. —Look, this stationer there, this clerk—I *had* to deal; he could have blown it all. It wasn't my idea. So I have the money. I can pay dock charges and I can deal for cargo."

"With sixteen lousy contraband thousand?"

"You think ten more is going to help? No. And if they catch me, you can believe they're going to inventory everything I've got; and they'd find me with more scrip than I'm supposed to have; and ten thousand in Pell currency, right? One question to comp and they'd have those serial numbers and a ten thousand transaction in your name. Take it from me. I know the routines."

"I'll bet you do."

"So you keep it. Against my problems, it's nothing, that ten. I'll get out of it my way." He picked up his jacket and put it on, checked his papers in his pocket. "I'll go take care of the finance, go to station offices. You just call it quits and go hang out with your cousins and say it's all nothing. Find somebody else to sleepover with and publicize it. Fast. That'll kill it. I know how to cover a trail. That, too."

"I wish you luck," she said, sounding earnest. "You'll need it."

He opened the door for her. Grinned, recovering himself. "Thanks," he said, and walked out, ahead of her in the hall, hands in pockets, a deliberate spring in his step.

Time to visit *Lucy*. Time to go under the eyes of the powers that be on Pell and try to pull it out of the fire. Or at least get some of the heat off. Station offices would unseal her for him if he could eel his way past a customs agent who might want to do a thorough check in his presence.

Then to get out of Pell with as much cash as he could save. Maybe check the black market—there was always that. Change the name and number out at Tripoint, trade black market at the nullpoints and hope no one cut his throat. Buy another set of forged papers. If he could get out with money; and if . . . a thousand things. His mind began to work again more clearly, with Allison Reilly set behind him. With bleak realities plain on the table.

He looked back. She was there, at the door of the sleepover, just watching. A craziness had come on him for a time. Self-destructive: she was right. On the one hand he wanted to survive; and on the other he was tired of trying, and it was harder and harder to think his way through the maze . . . even to recall what lies he had told and how they meshed.

There were troops here too. He saw them . . . a jolt. Not the green or the black of Union forces, but blue. Alliance militia. He recalled the buildup at Viking and the rumors of pirate-hunting and had a presentiment of times changing, of loopholes within which it had been possible for marginers to survive—being tightened, suddenly, and with finality.

He had a record at every station in Union now; and soon a record with the Alliance; and he was almost out of places.

"What happened?" Curran asked, joining her in the shadow of the sleepover doorway, and Allison frowned at the intrusion. "Been there," Curran said with a nod toward the bar next door. "Some of us had a little concern for it . . .

hung around. In case. What's he up to? You know the Old Man's going to ask."

"He's going back to his ship. I'm afraid it's a case of misplaced assumptions. We're quits."

"Allie, they've got a guard out there."

She straightened, dropped her arms from their fold. "What guard?"

"On his ship. That's what's had us upset. We weren't about to break in on you, but we've sure been thinking. That's military, that."

She hissed between her teeth, "More than customs seal?"

"More than customs. They say one of *Mallory*'s officers is on station."

"I heard that."

"Allie, if they haul him in, is there anything he can say he shouldn't?"

"No." She turned a scowl on her cousin, sharp and quick. "Are you making assumptions, Currie me lad? Don't Allie me."

"When our watch senior sleeps over with a man the militia's got their name on . . . we come asking questions. Third Helm has a stake here."

"You don't oversee me."

"That's thanks. —We've backed you. Get back to the ship. We're asking. Now."

She said nothing. Followed the distant figure with her eyes. There was not so much traffic now as mainday. A new set of residents had come out to work and trade in the second half of Pell's nevernight—more industrial traffic than in mainday; passersby wore coveralls more than suits, and traffic on the docks was heavy moving, big mobile sleds hauling canisters, whining their way along through a straggle of partying merchanters.

And troops.

And others. Pell orbited a living world. Natives worked on the station, small and furtive, wearing breather-masks that hissed when they breathed. They were brown-furred and primate . . . moved softly on callused bare feet. And watched, two of them perched on the canisters stacked nearest *Lucy*'s dock. She made out another of them near the security rail. They moved suddenly, took themselves elsewhere, a vanishing of shadows.

She shook her head slowly, took Curran by the arm and saw

the rest of her watch standing by, Deirdre and Neill. "Back," she said.

"He got a gun?"

"No," she said. "That, I know for sure. But we've no need to be bystanders, do we?"

VI

The customs seal was still in effect, *Lucy*'s access presenting deep shadow, a closed hatch where other ships had a cheerful yellow lighted access tube open. No lights here, only the customs barrier still in place, and grim dark metal of an idle gantry beyond—no cargo for *Lucy*, to be sure, but the abundant canisters of the ship in the next berth, which had been offloading, a busy whine of conveyers, a belt empty now, while they sorted out some snarl inside, perhaps. Native workers hovered about, idle . . . alien life, persistent reminder of possibilities. Man had found nothing else, but the quiet, avowedly gentle Downers of Pell.

It was perhaps out there, a star or two away. It might happen in his lifetime, some merchanter, disgruntled with things as they were, diverting his ship off to probe the deep . . . but the finding of nullpoints took probes, and probes took finance, and *Lucy* could never do it. Every route, everything that was settled in the Beyond rode that kind of maybe, that maybe this year . . . maybe someone . . . Sandor took some perverse comfort in that, that no one's prerogatives were that secure.

This running gnawed at him. And it was rout, this time. He was a contamination, a hazard. He thought about Allison Reilly and knew it for the truth, the things she had said.

Maybe he should have taken the money. Or anything else he could get.

He walked along the line of canisters, saw nothing out of the way—Downers peered down at him from a perch atop the cans, suddenly scampered out of sight. He looked about him, walked the shadows closer and closer to the access. *Lucy* was not a large problem for customs, nothing that deserved as much fuss as his anxiety painted. Likely—he earnestly hoped—they had gotten some junior agent to suit up and walk through the holds to check out his claim that they were empty. The plates under which the gold was hidden were inconspicuous in hundreds of other like places, in the empty cavern of the badly lighted hold. They had looked, that was all, gone offshift—it was alterday.

He walked around the bending of the huge can-stacks, came face to face with blue uniformed militia, two grim-faced men. Blinked, caught off balance for the moment, then shrugged and strolled the other way, suddenly out of the notion to prowl about the customs barrier.

So. Too many troops, everywhere. Viking, and here. He shifted his shoulders, persuaded his frayed nerves to calm. Better to go to the offices, get it settled up there and not go try security out here. He walked lightly still, the more so when he had gotten the shock out of his system, tucked his hands into his pockets and looked about him as he walked, anonymous again, among the passing mobile sleds, the pass-ersby that were mostly spacers or dockworkers—flinched once when a knot of stationers pointed at him and talked among themselves. But the mainday crowds were gone: the stationers who had seen his face on vid and gathered on the dock were decently in their beds, with the alterday shift awake. No one troubled him. He sealed off the experience back there, sealed off the nightmare of the docking, sealed off too the sleepover with Allison Reilly, getting himself focused again, sorting his wits into order. He might be on any station, at any year of his adult life. He had done the like over and over. His knees still felt like rubber, but that was hunger: he fished up the crushed sandwich out of his pocket—a prudent idea, that, after all; and that was his breakfast, dry, pocket-squelched mouthfuls while he walked the edge of the loading zones and headed for blue dock and the offices.

The Combine had me carry the gold in case, sir—personal funds, no, sir, not transporting for general trade. He started composing his arguments in advance, against every eventuality they might haul up. The unsettled state of affairs, sir, the military—

No. Maybe not such a good idea to invoke that particular reason unless he had to. Unsettled state of affairs was close enough.

And with luck, they had not found the cache in the hold at all; with luck, he could pay his dock charges and get out of here with some show of trying to arrange cargo. Best not to contact the black market here: they were likely to check him closer going out than coming in. But he could change *Lucy*'s name again, out at Tripoint—could risk a blown ship or a cut throat and do some nullpoint trading, sans customs, sans police, lying off at some place like Wesson's and waiting for some ship that might be willing to trade with a freelancer, and better yet, some other marginer who might deal in forged paper. Risky business. Riskier still . . . with the military stirring about. An operation to tighten loopholes in which piracy was possible—also tightened loopholes in which marginers survived.

Union and Alliance in cooperation. He had never foreseen that.

He swallowed the last of the dry sandwich, wadded the wrapper and thrust it back into his pocket, spacer's reflex. The section seal was ahead, the office section, the military dock where militia were even more in evidence. He watched the overhead signs to find his way, finally located the customs office adjunct to the Dock Authority, halfway down the dock, and walked through the door. It was getting close to mainday. A line of applicants stood inside, spacers and ships' officers with their own difficulties. A sign advised a separate window, a different procedure for ship clearance.

He fished his papers out of his pocket and presented them at the appropriate window, and the young woman looked him in the eyes and glanced down again at the ID and *Lucy*'s faked papers. "Captain Stevens. There's a call in for you."

It started his heart to pounding; any anomaly would, in places such as this. "What ship?"

"Just a moment, sir." She left the counter, took the papers with her. Terror verged on panic. He would have bolted, perhaps, with the papers—

No. He would not. With the security seal on *Lucy* there was no way. A long counter, a bored clutch of clerks and business as usual, separated him from his title to *Lucy*, and making a row about it would draw attention. He leaned there, locked his hands on the counter to brace himself in his studied weariness and exasperation, hoping, still dimly hoping, that it was Allison Reilly with a parting message—(but she would not, never would, wanting no connection with him)—and they would give him his papers back and unlock his hatch for him. He cursed himself for ever agreeing to that seal; but he had been tired, his mind had been on Allison Reilly and his wits were not what they had been.

The official came back. His heart leapt up again. He leaned there trying to look put upon. "I'm really pretty tired," he said. "I'd like to get that message later if I could." That was what he should have said in the first place. That he finally thought of it encouraged him. But she looked beyond his shoulder at someone who had come up behind him, and that little shift of the eyes warned him. He turned about, facing station police.

It was not the scenario he had planned—his back to a customs counter, an office full of people who had no involvement in the situation; no gun in his pocket, *Lucy's* papers in someone else's possession, his ship locked against him. "Captain Stevens," the policeman said. "Dockmaster wants to see you."

Perhaps his face was white. He felt himself sweating. "It's alterday."

"Yes, sir. Will you come?"

"Is something out of order?"

"I don't know, sir. I'm just asked to bring you to the offices."

"Well, look, I'll get up there in a minute. I need to settle something here with customs."

"My orders are to bring you now. If you would, sir."

"Look, they've got my papers tangled up here.—Ma'am, if I could have my papers back—" He turned belly to the counter again, expecting a heavy hand and cuffs on the instant. He tried, all the same, and the woman handed him the papers, which he started to put into his inside breast pocket. The officer stopped that reach with a grip on his wrist, patted his coat with a small deft movement even those standing closest might have missed, patted the other two pockets as well. "That's all right, sir," the officer said. "If you'll come along now."

He put the papers in his pocket, left the counter and went. The policeman laid no hand on him, simply walked beside him. But there was no escaping on Pell.

"This way." The officer showed him not to the main elevators in the niner corridor, but to a service elevator on the dock. Other police waited there, holding the door open.

"I think I have a right to know what this is about," Sandor protested, not sure that Union rights applied here at all, this side of the Line.

"We don't know," the officer in charge said, and put him into the lift with the other police, closed the door behind. "Sir."

The lift whisked them up with a knee-buckling force, two, four, six, eight levels. Sandor put his hands toward his pockets, nervous habit, remembered and did it anyway, carefully. The door opened and let them out into a carpeted corridor, and one of the police took a scanner from his belt and took him by the arm, holding him still while he ran the detector over him. Another finished the job, waist to feet.

"That's fine," the officer said then, letting him go. "Pardon, sir."

Maybe he had rights this violated. He was not sure. He let them take his arm and guide him down the corridor, a corporation kind of hall, carpeted in natural fiber, with bizarre carvings on the walls. The place daunted him, being full of wealth, and somewhere so far from *Lucy* he had no idea how to get back. Perhaps it was the shock of the strung-together jumps he had made getting here; maybe it was something else. His mind was not working as it ought; or it lacked possibilities to work on. His hands and feet chilled as if he were operating in a kind of shock. He was threadbare and shabby and as out of place here as he would be in *Dublin*'s fine corridors. Lost. There was money here that normally ignored nuisances his size, and somehow the thought of arguing a three thousand credit account in a place like this that dealt in millions—

One of the police strode ahead and opened a door with a key card, let them into an office where a militia guard stood with a large, ugly gun at his side; and two more station security officers, and a man at a desk who might be a secretary or a clerk.

"Go on in," that one said, and pushed a button at the desk console. The militiaman opened the farther door and Sandor hesitated when the police did not bid to move. "Go on," the officer said, and he went, far from confident, down an entry corridor into a large room with a U-shaped table.

All its places were filled, mostly by stationers silver-haired with rejuv; but there were exceptions. The woman centermost was one, a handsome woman in an expensive green suit; and next to her was another, a militia officer in blue, a pale blond man with bleak pale eyes.

"Papers," the woman in the center said. He reached into his pocket and handed them to a security agent on duty in the room, who walked to the head of the U and handed them to her. She unfolded them in front of her and gave them a cursory scrutiny.

"Why am I here?" Sandor ventured, not loud, not aggressive. But it had never seemed good to back up much either. "They just asked me to come up here. They didn't say why."

She passed the papers to the militia officer beside her. She looked up again, hands folded in front of her. "Elene Quen-Konstantin," she identified herself, "dockmaster of Pell." And he recalled then what was told about this woman, who had defied a Union fleet. He swallowed his bluffs unspoken, taking her measure. "There's been some question about your operation, Captain Stevens. We're understandably a little anxious here. We have statements by some merchanters that you're under ban at Mariner, under a different name. On unspecified charges. This is hearsay. You don't have to answer the questions. But we're going to have to run a check. We're quite careful here. We have to be, under circumstances I'm sure I don't have to lay out for you. Your combine will be reimbursed for any unwarranted delays and likewise your housing and your dock charges will be at Pell's expense during the inquiry. Unless, of course, something should turn up to substantiate the charges."

It took a great deal to keep his knees steady. "There ought to be something a little more than hearsay for an impoundment. And the damage to my reputation—what repairs that?"

"This is Alliance space, Captain. You're not in Union territory any longer. Alliance sovereignty. You came here of your own decision, without a visa, which we allow. But you have to have one to operate here. I'm personally sorry for the inconvenience, and I assure you Pell's inquiry will be brief, three days at maximum. There are several merchanters in from Mariner. We'll be talking to them. You have a right to know that the investigation is proceeding and to confront complainants and witnesses whose testimony is filed to your detriment. You have a right to counsel; this will be billed to your combine, but should the charges prove false, as I said, Pell will stand good for the—"

"I don't have that kind of operation." Panic crept into his

voice. It was in no wise acting. "I'm an independent under Wyatt's umbrella. I pay all my own costs and I'm barely making it as it is. This is going to ruin me. I can't afford the time, not even a few days. That comes out of the little profit I do make, and you're going to push me right over into the loss column. They'll attach my ship—"

"Captain Stevens, if you'd allow me to finish."

"This is something trumped up by some other marginer who doesn't want my competition."

"Captain, this is not the hearing. You have a right to counsel before making statements and countercharges and I would advise you to be careful. There are penalties for libel and malicious accusation, and the ship making charges against you will likewise be detained, likewise be liable for damages if the accusation is proved malicious."

"And where do I get counsel? I haven't got the funds. Just company funds. What am I supposed to do?"

Quen looked down the table to her left. Someone nodded. "Legal Affairs will help you select a lawyer."

"And prosecute me too?"

"Captain, Pell is the only world in Alliance territory . . . unless you want a change of venue to Earth itself. Or extradition to Mariner. At your hearing you can make either request. But your appointed defender should make it only after you've had a chance to consider all the points of the matter. I repeat, this is not the hearing. This is only your formal advisement that allegations have been made, of general character and as yet undefined, but of sufficient concern to this station to warrant further investigation. Particularly since you are Union registry, since you're not familiar with Alliance law, I do suggest you refrain from comment until you have a lawyer."

"I'm not one of your citizens."

"Presumably you're seeking Alliance registry, which is the only way you can trade here. Now on the one hand, you'll be seeking to prove the charges false; and on the other, if they are proved false, if your record is established, then your registry would be a matter of form. So if there's really no problem, it should after all save you time you might spend waiting for forms and technicalities, and I might add, at station expense. If you hoped to clear all your papers and get cargo in a three-day stopover under normal circumstances, Captain, I'm afraid you were misled."

"If it's processed *in* that time and not after it—" He played for conciliation, took an easier stance, felt a line of sweat running down his face all the same.

"Quite so. I assure you it will be simultaneous."

"I appreciate it." He folded his hands behind him and tried to look comforted. He felt sick. "Where am I supposed to stay, then? I'd like to have access to my ship."

"Not yet."

"Accommodations dockside, then?"

"At any B class lodging."

"Captain." That from the militia officer. The voice drew his eyes in that direction. The blue uniform—was wrong somehow. Foreign. He was not used to foreignness. He had never imagined any current military force outside Union, which was all of civilization. The emblem was a sunburst on the sleeve, and several black bands about the cuff. "Commander Josh Talley, Alliance Forces. Officially—why *are* you here?"

"Trade."

"For what?"

"Is that," Sandor asked, looking back at Quen, "one of the things I should wait for a lawyer to answer? I don't see I have to make my business public."

"You're not obliged to answer. Use your own discretion."

He thought about it—looked back at Talley: a precise, military bearing, cold and clean, with a hardness unlike any merchanter he had ever seen. The eyes rested on him, unvarying, virtually unblinking, making him uneasy. "For the record," he said, "I get some latitude from my combine. I was on the Viking-Fargone run. It never paid; and I thought maybe I could widen my operation a little, set up an account here and do better on a cross-Line run . . . my discretion. I have a margin to operate in. I moved it. Am moving it."

"How much margin, Captain? Three thousand, as you claimed? And you look to compete with larger, faster ships? We're interested in the economics of your operation. What do you haul, when you can get cargo? Small items—of high value and low mass?"

Suddenly the room was all too close and the air unbearably warm. "I couldn't do much worse than where I was, that was all. Yes, I haul things like that. Station surplus. Package mail. Licensed pharmaceuticals. All clean stuff. Dried foods. Sometimes I carry passengers who aren't in a hurry and can't afford better. I'm slow, yes."

"And WSC has interest in a Pell base of operations?"

He weighed his answer, trying to remember what he might have said over the com when he was accounting for himself coming in. "Sir, I told you—my own risk. I figured I could get some station cargo. I heard it was good here."

"Captain, I know something about Union law. The legal liabilities and the risks of your operation don't leave much room for profit; and it seems to me very doubtful that your combine would leave a step like yours to an independent."

"It's not a company move. It's a simple shift of a margin account." He grew desperate, tried to make it sound like indignation. "I never violated the law and I came here in good faith. There's no regulation against it on Unionside."

"Financial arrangements on both sides of the line have been—loose, true. And you fall into a peculiar category. I perceive you're an excellent dockside lawyer. Most marginers are. And I'd reckon if your log and ledgers are put under subpoena . . . we'll find they don't exist, in spite of regulations to the contrary. In fact you'll keep no more records than the Mazianni do. In fact it's very difficult to tell a marginer from that category of ship—by the quality of the records they keep. What do you say, Captain? Could that account for your economics in a cross-Line run?"

If ever in his life he would have collapsed in fright it would have been then, under that quiet, precise voice, that very steady stare. His heart slammed against his ribs so hard it affected his breathing. "I'd say, sir, that I'm no pirate, and having lost my family to the Mazianni, I don't take the comparison kindly."

The eyes never flinched, never showed apology. "Still, there is no apparent difference."

"*Lucy* doesn't carry arms enough to defend herself." His voice rose. He choked it down to a conversational tone as quickly, refusing to lose control. "You admit she can't make speed. How is she supposed to be a pirate?"

"A Mazianni carrier could hardly pull up to a station for trade and conversation. But there *is* a means by which the Mazianni are trading with stations, in which they do scout out an area and the ships trading in it, mark the fat ones, and pick them off in the Between. Marginers undoubtedly figure in that picture, trading in the nullpoints, picking up cargo, faking customs stamps. Would you know any ships like that?"

"No, sir."

"She moves fast when she's empty, your *Lucy*."

"You can inspect her rig—"

"We have an unusual degree of concern here. The allegations made against you include a possible charge of piracy."

"That's not true."

"We advise you that the Alliance Fleet is making its own investigation, apart from Pell Dock Authority. That investigation will take longer than three days. In fact, it will be ongoing, and it involves a general warrant, along with a profile of your ship and its internal identification numbers, a retinal print and voice print, which we'll take before you return to dockside, and all this will be passed to Wyatt's Star Combine and Mariner through diplomatic and military channels. Should it later prove necessary, that description will be passed to all ports, both Union and Alliance, present and future. But you won't be detained on our account, once that printing has been done."

"And what if I'm innocent? What kind of trouble am I left with? That kind of thing could get me killed somewhere, for nothing, some stupid clerk punching the wrong key and bringing that up, some ship meeting me at a nullpoint and pulling that out of library—you're setting me up for a target." He cast a desperate look at Quen. "Can I appeal it? Have I got a choice?"

"Military operations," Talley said, "are not under civil court. You can protest, through application to Alliance Council, or through a military court. Both are available here at Pell, although the Council has finished its quarterly business and it's in the process of dispersing as ships leave. You'd have to appeal for a hearing at the next sitting, about three months from now. Military court could be available inside a month. You'd be detained pending either procedure, but counsel will be provided, along with lodging and dock charges, if you want to exercise that right. And you can apply for extensions of time if you need to call witnesses. Counsel would do that for you."

"I'll see what counsel says."

"That would be wise," Quen said. An aide had come in, padded round the outside of the U and slipped a paper under her hands. She read it and spoke quietly to the messenger, folded her hands over the paper on the table as the messenger slipped out again. "There is an intervenor in the case, Captain Stevens, if you're willing to accept."

"I don't understand."

"Reilly of *Dublin Again* has offered his onboard legal counsel. This would be acceptable to Pell."

The blood drained toward his feet. "Am I free to make up my own mind in the matter?"

"Absolutely."

"I'd like to talk to them."

"I think our business with you is done, pending your appointment with the military identification process."

"But maybe I don't want to go through that. Maybe—" He stared into a row of adamant faces. Stopped.

"Captain," Talley said, "you have your rights to resist it. The military has its rights to detain you. Your counsel can interview you in detention and advise you. If you wish."

He thought of jails, of a Dubliner arriving to fetch him out, one of Allison's hard-eyed cousins. "No," he said. "I'll go along with the ID."

"That ought to do it, then," Quen said, and looked aside at Talley. Talley nodded, once and economically. "Sufficient, then," Quen said. "Our hopes, Captain Stevens, that there's nothing but a mistake involved here. You're free to address the board in general. We'll listen. But I'd advise selecting your attorney before you do that. And prepare your statements with counsel's advice."

"I'll reserve that, then."

"Captain," Talley said, "if you'd go with the officer."

"Sir," he said, quietly, precisely. "Ma'am." He turned and walked out with the security officer, through the outer office and into the hall, trying in his confusion to remember where he was and which way the lift was and to reckon where he was being taken now. He was lost; he was panicked, inside corridors which were not *Lucy*'s, a geometry which was not the simple circle of dockside.

There was a small office down the corridor, two desks, a counter full of equipment. He stood, waited: a technician in militia blue showed up. "General ID," the officer said, and the tech took him in charge, walked him through it, one procedure and the next, even to a cell sample.

It was done then, irrevocable. The information was launched, and they would send it on. The tech gave him a cup of cold water, urged him to sit down. "No," he said. Maybe it was the look of him that won the sympathy. He failed at unconcern—looked back at the officer who had acquired a companion.

"Your party's waiting for you," the second officer said, "out by the lift."

Allison, he thought, at a new ebb of his affairs. He should have accepted jail; should have refused the typing. He had fouled things up. But confinement—being shut up in a cell for Dubliners to stare at—being shut inside narrow station walls, in places he knew nothing about—

The officer indicated the door, opened it for him, pointed down the hall to the left. "Around the corner and down."

He went, turned the corner—stopped at the sight of the silver-coveralled figure standing by the lift, a man he had never met.

But Dubliner. He walked on, and the dark-haired young man gave him no welcome but a cold stare. C. REILLY, the pocket said, on a broad and powerful chest. "Curran Reilly," the Dubliner said.

"Where's Allison?"

"None of your business. You're through getting into trouble, man. Hear me?"

"I'm headed down to the exchange. I'm not looking for any."

"You hold it." An arm shot out, blocking his arm from the lift call button. "You got any enemies in port, Stevens?"

"No," he said, resisting the impulse to swing. "None that I know about. What's your percentage in it?"

Curran Reilly reached in his coveralls pocket and pulled out several credit chits, thrust them on him and he took them on reflex. "You take this, go get breakfast, book into the same sleepover as last night. You don't go to the exchange. You don't go near station offices. You don't sign anything you haven't signed already."

"I've been printed."

"A great help. Really great."

He thrust the credits back. "Keep your handout. I've got my own funds."

"The blazes you have. Shut your mouth. You go to that

sleepover and stay there and that bar next door. We want to know right where to find you. We don't want any complications and we don't want anything else stupid on your part. Keep that money and don't try to touch what you arrived with. You've got enough troubles."

He stared into black and angry eyes, smothered his own temper, afraid to walk away. "So how do I find the place? I'm lost."

The Dubliner reached and pushed buttons on the lift call. "I'll get you there."

"Where's Allison?"

"Don't press your luck, mister."

"That's Captain, and I'm asking where Allison is. Is she in trouble?"

"Captain." The Dubliner hissed, half a laugh, and the scowl darkened. "Her business is her business and none of yours, I'm telling you. She's working to save your hide, and I'm not here because I like the company."

"She's not spending any money—"

"You've got one track in your mind, haven't you, man? Money. You're a precious dockside whore."

"Go—"

"Shut your mouth. You take our charity and you'll do as you're told." The car arrived and the door whipped open. The Dubliner held it for him and he got in, with rage half blinding him to anything but the glare of lights and the realization that they were not alone in the car. Curran Reilly stepped in: the door shut and the car shot away with them. A pair of young girls stood against the rail on the far side of the car; an old man in the front corner. Sandor put his hands in his pockets and felt the Reilly money in his left with the sandwich wrapper, with the adrenalin pulsing in him and Curran Reilly standing there like a statue at his right. The girls whispered behind their hands. Laughed in adolescent insecurity. "It's *him*," he heard, and he kept staring straight ahead, an edge of raw terror getting through the anger, because his face was known—everywhere. And he had to swallow whatever the Dubliner said and did because there was no other hope but that.

If the Reillys were not themselves plotting revenge, for the stain on their Name.

A long, slow trip on *Dublin*, Allison had warned him, if he crossed her cousins. Revenge might recover *Dublin*'s sullied Name, when the word passed on docksides after that.

But he went where he was told. He knew well enough what station justice offered.

VII

It was executive council on *Dublin*, and to be the center-piece of such a meeting was no comfortable position. Seventy-six of the posted and the retired crew . . . and the Old Man himself sitting in the center seat of the table of captains which faced the rest of the room: Michael Reilly, gray-haired with rejuv and frozen somewhere the biological near side of forty. Ma'am was in the first row after the Helm seats, in that first huge lounge behind the bridge that was the posteds lounge when it was not being the council room. And with Ma'am was the rest of Com; and Scan on the other side of the aisle, behind the rest of Helm, and that was Megan and Geoff and others. Allison sat with impassive calm, hands folded, trying to look easy in the face of all the power of *Dublin*, all the array of her mother and aunts and grandmother and cousins once and several times removed. She was all too conscious of Curran's empty seat beside hers, Helm 22; and Deirdre missing from 23; and Neill sitting in 24 and trying to look as innocent as she. The Old Man and the other captains had a nest of papers on the long table in front of them. She knew most of the content of them well enough. Some of it she did not, and that worried her.

The Old Man beckoned, and Will, who was the senior lawyer in the family, came up to the table and bent over there and talked a while to the captains in general. Heads nodded, lips pursed, a long slow conversation, and not a paper shuffled elsewhere in the room. The rest of the council listened, eavesdropping; and words fell out like *papers* and *liability*; and *piracy*, and *Union forces*.

Will went back to his seat then, and the board of captains straightened its papers while Allison tried not to clench her hands. Her gut was knotted up; and somewhere at her back was her mother, who had to be feeling something mortal at her daughter's insanity. People never quit their ships. Kin

87

stayed together, lifelong; and daughters and sons were there, forever. There was Connie left, to be sure—Connie, waiting elsewhere, not posted, and not entitled here. There were friends and cousins, Megan's support at a time like this. Allison was numb, convinced that she was committing a betrayal of more than one kind—and still there was no more stopping it than she could stop breathing. Win or lose, she was marked by the attempt.

"Your entire watch," the Old Man said, "21, isn't represented here."

"Sir," she said quietly, "they're settling a situation involving *Lucy*. Before it gets out of hand."

"I'll refrain from comment," the Old Man said. "Mercifully."

"Yes, sir."

"I'm going to approve the request for financing. Contingent on the rest of your watch applying for this transfer as you represent."

"Yes, sir." A wave of cold and relief went through her. "Thank you, sir."

"You've phrased this as a temporary tour."

"Yes, sir."

"You'll retain your status then. Your watch in Helm will not be vacated."

"Yes, sir," she said. That was the risk they had run. Council supported them, then. "Thank you for the others, sir."

"I'll be talking to you," the Old Man said. "Privately. Now. Council's dismissed. Come to the bridge."

"Sir," she said very softly, and caught Neill's eye, two vacant seats removed, as others began to rise—Neill, whose brow was broken out in sweat. He gave her a nod. She got up, looked back across the rows of chairs for Megan and Geoff, and met her mother's stare as if there were no one else in the room for the moment. Her mother nodded slowly, and it sent a wave of anguish through her, that small gesture: it was all right; it was—if not understood—accepted. *Thank you*, she said: her mother lipread. Then she turned away toward the forward door the Old Man had taken, which led down the corridor to the bridge.

Little was working . . . in this heart of hearts of *Dublin*, most of the boards dark and shut down. Most of the work they did now besides monitor was connected to the cargo facility and to the com links with station. The Old Man had taken his seat in his chair among the rows and rows of dormant instruments and controls, with the few on-duty crew working in the far distance forward on the huge bridge. She went up to that post like a petitioner going to the throne, that great gimballed black chair in the pit which oversaw anything the captain wanted to look at. Anywhere. Instantly.

"Sir," she said.

The Old Man stared at her—white-haired and powerful and young/old with rejuv that took away more hope than it gave . . . for the ambitious young.

"Allison." Not Allie; Allison. She was always that with him. He rested his elbows on the arms of the chair and locked his hands on his middle. "You'll be interested to know that it's all stalled off. *Dancer*'s the ship that made the complaint. I've talked to their Old Lady. Says she doesn't have anything personal involved, and there hasn't been word of other witnesses. I take it you're still set on this."

"Yes, sir." Soft and careful. "By your leave, sir."

He stared at her with that humorless and unflappable calm that came of being what he was. "Sit down. Let's talk about this."

She had never sat in the Old Man's presence, not called in like this. She looked nervously to her left, where a small black cushion edged the main vid console, there for that purpose. She settled, hands on her knees, eye to eye with Michael Reilly.

"Applying to take a tour off *Dublin*," the Old Man said. "Applying for finance into the bargain. Let me see if I can quote your application: 'a foot in Pell's doorway, a legitimate Alliance operation . . . outweighing other disadvantages.' You know where the sequence of command falls, 21, if we buy into another ship. Could that possibly have occurred to you?"

"I know that council could have voted it down, and Second Helm approved."

"If I thought you were the mooncalf dockside paints you, I'd give you the standard lecture, how a transfer is a major step, how strange it can be, on another ship, away from everything you know, taking orders from another command and coping with being different in a crew that—however

friendly—isn't yours. But no. I know what you're in love
with. I know what you're doing. And I'm not sure you do."

"There's worse can happen to him than *Dublin*'s backing."

"Is there? You look at your own soul, Allison Reilly, and
you tell me what you'd do and what you're buying into. You
come making requests we should throw our Name behind a
ne'er-do-well marginer, we should stop a complaint an honest
ship has filed—all of that. And I'll remind you of something
you've heard all your life. That every Dubliner is born with
one free judgment call. Always . . . just one. Once, you've
got the right to yell trouble on the docks and have the Old
Man blow the siren and bring down every mother's son and
daughter of us. And every time you do it right, that buys you
only one more guaranteed judgment call. No Dubliner I can
think of has taken much more on himself than you. You
know that?"

"I know that, sir."

"And you apply to keep your status."

"To guarantee the loan, sir, begging your pardon."

"Not so pure, 21."

"Not altogether, no, sir."

"You're jumping over the line of succession; you're ignoring the claims your seniors might make ahead of you, if we
bought that ship outright. Alterday command right off, isn't
it, and not waiting the rest of your life without posting. It's a
maneuver and every one of us knows it. It's a bald-faced con-
niving maneuver that oversets those with more right, and
you're doing it on a technicality. And how do I answer that?"

Her heart was beating more than fast, and heat flooded her
face. "I'd say they voted and passed it, sir. I'd say they have
the same chance I'm taking, and there's dozens more marginers like *Lucy*. Maybe they don't want to take that kind of
chance; and maybe they don't want it that bad. I do. Those
with me do. Third Helm's alterday watch—has stayed unitary
blamed long, sir; and begging your pardon, sir, it functions."

"It functions," Michael Reilly said, looking into her eyes
with eyes that missed nothing, "because they've got one
bastard of a number one who's been number one in her
watch too long, who's infected with godhood and who finds
the stage too small."

"Sir—"

"Let me tell you about smallness, 21. That ship you're going to is small. There's no privacy, no amenities. No luxuries. No safeties and no relief and no backup."

"Better to reign in hell—"

"Yes. I thought so. And what about this Stevens?"

"He's better off with us."

"Is he?"

"Than being beached here with Pell owning his ship, yes, sir."

The Old Man nodded slowly. "He'll thank you—about that far. And what will you assign him—when you've got his ship?"

"That becomes a council problem, sir, as I believe."

"Let me tell you something, young ma'am." Michael Reilly leaned forward and jabbed a forefinger at her. "That lies in your watch. Don't you hand it to council to settle. Clear?"

"Clear, sir."

"So." He turned to the console beside him, searched among the papers there, powered the chair back around again and offered her a handful of them. "There's a communication from *Dancer*. They'll withdraw the charge without protest. Understandable nervousness on their part . . . finding a ship in port they know isn't clean. But that's no hide off them, if we guarantee it's been taken thoroughly in hand. The word's gone out by runner: no one else will file a complaint on that ship without going through *Dublin* first, and they've had an hour now to think it over. Something would have come in if it was going to, so I tend to agree with your judgment, that it's a financial problem the man has, no merchanter grudge. So he's clear in that respect. About the military, *that* inquiry can't be stopped; and that's going to be another problem that lies in your watch."

"Yes, sir."

"There's a voucher that will pay the dock charge; and a document of show-cause from Will that's going to clear up the matter with Pell Dock Authority. They'll have to come up with an official complaint with witnesses or drop the charge on the spot and free up the ship, and since *Dancer*'s not going to stand behind the charge, it's going to die. So *Lucy*'s cleared, at least on civil charges. There's the loan agreement, for dock charges and cargo; and whatever else is reasonable in the way of outfitting. Do it proper, if you're going to rig out; no need economizing. And you remember what I told you. You come between somebody and his ship, you take that from him, and you know, in your heart of hearts you know what you're doing. And we know. And he will. You remember that. You remember your Name, and you remember who you are."

"Yes, sir," she said softly.

"Dismissed."

She took the precious papers, stood up, nodded in respect and walked for the door—stopped for a moment, a look back at the bridge, the spacious, modern bridge of *Dublin*, the real thing that she had desired all her life. A knot swelled up in her throat, a final anger, that there was no hope of this—that it had to be the sordid, aged likes of *Lucy*, because that was the only way left for *Dublin*'s excess children.

She went to say good-bye, to begin the good-byes, at least, a courtesy to Megan and Connie and Geoff and Ma'am, which was not as hard as that to *Dublin* herself.

VIII

There looked to be no change out across the docks. Sandor kept his eye on *Lucy*'s berth, covertly, from the doorway of the sleepover. Workers moved, pedestrian traffic went its unconcerned way up and down—mainday now, and he kept his face in the shadows. Downers shrilled and piped their gossip, busy at tasks like human dockworkers, moving canisters onto ramps or off, making distant echoes over the drone and crash of machinery.

He entertained wild thoughts . . . like waiting until station lights dimmed again in the half hour of twilight which passed mainday to alterday: like slipping over to that security barrier and decking some unfortunate workman—seeing if he could not liberate a cutter to get past that lock they had on *Lucy*'s hatch. Improbable. He thought even of going to some other marginer and pleading his way aboard as crew, because he was that panicked. The thought whisked through his mind and out again, banished, because he was not going to give *Lucy* up. He would try the cutter first; and they would take him in for sure then, with a theft and maybe an assault charge to add to the complaints already lodged against him.

Antisocial conduct. Behavior in willful disregard of others' rights. That was good for a lockup. Behavior in willful disregard of others' lives: that was good for a mindwipe for sure. Rehabilitation. Total restruct.

A cutter was as good as a gun, when it came to someone trying to get it away from him. It might bring about shooting. He thought that he preferred that, though he balked at the idea of using a cutter on any living thing. He was not made for this, he thought, not able to kill people; the thought turned him cold.

There was *Dublin*, and whatever hope that gave. He held onto that.

Militia passed in a group, male and female, blue-uni-

93

formed: he retreated inside the foyer and waited until they had gone their way with some other business in mind. Militia. Alliance Forces, Talley had said. Alliance Forces. There was talk that the militia of Pell had at its core a renegade Mazianni carrier; one of Conrad Mazian's captains—Signy Mallory of _Norway_, who had fought for the old Earth Company . . . the name the Mazianni used while they were legitimate; but a Mazianni captain all the same. Talley . . . upstairs: that was an officer of what Pell called its defense, maybe a man who had worked with Mallory. _That_ was what was doggedly investigating him, a pirate hunting other pirates, who played by civilized rules in port.

But outside port—even if some miracle got him clear of Pell—

A flash across his vision, of armored troops on _Lucy_'s bridge, of fire coming back at them, and the Old Man dying; and his mother; and the others—of being hit, and Ross falling on him—

And Jal screaming for help, when the troopers dragged him back through that boarding access and onto their ship; Jal and the others they had taken aboard, for whatever purposes they had in mind. . . .

The Alliance played politics with Union; and maybe they wanted, at the moment, to manufacture a pirate threat to Pell interests, to justify the existence of armed Alliance ships. And if they hauled him in—the mindwipe could make sure he told the story they wanted. A paranoid fancy. Not likely. But he was among strangers, and too many things were possible . . . where pirates hunted pirates and might want to throw out a little deceiving chaff.

A step approached him on his left. He looked about and a hand closed on his arm and he looked straight into the face of Allison Reilly. "Told you to stay inside," she said.

"So I'm here." The shock still had his pulse thumping. "Find out anything?"

She pulled papers from her pocket, waved them in front of him. "Everything. It's covered. I've got you off clear."

He shook his head. The words went through without touching. "Clear."

"_Dublin_ got _Dancer_ to withdraw the allegations. We've got a show-cause order for station and they're not going to be able to come up with anything to substantiate it. We just filed the papers. And this—" She thrust one of the papers at him.

"That's an application for your Alliance registry and trade license. And *Dublin*'s standing witness. That'll get you clear paper for this side of the Line. That's to be signed and filed, but it's all in order: our lawyer set it up." A second paper. "That's a show-cause for customs, to get that seal off. They can't maintain that without the charge from *Dancer*. This—" A third paper. "A loan, enough for dock charges, refitting, and cargo. I've got you crew. I've got you all but cleared to pull out of here. A way to outfit with what you need. Are you following me?"

He blinked and tried. Stopped believing it and looked for the strings: it was the only thing to do when things looked too good. "What's it cost?" he asked. "Where's the rest of it? There is a rest of it."

She nodded toward the bar next door. "Come on. Sit down and look through it."

He went, dragged by the hand, into the noise and closeness of the smallish bar, sat down with her at a table by the door where there was enough light to read, and spread out the papers. "Beer," she ordered when the waiter showed, and in the meantime he picked up the loan papers and tried to make sense of them. Clause after clause of fine print. Five hundred thousand credit cargo allowance. A hundred thousand margin account. He looked at numbers stacked up like stellar distances and shook his head.

"You're not going to get a better offer," she said. "I'll tell you how you got it. I'm going with you. The whole Third Helm alterday watch of *Dublin* is signing with you for this tour. Crew that knows what they're doing. I'll vouch for that. My watch. And it's a fair agreement. You say that your *Lucy* can make profit on marginer cargoes. What do you think she could do given real backing?"

That touched on his pride, deeply. He lifted his head, not stupid in it, either. "I don't know. My kind of operation I know—how to get what's going rate on small deals. *Lucy*'s near two hundred years old. She's not fast. I strung those jumps getting here. Hauling, she's slow, and you come out of those jumps feeling it."

"I've seen her exterior on vid. What's the inside rig?"

He shrugged. "Not what you're used to. Number one hold's temperature constant to 12 degrees, the rest deep cold; fifteen K net—It's not going to work. I can't handle that kind of operation you're talking about."

"It'll work."

"I don't know why you're doing this."

"Business. *Dublin*'s starting up operations here, wants a foot on either side of the line; putting you on margin account is convenient. And if it helps you out at the same time—"

The beers came. Sandor picked his up and drank to ease his dry mouth, gave the papers another desperate going over, trying to find the clause that talked about confiscations, about liability that might set him up for actions, about his standing good for previous debts.

"A few profitable runs," she said, "and you build up an account here and you clear the debt. You want to know what *Dublin* clears on a good run?"

"I'm not sure I do."

"It's a minor loan. Put it that way. That's the scale we're talking about. It's nothing. And there's a ten-year time limit on that loan. Ten years. Station banks—would they give you that? Or any combine? You work that debt down and there's a good chance you could deal with *Dublin* for a stake to a refitting. I mean a real refitting. No piggyback job. Kick that ancient unit off her tail and put a whole new generation rig on. She's a good design, stable moving in jump; some of the newest intermediate ships on the boards borrow a bit from her type."

"No," he said in a small voice. "No, you don't get me into that. You don't get your hands on her."

"You think you can't do it. You think you'll fail."

He thought about it a moment.

"What better offer," she asked him, "have you ever hoped to have? And if charges come in, who's going to stand with you? Hmn? You sign the appropriate papers, you take the offer.—I've gone out on a line for you; and for me, I admit that. I get a post I can't get on my ship. So we both take a risk. I don't know but what there's worse to you than you've told. I don't know who your enemies might be; and I wouldn't be surprised if you had some."

He shook his head slowly. "No. I don't. Hard as it may be to believe, I've never made any I know of."

"Smart, at least."

"Survival.—Reilly: if I sign those papers, I'm telling you—there's one captain on *Lucy*, and I'm it."

"There's nothing in those papers that says anything to the contrary."

He drank a long mouthful of the beer. "We get a witness on this?"

"That's the deal. Station offices."

He nodded slowly. "Let's go do it, then."

It made him less than comfortable, to go again into station offices, to confront the dockmaster's agents and turn in the applications that challenged station to do its worst. The documents went from counter to desk behind the counter, and finally to one of the officials in the offices beyond—a call finally into that office, where they stood while a man looked at the papers.

"How long—" Sandor made himself ask, against all instincts to the contrary. "How long to process those and get the seal clear? I'd like to start hunting cargo."

An official frown. "No way of knowing."

"Well," Allison said, "there's already a routing application in."

A lift of the brows, and a frown after. None too happy, this official. "Customs office," he said, punching in on the com console. "I have *Lucy*'s Stevens in with forms."

And after the answer, another shunting to an interior office, more questions and more forms.

Nature of cargo, they asked. Information pending acquisition, Sandor answered, in his own element. He filled the rest out, looped some blanks, letting station departments chase each other through the maze. *Clear* was a condition of mind, a zone in which he had not yet learned to function.

Legitimate, he kept telling himself. These were real papers he was applying for. Honest papers. In the wrong name, and under a false ID, and that was the stain on matters: but real papers all the same.

They walked out of the customs office toward the exchange, and when he got to that somewhat busier desk, to stand in line with others including spacers with onstation cards to apply for . . . Allison snagged his arm and drew him over to the reception desk for more inner offices.

"Sir?" the secretary asked, blinking a little at his out at the elbows look and the silvery company he kept.

Embarrassed, Sandor searched for the appropriate papers. "Got a fund transfer and an account to open."

"That's Wyatt's?" *Everyone* knew his business. It threw him off his stride. He put the loan papers on the desk.

"No," he said, "that's an independent deal."

"*Dublin* has an account with Wyatt's." Allison leapt into the fray. "This is a loan between *Lucy* and *Dublin*. The ship is collateral. Captain Stevens hopes to straighten it up with his own combine, but as it is, *Dublin* will cover any transfer of funds that may be necessary: escrow will rest on Pell."

"What sum are we talking about?"

"Five hundred thousand for starters."

"I'll advise Mr. Dee."

"Thank you," Allison said with a touch of smugness, and settled into a waiting area chair. Sandor sat down beside her, wiped a touch of sweat from his temples, crossed his ankles, leaned back, willed one muscle after another to relax. "You let me do the talking, will you?" he asked her.

"You take it slow. I know what I'm doing."

His fingers felt numb. A lot of him did. *Clear*, he thought again. There was something wrong with such a run of luck. Ships that tossed off half a million as if it were pocket change—rattled his nerves. He felt a moment of panic, as if some dark cloud were swallowing him up, conning him into debts and ambition more than he could handle. He had no place in this office. It was like stringing jumps and accumulating velocity without dump—there was a point past which no ship could handle what it could acquire.

"Captain." The secretary had come back. "Mr. Dee will see you."

He stood up. Allison put her hand on his back, urging him, intended for comfort, perhaps, but it felt like a fatal shove.

He walked, and Allison went behind him. He met the smallish man in his office . . . a wise, wrinkled face, dark almond eyes that went to the heart of him and peeled away the layers. So, well, one sat down like a man and filled out the forms and above all else tried not to look the nervousness he felt.

"You'll have claims from WSC," Dee advised him.

"Minor," Allison said.

Again a stab of those dark, fathomless eyes. An elderly finger indicated the appropriate line and he signed.

"There we go," Allison said, approving it. He shook hands with the banker and realized himself a respectable if mortgaged citizen. Allison shook hands with Dee and Dee showed them to the outer office in person. They were someone. He was. He felt himself hollow centered and scared with a different kind of fear than the belly-gripping kind he lived in on stations: with a knowledgeable, too-late kind of dread, of having done something he never should have done, a long time back, when he had walked into a bar on Viking and tried to buy a Dubliner a drink.

"You come," Allison said as they walked out empty of their bundle of applications, with a set of brand new credit cards and clear ship's papers in exchange. "Let's get some of the outfitting done. I don't know what you're carrying in ship's stores. Blast, I'll be glad to get that customs lock off and have a look at her."

"Got some frozen stuff. I outfitted pretty fair for a solo operation at Viking."

"We've got five. What's our dunnage allotment?"

"I really don't think that's a problem."

"Accommodations?"

"Cabins 2.5 meters by 4. That's locker and shower and bunk."

"Sleep vertical, do you?"

"Lockers are under and over the bunk."

"Private?"

"Private as you like."

"Nice. Good as *Dublin*, if you like to know."

He considered that and expanded a bit. "If you have extra—there's always space to put it. Storage is never that tight."

"Beautiful.—Hey." She flagged one of the ped-carriers that ran the docks, a flatbed with poles, hopped on: Sandor followed, put his own card in the slot as it whisked them along the station ring with delirious ease. He had never ridden a carrier; never felt he could afford the luxury, when his legs could save the expense. All his life he had walked on the docks of stations, and he watched the lights and the shops blur past, still numb in the profusion of experience. "Off!" someone would sing out, and the driver would stop the thing just long enough for someone to step down. "Off!" Allison called, and they stepped off on white dock, in the face of a large pressure-window and a fancy logo saying WILSON, and in finer print, SUPPLIER. It was all white and silver and black inside. He swore softly, and let Allison lead him into the place by the hand.

Displays everywhere. Clothing down one aisle, thermals and working clothes and liners and some of them in fancy

colors, flash the like of which was finding its way onto docksides on the bodies of those who could afford it. New stuff.
All of it. He looked at the price on a pair of boots and it was
150. He grabbed Allison by the arm.

"They're thieves in here. Look at that. Look, this isn't my
class. *Lucy* outfits from warehouses. Or dockside."

She wrinkled her nose. "I don't know what you're used to,
but we're not going to eat seconds all the way and we're not
using cut-rate stuff. You don't get class treatment on dockside
if you don't have a little flash. And we'll not be dressing
down, thank you; so deaden your nerves, Stevens, and buy
yourself some camouflage so you don't stand out among your
crew."

He looked up the aisle at clothes he could not by any
stretch of the imagination see himself wearing, stuffed his
hands in his pockets. The lining on the right one was twice
resewn. "You wear that silver stuff into *Lucy*'s crawlspaces,
will you? You fit yourselves out for work, Reilly."

"There's dockside and there's work. Find something you
like, hear me?"

He studied the aisle, nothing on racks, no searching this
stuff for burn-holes and bad seams. One asked, and they
hunted it out of computerized inventory. "So I get myself the
likes of yours," he muttered, thinking he would never carry it
well. "That satisfy you?"

"Good enough. What kind of entertainment system does
she carry?"

"Deck of cards," he muttered. "We can buy a fresh one."

She swore. "You have to have a tape rig."

"Mariner-built Delta system."

"Lord, a converter, then. We'll bring our own tapes and
buy some new."

"I can't afford—"

"Basic amenities. I'm telling you, you want class crew, you
have to rig out. What about bedding?"

"Got plenty of that. Going to have to stock up on lifesupport goods and some filters and detergents and swabs—before
we get to extravagances. I'd like to put a backup on some
switches and systems that aren't carrying any right now."

A roll of Allison's dark eyes in his direction, stark dismay.

"Two of them on the main board," he added, the plain
truth.

"Make a list. This place can get them."

"Will. Going to be nice, isn't it, knowing there's a fail-safe?"

He walked down the aisle alone, looking at the clothes. And all about him, over the tops of the counters, were other displays . . . personal goods, bedding, dishes, tapes and games, utility goods, cabinets, ship's furnishings, interior hardware, recycling goods, tools, bins, medical supplies, computer softwares. Music whispered through his senses. He turned about him and stared, lost in the glitter of the displays he had never given more than a passing glance to—had never come *in* a place like this, where his kind of finances could get a man accused of theft.

A kind of madness afflicted him suddenly, like nerving himself for a bad jump. "Help you?" a clerk asked down his nose.

"Got to get some clothes," he said. And yielding to the recklessness of the moment: "Like to have it match, jacket and the rest. Some dockside boots. Maybe a few work clothes." Allison was out of sight: that panicked him in more than one sense. She was probably off buying something. And the clerk was giving him that look that bartenders gave him. He pulled his new card from his pocket. "Stevens," he said, and clerkly eyes brightened.

"You're the one that came in yesterday."

"Yes, sir." Lord, was it only yesterday? His shoulders ached with the thought. "Got in with nothing but my account money and I need a lot of things."

The eyes brightened further. "Be happy to help you, Captain Stevens."

Flash coveralls. A 75 credit pair of boots; a jacket; a stack of underwear. He looked at himself in the fitting room, haggard and wanting a shave, and took off the fine clothes and ordered it all done in packages.

And he found Allison Reilly at the commodities counter, perched on a stool and going through the catalogue. "Ordered anything?" he asked with a sinking feeling.

"Making a list." She tapped the screen in front of her, a display of first line meals with real meat and frozen fruits and boxed pastries.

"Chocolates," he added in a sense of fantasy. He had had chocolate once.

"Chocolate," she said. "There we go."

"Cancel that. It's too expensive."

"Chocolate and coffee. Real stuff. Leave it to me."

"Allison—do you—get this stuff usually?"

He would have cut his throat rather than ask an hour ago. He looked into her face and suspected something as childish as his chocolates.

"For special days," she admitted. "I got some staple stuff too."

"I have 75 standard frozens. You can wipe that off."

"Good enough." She wiped the stylus over part of the order. "What about those hardware items we need?"

We, it was. He took up the seat next to her and keyed up the catalogue. "I can get better prices," he muttered.

"There's a discount system. Do your whole rig here and you get some off."

"Better." After the moment's euphoria, his stomach was upset. He ticked through the things they really needed. He felt conspicious sitting here, at the counter in this place, dressed as he was. The list went on growing, more and more expensive, because systems were, more than crew luxuries.

"That do it?" Allison asked finally.

He punched for the total. 5576.2 came up on the screen. He shook his head in shock. "Can't go that."

"Five of us, remember? And the hardware. That's not out of line. Put the card in, there."

He shoved it into the slot. It registered. THANK YOU, the screen said. He stared at it like some oncoming mass.

Took his card back.

She patted his shoulder. "Haircut for us both," she said. "And clean up. We're meeting someone for dinner."

"Who?"

"The rest of us, who else? And why don't you get yourself a proper patch, while we're at it? I looked in the directory. There's this place does them to order, all computer set up. Anything you like, on the spot. It's really amazing how it works."

"Lord, Reilly—does it matter?"

"I'd think it would." She touched the misembroidered nymph on his sleeve. "You could do yourself a class job. Or they've got the over-the-counter stuff. If you really want."

That was low. He scowled and she never flinched. "Mind your business," he said. "If I like the tatty thing it's my business."

"You're really going to go blank like that. They'll think you're a pirate for sure."

"I'll just get me a handful of the tatty ones. Thanks."

Lips pursed. So she knew how far she had pushed.

"The name's not Stevens," she said.

"That's what you're asking, is it?"

"Maybe."

"That's my business." And after a moment: "I'll get some blamed patch. I don't care what. But no shamrock. I'll promise you that."

"Didn't think so."

He nodded, gathered up his packages, all of them but the stuff they had ordered on catalogue, that would see ship delivery when they made the loading schedule.

When.

IX

He had his doubts—had them following Allison to the patcher; and getting trimmed and shaved and lotioned at the barber—his first time, for a haircut that gave him a sleek, blond look of affluence. Doubts again in sleepover, spoiling the hour he snatched for sleep: his privacy, he kept thinking; the life that he had—It was a miserable life, but he controlled it; there was comp, with its peculiarities; and the sealed rooms that these Dubliners would demand to open. There were things they would hear and see that were worse than public nakedness to him; that undercut his pride, and rifled through his memories.

But it had to be, he reasoned with himself. He had never had such a chance. Never could dream of such a chance. He looked at Allison looking at him in the mirror—and the warmth of that drove the chill away. "You look good," she said, to the silver-suited image of him, and he faced about toward her with a surge of confidence that sent some feeling back into his hands and feet. "Reckon so?" he asked.

"No question."

So it fed him his courage back. He drew a deeper breath, reassessed himself and the pathetic ridiculousness, the childishness of the things stored in comp, the nature of the sealed compartments and the relics he lived among. So if she thought that, so if she *felt* that, then she would not laugh—and the others, these strangers they went to meet—she could handle. As long as she was with him; as long as she found nothing humorous in a man trying to be what he was not—who listened to voices instead of family, who had never had the strength to clear out all the debris of the past; who kept a secret voice that talked to a child who should have long ago grown up; excruciating things. A lifetime of illusions.

There was always the alternative, he reminded himself. He could wait for the military; in his mind he heard the laughter of the dockside searchers who might get into such privacies. Or the techs who might strip his mind down, when his scams caught up to him, discovering the twisted child he was. They would put it all together, taking it all apart; and the thought of that—of the questions; the exposure of himself—

He wore a patch, had sewn it on: LUCY, it said, white letters on a black, blue-centered circle; and that was as close as he dared come to the old one. It looked naked, too, without the swan in flight that belonged there. But someone might know *Le Cygne*, and Krejas; and he and Ross and Mitri had always agreed, in all the scams, to keep the Name out of it. So it was not possible now to go to station offices and say—I lied; change the name; put it the way it ought to be. That would finish everything.

And maybe, he thought, a lifetime would get him used to looking at the patch that way.

"Coming?" Allison asked him.

He walked into the restaurant arm in arm with Allison—one of those places he expected of Allison, ornate and expensive, where flash and fine cloth belonged, and stationer types occupied tables alongside spacers of the big ships, men and women with officers' stripes: a lot of silver hair in the place. A lot of money. A waiter intercepted them—"Reilly," Allison said; and the waiter nodded deferentially and showed them the way among serpentine pillars to the recesses of the place, deep shadows along the walls.

A silver company occupied the table he located for them, a company that rose when they arrived—Sandor did a quick scan of lamp-lit faces, heart thumping, hand already extending in response to offered hands and a murmur of courtesies—and found himself face to face with Curran Reilly.

No hand offered there. Nothing offered. "Curran," Allison said. "Helm 22 of *Dublin*, my number two. Captain Stevens of *Lucy*. But you'll have met."

"Yes," Sandor said, the adrenalin hazing everything else; and in belated time, Curran Reilly took the hand he offered, a dry palm clenched about his sweating one. A grip that he expected, hard and unfriendly like the stare. And other hands, then, earlier offered. "Deirdre," Allison said, "number three"—a freckled, solid woman, dark-haired like all the Reillys, but with a grin that went straight to the heart, punctured his anger and half made up for Curran. Happiness. He was not accustomed to cause that in people.

"Neill," Allison said of the third, another offered hand; a lank and bearded man with an earnestness that persuaded him Curran was at least unique in the lot. "Neill," he murmured in turn, looked at the others. The waiter hovered, offering chairs. They settled again, himself between Allison and Deirdre, facing Curran and Neill.

"Would you like cocktails?" the waiter asked.

"Drinks with dinner," Allison said. "That's all right with everyone?"

Nods all about. The waiter whisked forth a set of menus, and for a merciful time there was that amenity among them.

He was buying; he reckoned that. The prices were enough to chill the blood, but he nerved himself and ordered the best, maintained a smile when his guests did. It was, after all, one night, one time—an occasion. He could afford it, he persuaded himself. To please these people. To give them what they were accustomed to having. On their own money.

The waiter departed. A silence hung there. "Got everything in order?" Curran asked Allison finally.

"All settled."

"Megan sends her regards."

A silence. A glance downward. Sandor had no idea who Megan might be; no one offered to enlighten him. "I'll talk to her," Allison said. "It's not good-bye, after all. We'll be meeting on loops."

"I think she understands," Deirdre said. "My people—they know. They know why."

"Everyone knows *why*," Allison said. "It's forgiving it." She laid her hand briefly on Sandor's arm. "Ship politics." To the others: "—We got the outfitting done. First class."

"What kind of accommodations have we got?" Neill asked.

The adjoining table filled, with all attendant disorganization. Sandor sat and listened to Reillys talk among themselves, plans for packing, for farewells, discussion of what supplies they had laid in. "Private cabins and no dunnage limit?" Deirdre exclaimed, eyes alight. "I'd thought we might be tight."

"No limit within reason," Sandor said, breaking out into the Reilly dialogue—expanded at the reaction that got from the lot of them. "That's one advantage of a small-crew ship, few as there are. Bring anything you like. Any cabin you like."

"You and Allison plan to double up?" Curran asked.

It was not the question; it was the silence that went after it. The look in Curran's eyes.

"Curran," Allison said.

"Just wondering."

The meal started arriving, wine first; the appetizers when they had scarcely settled from that. Sandor sat and smoldered, out of appetite with the temper that was boiling in him. "I'll tell you," he said, jabbing a serving knife in Curran's direction as the waiter passed finally out of earshot, "Mr. Reilly, I think you and I have a problem. I'm not sure why. Or what. But it started up there in blue section this morning and I'm not going to have it go on."

"Stevens," Allison said.

"I think we'd better settle it."

"All right," Curran said softly. "The number one says you're all right, that goes with me. Let's start from zero."

"My rules, mister."

"Absolutely," Curran said. "Chain of command. As soon as we get that lock off."

"Ought to be soon," Allison said. "How about that routing application?"

"Got it," Curran said. His sullen face lighted instantly. "Clear. We're routed to Venture and Bryan's, Konstantin Company commodities, on *Dublin*'s guarantee."

Sandor had ducked his head to eat and stay out of it. He looked up again. "You're talking about our route and cargo."

"Right."

"You take it on yourself—"

"Part of the package."

"No. Not part of the package. You don't set up routes or make agreements."

"Come down, man. We've got you a deal better than you could get. A deal that's guaranteed profit. With a station commerce load that doesn't cost you, and guaranteed rate for the delivery. How do you do better than that?"

"I don't care what you've got. No. I decide where *Lucy* goes and if she goes."

"Slow," Allison said, patted his arm, once, twice. "Hold it. Listen: it *is* part of the package. I was going to tell you. It's a good deal. The best. The Hinder Stars opening up again, the stations being set up to operate—you know what a chance it is, to get in on the setup of a station? *Dublin* herself is taking on cargo and looping back to Mariner. But we go out to the Hinder Stars. Toward Sol. You see how it works? That's Sol trade: luxuries, exotics. We take a station load out and do small runs; and as the Sol trade starts coming in, we start picking up Sol cargo. We run small cargo at first, then see about doing that conversion that'll boost her up to speed. . . ."

"You've got that planned too."

"Because I know this kind of economics, if you don't. We're not talking about dockside trading. We're talking about running full and being where trade can build."

"We get backing that way," Deirdre said. "Eventually we schedule to catch *Dublin*'s Pell loop and funnel Sol goods into Union territory; and that's big profit. *Dublin*'s not doing a total act of charity."

"They'll cut our throats. Alliance traders. Locals won't stand for that."

"Stop thinking like a marginer," Allison said. "You're linked to the *Dublin* operation. They won't touch us the way they won't touch *Dublin* herself. And after one run, we'll be local. We'll have Alliance paper."

"And I take what deals *Dublin* offers."

"Fair deals."

He thought about it a moment, avoiding the sight of Curran Reilly, took a drink of wine. "Hinder Stars," he said, thinking that if there was a place least likely for his record to catch up to him it had to be that, the forgotten Earthward stations. Sol goods, expensive for their mass. Rarities and luxuries. "So *Dublin* wants a trade link."

"Believe it," Allison said. "Both sides of the Line are interested . . . Pell, absolutely; Union, in keeping the flow of trade across the Line. You think Union wants Pell and Sol in bed together alone? No. Union's supporting Unionside merchanters that want to trade across the Line; and there's nothing that says we can't set up an operation on this side."

"We."

"Any way you like it. You needed the bailout. And we saw the advantage. You. We. You and the lot of us on *Lucy* can develop a new loop that's going to pay."

He thought about it again, excited in spite of himself. "You plan to stay on—how long?"

"We don't necessarily plan to go back. It's like I said . . . too far to the posted ranks. We're coming to stay."

He nodded slowly. "All right," he said, even including Curran in that. "All right, I'll take your deal. And the lot of you.—What about charts?"

"Got that arranged," Curran said. "No problem with that."

"From what I know," Allison said, "we're going to have a double jump to Venture and a double to Bryant's."

"Lonely out that direction."

"Pell's got some sort of security out that way."

"Patrol?"

"They don't say. They just put out they've got it watched."

"Comforting." He doubted it all. It was likely bluff. Or Pell was that determined to keep the Sol link open.

He looked up again, at the strangers who looked to share with him, to come onto *Lucy*'s deck—permanent company. So they were not all what he would have chosen. But with a Curran came a Deirdre, whose broad, cheerful self he liked on sight; and Neill Reilly, who had said little of anything and who seemed set in the background by all the others—They were Family, like any other, the rough and the smooth together. He had not known that kind of closeness . . . not since Ross. He wanted it, and Allison, with a yearning that welled up in his throat and behind his eyes and throughout. And it was his. It came with the wealth, the luck he still could not imagine. But it was real. It was all about him. He made himself relax, limb by limb, up to the shoulders, looked across the table at his acquired crew and felt something knotted up inside unsnarl itself.

And when dinner was done, down to a fancy fruit dessert, when they had drunk as much as merchanters were apt to drink on liberty—they found things to laugh at, Dubliner anecdotes, tales on each other. He laughed and wiped his eyes, as he had not done in longer than he had forgotten.

The bill was his: he took it without flinching, gave a tip to the waiter—left a happy man in their wake and strolled out into the chill air of the dockside with his flock of Dubliners.

"Go to the offices," he suggested, "see if we can't get the lock off my ship."

"Let's," Allison agreed. "Is it past alterdawn? We can get something done."

"Get a ped carrier," Deirdre said.

"Walk," said Neill. "We might be sober when we get there."

They walked, along the busy docks, past *Lucy*'s barriered berth, weaving a good deal less when they had covered all of green dock, sweating a bit when they had come into blue, and near the customs offices.

But he came differently this time, in company, with the knowledge of *Dublin*'s lawyer behind them, and papers on file that put him in the right. He walked up to the desk and faced the official with a plain request, brought out the papers. "I need the lock off," he said. "We seem to have everything else straightened away but that."

"Ah," the official said. "Captain Stevens."

"Can we get it taken care of?"

The official produced a sealed envelope, passed it over.

"What's this?"

"I've no idea, sir. I'm told it relates to the hold order."

He was conscious of the others at his back—refused to look at them, tore open the seal on the message slip and read it once before it sank in. "Report blue dock number three," he read it, looking back at Allison then. "*AS Norway*, Signy Mallory commanding."

Curran swore. "Mallory," Allison said, and it might as well have been an oath. "On Pell?"

"Arrived two hours ago," the official said, a roll of the eyes toward the clock. "The message is half an hour old."

"What's the military doing in this?" Curran asked. "Those papers are clear."

"I don't know, sir," the official said. "Answering ought to clear it up."

The fear was back, familiar as an old suit of clothes. "I'd better get out there and take care of this," Sandor said. "I don't see there's any reason for you to go."

They walked out with him, that much at least, back out onto the dock facing the military ships . . . the schedule boards showed it plainly: NORWAY, the third berth down occupied now, conspicuously alight. He looked at the Dubliners, at worried faces and Curran's scowl.

"Don't know how long this may take," he said. "Allison, maybe I'd better call you after I get back to the sleepover. Maybe you'd better go on back to *Dublin*."

"No," Allison said. "If you don't get out of there fairly soon, we'll be calling some legal help. They don't bluff us."

That was some comfort. He looked at the rest of them, who showed no inclination to take any different course. Nodded then, thrust his hands into his pockets, crumpling the message in the right.

He prepared arguments, countercharges, mustered the same indignation he had used on authorities before. It was all he knew how to do.

But it was hard to keep the bluff intact walking up to the lighted access of *Norway*, where uniformed troops—these *were* troops, far different from any stationside militia—took him in charge and searched him. They were rejuved, a great number of these men and women—old enough to have fought in the war, silver-haired and some of them marked with scars no stationsider would have had to wear. They were not rough with him in their searching, but they were more thorough than the police had been. They frightened him, the way that ship out there frightened him, behind that cheerful lighted access, a huge carrier bristling with armaments, a Company ship, from another age. They brought him toward the ramp that led up into the access. And standing in the accessway . . . Talley, grim and waiting for him.

He kept walking. So the man was part of this action. He was somehow not surprised. The Dubliners, he was thinking, ought to get back to their ship. The military would think twice about demanding that a merchanter family of the Reillys' size give up some of its own to questioning. But alone, far from *Dublin*, they were vulnerable, unused to authorities who ran things as they pleased.

He encountered Talley, a bleak, pale-eyed stare from the Alliance officer, a nod in the direction he should go. So he had acquired a certain importance: a man with commander's rank took him in personal charge and escorted him into the heart of this narrow-accessed monster. Dim corridors: a long walk to a wider area and a lift to the upper levels. He stared through Talley on the way up in the car. Conversation could do him no good. One never gave anything away. One always regretted it later.

A walk afterward down a narrower corridor—bare, dull metal everywhere, nothing so cheerful as *Lucy*'s white, age-scarred compartments. Coded identifications on the exposed lines, on the compartments. Everything was efficiency and no comfort. They reached the door of an office and got a come-ahead light: the door opened, and Talley brought him through.

"Captain," Talley said, "Stevens of the merchanter *Lucy*."

The silver-haired woman was already looking at him across her desk, already sizing him up. "Mallory," she identified herself. "Sit down, Captain."

He pulled the chair over and sat facing her across the desk, while Talley settled himself against the cabinet, arms folded. Mallory pushed her chair back from the desk and leaned back in it—rejuved, young/old, staring at him with dark eyes that said nothing back.

"You're getting clearance to go out," she said. "On the Venture run. I understand there's some question about your ID, Captain."

His wits deserted him. It was not the question. It was the source. One of the nine captains, one of the Mazianni from the war years, who had gotten supply by boarding merchanters, by taking supplies and personnel. Who had killed. It might have been this one, those years ago, this ship that had locked onto *Lucy* and boarded. He might be that close to the captain who had ordered it, among troops who had been inside the armor, who had killed all his family. He had thought if he met one of them he would kill barehanded, and he found himself sitting still and staring back, paralyzed by the quiet, the tenor of the moment.

"You don't have any comment," Mallory said.

"I thought it was settled."

"*Is* there an irregularity, Captain?" Softly. Staring straight at him.

"Look, I just want the lock off my ship. I've got a cargo lined up, I've got everything else in order. Because some muddled-up merchanter mistakes my ship. . . ."

"Let me see your papers, Captain."

It took the breath out of his argument. He hesitated, off his mental balance, pulled them out of his pocket and leaned forward as she did, passing them into her extended hand across the desk, close, that close to touching. She leaned back easily, looked through them, lingered over them.

"But these are new," she said. "Except for the title papers, of course." She felt of the older paper, the title, itself false. "You know this kind of paper gets traded on the market. Has to get from one station to the other, after all; and across docks, and I know places where you can get it. Don't you, Captain?"

"I'm legitimate."

"So." She passed the papers back to him, and he thrust them quickly back into his pocket, his fingers gone cold. "So. Linked up with *Dublin Again*, are you? A very respectable operation. That does say something for you. Unionsider."

"I plan to operate here. On the Alliance side."

"Oh, relations are very good with Union at the moment. They're supplying ships and troops all along the Line. We have no quarrel with Union origins. You plan to stay here, do you? Operate as *Dublin*'s pipeline out of the Sol trade?"

"I don't know how things will work out." He stepped slowly through the argument, aware of maneuvering on the other side, not understanding it. Mallory was not taken in. Was prodding at him, to find some provocation.

"Your certification comes through us," she said. "We've got a problem, Captain. We've got Mazianni activity between us and Sol, into the Hinder Stars. Does that bother you?"

"It bothers me."

"They'd like to cut us off, you understand. It's a lot of territory to patrol. And they win, simply by scaring merchanters out of that run. We've got two stations coming back into operation, and we're doing what we can to keep the zones clear. We'll be out at the nullpoints, making sure you're not ambushed there. We've got a rare agreement on the other side of the Line. Union's sealing up Tripoint and Brady's and any other point you can name." The eyes shot up to lock on his, abrupt and invasive. "You play the shy side of legal, do you? Marginer. I'll reckon you're no stranger to the fringes. Lying off in space. Operating out of the nullpoints. Doing trading on the side, without customs looking on. I'll bet you have a fine sense of what's trouble and what's not. A fine sense."

He said nothing. Tried to think of an excuse to look away and failed in that too.

"Might stand you in good stead," she said. "It's a place out there—that makes raw nerves survival-positive. We'll be there, Captain. I really want you to know that."

It was delivered very softly, with the same stare. It promised—he had no idea what.

"You can go," she said. "You'll find the obstacles clear. But I have news for you. Your Konstantin Company cargo is cancelled. You'll be carrying military cargo. You'll be paid hazard rate. An advantage. You'll be taking it aboard in short order and undocking at 0900 mainday."

"Like that."

"Like that."

"I thought—I was under military investigation."

"You are," she said. "Good evening, Captain."

"Maybe I don't want this. Maybe I want to change my mind."

"Do you, Captain? I'd prefer not."

The silence hung there. "All right," he said. "You protect us, do you?"

"As best we can, Captain."

Never Stevens. She never used the name. He stood up, nodded a reflexive courtesy. Not a response: dead eyes stared into him. He turned then and walked out, and Talley followed him into the corridor, hand-signaled a trooper who came down the corridor to walk him out.

Down the lift and out to the ramp again, the cold of the dockside coming as a shock after the metal closeness of the warship. He walked down the slant past the guard that stood there, past uniformed troops and idle, hard-eyed stares. . . . He reached the dockside and walked away, taking larger breaths the farther he got from the perimeter. He felt as if he had been picked up and shaken. Dropped hard.

He saw the Dubliners waiting for him, out by the lighted fronts of the offices. Allison and the others. He went toward them with the consciousness that the military might be watching his back, taking notes on his associations.

"What was it?" Allison asked. "Trouble?"

He shook his head and swept them up with a motion of his arms. "Come on. We've got our clearance. They're going to load."

"Like that?"

"Like that." He looked at Curran as the five of them headed down the dock at a good pace. "The Konstantin cargo just got cancelled. We've been handed military stuff. Hazard rate. Immediate loading, undocking at 0900 mainday."

"Military." For once Curran was taken aback. "What, specifically?"

"No word on that. I talked with Mallory. The lock was hers. The cargo's hers. I think she wants rumors spread, or she wouldn't spill what she spilled."

"Like what?"

"That Union's occupying the nullpoints along the Line, hunting Mazianni, and Alliance is doing the same."

"Lord, you've got to tell that to the Old Man."

He walked along in a moment's silence—that it took that much for them to suggest him and the Reilly talking face to face. They were scared. He saw that. Deirdre's face had lost all its cheer, pale under its freckles. Allison's—had a hard-eyed wariness like Curran's. Neill just looked worried. "I'll make a call from *Lucy*," Sandor said. "When I get clear and boarded."

"They're on a hunt?" Neill asked.

"I think I was told what she wants told in every bar on dockside. And I don't know what the percentage is."

"She say anything else?" Curran asked.

"She knows about the deal. She talked about the profit there might be for a route from Sol into Union. Direct to the point. Said they're going to be at the nullpoints of the Hinder Stars, keeping an eye on things."

"For sure?" Allison said.

"I don't trust anything I was told.—I know I want to be down there if they're taking the security seal off the hatch. I want to see what they've had their fingers into on my ship."

"We're going to take a look and go straight back to *Dublin*," Allison said, "as soon as we're sure we've got that lock open. Got some good-byes to say, all of us. If they're going to load for a 900 undock, then you can use some crew over there."

"Could," he agreed. "Could."

He had help, he was thinking, an unaccustomed comfort. He had his Dubliners who were not leaving him at the first breath of trouble. He felt a curious warmth in that thought.

Legitimate, he kept reminding himself. With connections. Mallory could not touch him. Might not want to, wanting to keep on the good side of a powerful Unionside merchanter, with all its connections.

He tried to believe that.

But he had looked Mallory in the eyes, and doubted everything.

Downers surrounded the lock, the barriers having been removed . . . Downers in the company of one idle dockworker,

who rose from the side of the ramp and gave them all a looking at. "Business here," the man asked.

"Stevens," Sandor said. "Ship's owner."

The dockworker held out his hand. "Be happy to turn her
over to you, sir, with ID. Otherwise I have to report."

It was insane, such bizarre security interwoven with the
real threat of Alliance military. It was Pell, and they did
things in strange ways. He took out his papers and showed
them.

"He good?" a Downer asked, breather-masked and popping
and hissing in the process. Round brown eyes looked at them,
one Downer, a whole half-circle of Downers.

"Good paper," the dockworker confirmed. "Thank you, sir.
Good day to you, sir; or good night, whichever."

And the dockworker collected his assortment of Downers,
who bowed and bobbed courtesies in the departure, trooped
off with shrill calls and motion very like dancing.

"Lord," Allison said.

"Pell," Sandor said. He turned, led the way up the ramp in
deliberation, into the lighted access, with thoughts now only
for his ship. He walked the tube passage, into the familiar
lock. Home again. He kept going to the lift—five of them to
fill the space, to make an unaccustomed crowd in the narrow
corridors. The lift let them out on the main level, into the
narrow bowed floor of the indock living quarters and the
bridge; and he stood by the lift door and watched them walk
about the little zone of curved deck that was accessible . . .
silver-clad visitors come home to scarred *Lucy*, to pass their
fingers over her aged surfaces, to touch the control banks and
the cushions, to look this way and that up the inaccessible
curve of her cabin space and storage corridors, wondering
aloud about this and that point of her design. He was anxious
in that scrutiny, watched their faces, their smallest reactions,
more sensitive than if they had been looking him over.

"Not so comfortable in dock," Allison said, "but plenty of
room moving." She fingered the consoles. He had cleaned the
tape marks off because of customs, disposed of all the evidence: but she found a sticky smudge and rubbed at it. She
looked back at him. "She's all right," she pronounced. "She's
all right."

He nodded, feeling the knot in his chest dissolve.

"Handle easy?" Curran asked.

"A crooked docking jet. That's her only wobble. I use it."

"That's all right," Curran said, surprisingly easy.

"You going to call the Old Man?" Allison asked.

". . . it's likely," he said into the com, "that all of it's planted rumors. But if you're headed for Union space, sir—it seemed you might want to know what was said."

"Are you in trouble with them?" the voice came back to him.

"It's still possible, yes, sir." And aware of the possibility the transmission was tapped, shielded-line as it was: "I hope they get it straightened up."

A silence from the other end. "Right," Michael Reilly said. "You'll be taking care, Captain."

"Yes, sir."

"Thanks for the advisement."

"Thank you, sir."

"Yes," the Reilly said, "you might do that."

"Sir."

"Information appreciated, *Lucy.*"

"Signing off, *Dublin.*"

He shut it down, alone in the quiet again. The Dubliners were on their way back to their ship. For good-byes. For gathering their baggage. He sat in the familiar cushion, staring at his reflection in the dark screens and for a moment not recognizing himself, barbered and immaculate and in debt over his head.

Mallory's face kept coming back at him, the scene in her onship office. Talley's face, and the meeting on Pell. The old fear kept trying to reassert itself. He kept trying to put it down again.

He clasped his hands in front of him on a vacant area of the console, lowered his head onto his arms, tried for a moment to rest and to recall what time it was—a long, long string of hours. He thought that he had slid mostly into the alterday cycle; or somehow he had forgotten sleep.

He did that, slept, where he sat.

It was com that woke him, the notice from dockside that he had cargo coming in, and would he prepare to receive.

X

Leaving *Dublin* was a tumult of good-byes, of cousin-friends hugging and looking like tears; Ma'am with a look of patience; and Megan and Connie—Connie snuffling, and Megan not—Megan with that data-gatherer's focus to her stare that most acquired in infancy, who got posted bridge crew, wide-scanning the moment, too busy inputting to output, even losing a daughter. And in that, they had always understood each other—no need for fuss, when it stopped nothing. Allison hugged her pregnant sister, listened to the snuffles: hugged her mother longer, patted her shoulder. "See you," she said. "In not so many months, maybe."

"Right," her mother said. And when she had begun picking up the duffel and other baggage in a heap about her feet: "Don't take chances."

"Right," she told Megan, and shouldered strings and straps and picked up the sacks with handles. She looked back once more, at both of them, nodded when they waved, and then headed out of the lock and down the access tube to the ramp, leaving her three companions to muddle their own way off through their own farewells.

Her leaving had an element of the ridiculous: instead of the single duffel bag she might have taken, she moved all her belongings. It was not the way she had started. But she found excuses to take this oddment and that, found sacks and bags people were willing to part with, and ended up going down the ramp and across the docks loaded with everything she owned, a thumping, swinging load she would have done better to have called a docksider to carry. But it was not that far to walk; and the load was not that heavy, distributed as it was. She had her papers, her IDs and her cards and a letter-tape from Michael Reilly himself that advised anyone they cared to have know it, that *Lucy* was an associate of *Dublin*

118

Again—in case, the Old Man put it, you have credit troubles somewhere.

God forbid they met someone with some grudge Stevens had deserved for himself in his previous career.

Or trouble with the military out there. She was far less sanguine about the voyage than she had been when she conceived it. The neat control she had envisioned over the situation had considerably unraveled.

But she went, and the others would, for the same reasons, and if it should get tight out there, then they would handle it, she and her cousins. To sit a chair before she died of old age—it was that close; and no threat, no sting of parting was going to take it from her.

She kept walking—the first, she knew, of her unit to leave *Dublin*, headed for *Lucy*'s dock. She had had to go up the emergency accesses to get her belongings, and pack while clambering back and forth down the angle of deck and bulkhead, no easy proposition: was tired and had visions of bed and sleep. There was no question of spending her last night on *Dublin*. There was no room, the onboard sleeping accommodations filled with others with more seniority. Her leaving had the same exigencies as her life aboard, no room, never room; and she made her overloaded way down the dockside with a knot in her throat and a smothered anger at the way of things, worked the anger off in the effort of walking, burdened as she was. So good-bye, for once and all. It hurt; she expected that. So did giving birth, and other necessary things.

There was *Lucy*'s berth at last, aswarm with loading vehicles, with lights and Downers and dockers. Chaos. The sight unfolding past the gantries drained the strength out of her. She stopped a moment to take her breath, then started doggedly toward the mess, closer and closer. There was Stevens, out there on the dockside, in a disreputable pair of coveralls, shouting orders for the dockers who were rolling canisters onto the loading ramp in rapid sequence.

She walked into it, into a sudden confluence of Downers who tugged at the straps and sacks. "Take, take for you," they piped, and she tried to keep them. "It's all right," Stevens called to her: she surrendered the weight. "Air lock," she instructed the Downers, shouting over the clank of loading ramps and canisters, and they whistled and bobbed and scampered off with the load, blithe and light. Her knees ached.

"When did this start?" she asked Stevens, who looked wrung out.

"Too long ago. Listen, I've got a call the supplies are coming in any minute. You want to do me a favor, get on that. Ship's stores are core, bridge-accessed for null *G* stuff; or stack it in the lift corridor if it's personal and heated-area stuff; and in the core if it's freezer stuff too, because we can't get at the galley yet. You'll have to suit up."

"Got it." She gathered her reserves and headed up the ramp to look it over. It was going to be that way, she reckoned, for the next few hours; and with luck the rest of the unit would come trailing in shortly.

She hoped.

And the supplies started coming.

Curran and Neill came in together, with notions of sleep abandoned; Deirdre came trailing in last, with most of the real work done, and Stevens a shell of himself, his voice mostly gone, checking the last of the loading with the docker boss, signing papers. Most of it was his job—had to be, since he was the only one who knew the ship,. the shape of the holds and where the tracks ran and how to arrange the load for access at Venture.

They all trailed into the sleeping area finally, sweating and undone, Stevens bringing up the rear. Allison sat down on one of the benches, collapsing in the clutter of personal belongings she had struggled to get to main level—sat among her cousins likewise encumbered and saw Stevens cast himself down at the number four bridge post to call the dockmaster's office and report status; to feed the manifest into comp finally, a matter of shoving the slip into the recorder and waiting till the machine admitted it had read it out.

So they boarded. They sat there, in their places, too tired to move, Neill stretched out on a convenient couch with a soft bit of baggage under his head.

"Still 0900 for departure?" Allison asked. "Got those charts yet?"

Stevens nodded. "Going to get some sleep and input them."

"We've got to get our hours arranged. Put you and Neill and Deirdre on mainday and me and Curran on alterday."

He nodded again, accepting that.

"It's 0400," he said. "Not much time for rest."

She thought of the bottle in her baggage, bent over and

delved into one of the sacks, came up with that and uncapped it—offered it first to Stevens, an impulse of self-sacri-
fice, a reach between the sleeping couches and the number
four post.

"Thanks," he said. He drank a sip and passed it back; she
drank, and it went from her to Curran and to Deirdre: Neill
was already gone, asprawl on the couch.

No one said much: they killed the bottle, round and
round, and long before she and Curran and Deirdre had
reached the bottom of it, Stevens had slumped where he sat,
collapsed with his head fallen against the tape-patched plastic,
one arm hanging limp off the arm of the cushion. "Maybe we
should move him," Allison said to Curran and Deirdre.

"Can't move myself," Curran said.

Neither could she, when she thought about it. No searching
after blankets, nothing to make the bare couches more comfortable. Curran made himself a nest of his baggage on the
couch, and Dierdre got a jacket out of her bags and flung
that over herself, lying down.

Allison inspected the bottom of the bottle and set it down,
picked out her softest luggage and used it for a pillow, with a
numbed aching spot in her, for *Dublin*, for the change in her
affairs.

The patches in the upholstery, the dinginess of the paneling
. . . everything: these were the scars a ship got from neglect.
From a patch-together operation.

Lord, the backup systems Stevens had talked about: they
were going out at maindawn and there was no way those systems could have been installed yet. He meant to get them in
while they were running: probably thought nothing of it.

Military cargo. The cans they had taken on were sealed.
Chemicals, most likely. Life-support goods. Electronics.
Things stations in the process of putting themselves back in
operation might desperately need.

But Mallory being involved—this military interest in
Lucy—she felt far less secure in this setting-out than she had
expected to be.

And what if Mallory was the enemy he had acquired, she
wondered, her mind beginning to blank out on her, with the
liquor and the exhaustion. What if he had had some previous
run-in with Mallory? There was no way to know. And she
had brought her people into it.

She slept with fists clenched. It was that kind of night.

XI

Moving out.

Sandor sat at the familiar post, doing the familiar things—held himself back moment by moment from taking a call on com, from doing one of the myriad things he was accustomed to doing simultaneously. No tape on the controls this run: competent Dubliner voices, with that common accent any ship developed, isolate families generations aboard their ships—talked in his left ear, while station com came into his right. Relax, he told himself again and again: it was like running the ship by remote, with a whole different bank of machinery . . . Allison sat the number two seat, and the voices of Curran and Deirdre and Neill softly gave him all that he needed, anticipating him. Different from other help he had had aboard—anticipating him, knowing what he would need as if they were reading his mind, because they were *good*.

"There she goes," Allison said, putting *Dublin* on vid. "That's good-bye for a while."

Another voice was talking into his right ear, relayed through station: it was the voice of *Dublin* wishing them well.

"Reply," Allison said to Neill at com; and a message went out in return. But there was no interruption: no move faltered; the data kept coming, and now they did slow turnover, a drifting maneuver.

"Cargo secure," the word came to him from Deirdre. "No difficulties."

"Got that. Stand by rotation."

"Got it."

He pushed the button: the rotation lock synched in, and there began a slow complication of the cabin stresses, a settling of backsides and bodies into cushions and arms to sides and minds into a sense of up and down. They were getting acceleration stress and enough rotational force to make the whole ship theirs again. "All right," he said, when their status was relayed to station, when station sent them back a run-clear for system exit. "We get those systems installed. Transfer all scan to number two and we'll get it done."

"Lord help us," Curran muttered—did as he was asked and carefully climbed out of his seat while Sandor got out of his. "You always make your repairs like this?"

"Better than paying dock charge," Sandor said. "Hope they gave us a unit that works."

A shake of Curran's head.

They had time, plenty of time, leisurely moving outbound from Pell. The noise of station com surrounded them, chatter from the incoming merchanter *Pixy II*, a Name known all over the Beyond; and the music of other Names, like *Mary Gold* and the canhauler *Kelly Lee*. And all of a sudden a new name: "*Norway*'s outbound," Neill said.

For a moment Sandor's heart sped; he sat still, braced as he was against the scan station cushion—but that was only habit, that panic. "On her own business, I'll reckon," he said, and set himself quietly back to the matter of the replacement module.

The warship passed them: as if they were a stationary object, the carrier went by. Deirdre put it on vid and there was nothing to see but an approaching disturbance that whipped by faster than vid could track it.

"See if you can find out their heading," Allison asked Deirdre.

Station refused the answer. "Got it blanked," Deirdre said. "She's not tracked on any schematic and longscan isn't handling her."

"Bet they're not," Sandor muttered. "Reckon she's on a hunt where we're going."

No one said anything to that. He looked from time to time in Allison's direction—suspecting that the hands on *Lucy*'s controls at the moment had never guided a ship through any procedure: competent, knowing all things to do, making no mistakes, few as there were to make in this kind of operation that auto could carry as well. He did not ask the question: Allison and the others had their pride, that was certain—but he had that notion, from the look in Allison Reilly's eyes when control passed to her, a flicker of panic and desire at once, a tenseness that was not like the competency she had shown before that.

So she had worked sims, at least; or handled the controls of an auxiliary bridge on a ship the size of *Dublin*, matching move for move with *Dublin* helm. She was all right.

But he got up when he saw her reach to comp and try to key through to navigation, held to the back of her cushion. "You don't have the comp keys posted," she said. "I don't get the nav function under general op."

"Better let me do the jump setup," he said. "This time. I know her."

She looked at him, a shift of her eyes mirrored in the screen in front of her. "Right," she said. "You want to walk me through it?"

He held where he was, thinking about that, about the deeper things in comp.

(Ross. . . . Ross, now what?)

"You mind?" she asked, on the train of what she had already asked.

So it came. "Let me work it out this time," he said. "You're supposed to be on alterday. Suppose you take your time off and go get some sleep. You're going to have to take her after jump."

"Look, I'd like to go through the setup."

"Did I tell you who's setting up the schedules on this ship? Go on. Get some rest."

She said nothing for the moment, sitting with her back to him. He stayed where he was, adamant. And finally she turned on the auto and levered herself out of the cushion. Offended pride. It was in every movement.

"Cabins are up the curve there," he said, trying to pretend he had noticed none of the signals, trying to smooth it over with courtesy. It hurt enough, to offer that, to open up the cabins more than the one he had given to his sometime one-man crews. ("I sleep on the bridge," he had always said; and done that, bunked in the indock sleeping area, catnapped through the nights, because going into a cabin, sealing himself off from what happened on *Lucy*'s bridge—there was too much mischief could be done.—"Crazy," they had muttered back at him. And that thought always frightened him.) "Take any one you like. I'm not particular.—Curran," he said, turning from Allison's cold face—and found all the others looking at him the same way.

("Crazy," others had said of him, when he occupied the bridge that way.)

"Look," he said, "I'm running her through the jumps this go at it. I know my ship. You talk to me when it gets to the return trip."

"I had no notion to take her through," Allison said. "But I won't argue the point."

She walked off, feeling her way along the counter, toward the corridor. He turned, keyed in and took off the security locks all over the ship, turned again to look at Curran, at the others, clustered about the console where they were installing the new systems. He had offended their number one's dignity: he understood that. But given time he could straighten comp out, pull the jump function out of Ross's settings. And the other things . . . it was a trade, the silence Ross had filled, for live voices.

Putting those programs into silence—sorting Ross's voice out of the myriad functions that reminded him, talked to him—(Good morning, Sandy. Time to get up. . . .)

Or the sealed cabins, where Krejas had lived, cabins with still some remnant of personal items . . . things the Mazianni had not wanted. . . . things they had not put under the plates. And the loft, where Ma'am and the babies had been. . . .

"Curran," he said, daring the worst, but trying to cover what he had already done, "you're on Allison's shift too. Any cabin you like."

Curran fixed him with his eyes and got up from the repair. "That's in," Curran said. Being civil. But there was no softness under that voice. "What about the other one?"

"We'll see to it. Get some rest."

We. Neill and Deirdre. Their looks were like Curran's; and suddenly Allison was back in the entry to the corridor.

"There's stuff in there," she said, not complaining, reporting. "Is that yours, Stevens?"

"Use it if you like." It was an immolation, an offering. "Or pack it when you can get to it. There's stuff left from my family."

"Lord, Stevens. How many years?"

"Just move it. Use it or pack it away, whichever suits you. Maybe you can get together and decide if there's anything in the cabins that might be of use to you. There's not that much left."

A silence. Allison stood there. "I'll see to it," she said. She walked away with less stiffness in her back than had been in the first leaving. And the rest of them—when he looked back—they had a quieter manner. As if, he thought, they had never really believed that there had been others.

Or they were thinking the way other passengers had thought, that it was a strange ship. A stranger captain.

"Going offshift," Curran said, and followed Allison.

Neill and Deirdre were left, alone with him, looking less than comfortable. "Install the next?" Neill said.

"Do that," Sandor said. "I've got a jump to set up."

He turned, settled into the cushion still warm from Allison's body. *Lucy* continued on automatic, traversing Pell System at a lazy rate.

Of *Norway* there was now no sign. Station was giving nothing away on that score.

A long way, yet, for the likes of a loaded merchanter, to the jump range. Easy to have set up the coordinates. He went over the charts, turned off the sound on comp, ran the necessities through—started through the manual then, trying to figure how to silence comp for good.

(I'll get it on tape, Ross. For myself. Lose no words. No program. Nothing. Figure how to access it from my quarters only.)

But Ross knew comp and he never had, not at that level; Ross had done things he did not understand, had put them in and wound voice and all of it together in ways that defied his abilities.

(But, Ross, there's too much of it. Everywhere, everything. All the care—to handle everything for me—and I can't unwind it. There's no erase at that level: not without going into the system and pulling units. . . .

(And *Lucy* can't lose those functions. . . .)

"We got it." Neill was leaning on the back of the cushion, startled him with the sudden voice. "Got it done.—Is there some kind of problem, there?"

"Checking."

"Help you?"

"Why don't you get some sleep too?"

"You're in worse shape."

"That's all right." A smooth voice, a casual voice. His hands tended to shake, and he tried to stop that. "I'm just finishing up here."

"Look, we know our business. We're good at it."

"I don't dispute that."

Deirdre leaned on the other side of the cushion. "Take some help," she said. "You can use it."

"I can handle it."

"How long do you plan to go on handling it?" Neill asked. "This isn't a solo operation."

"You want to be of help, check to see about those trank doses for jump."

"Is something wrong there?"

"No."

"The trank doses are right over there in storage," Neill said. "No problem with that."

"Then let be."

"Stevens, you're so tired your hands are shaking."

He stared at the screens. Reached and wiped everything he had asked to see. The no-sound command went out with it. It always would. It was set up that way.

"Why don't you get some rest back there?"

"I've got the jump set up," he said. He reached and put the lock back on the system; that much he could do. "You two take over, all right?" He got up from the chair, stumbled and Neill caught his arm. He shook the help off, numb, and walked back to the area of the couches to lie down again.

They would laugh, he thought; he imagined them hearing that voice addressing a boy who was himself, and they would go through all of that privacy the way they went through the things in the cabins.

He should never have reacted at all, should have taken the lock off and let her and the others hear it as a matter of course. But they planned changes in *Lucy*; planned things they wanted to do, destroying her from the inside. He sensed that. And he could not bear them to start with Ross.

He was, perhaps, what the others had said, crazy. Solitude could do that, and perhaps it had happened to him a long time ago.

And he missed Ross's voice, even in lying down to sleep. What he discovered scared him, that it was not their hearing the voices in *Lucy* that troubled him, half so much as their discovering the importance the voices had for him. He was not whole; and that had never been exposed until now—even to himself.

He did not sleep. He lay there, chilled from the air and too tired to get up and get a blanket; tense and trying in vain to

relax; and listening to two Dubliners at *Lucy*'s controls, two
people sharing quiet jokes and the pleasure of the moment.
Whole and healthy. No one on *Dublin* had scars. But the war
had never touched them. There were things he could have
more easily said to Mallory than to them, in their easy trivial-
ity.

Mallory did not know how to laugh.

They reached their velocity, and insystem propulsion shut
down; Allison felt it, snugged down more comfortably in the
bed and drifted off again.

And waked later with that feeling one got waking on
sleepovers, that the place was wrong and the sounds and the
smells strange.

Lucy. Not *Dublin* but *Lucy.* Irrevocable things had happened. She felt out after the light switch on the bed console,
brightened the lights as much as she could bear, rolled her
eyes to take in the place, this two meter by four space that
she had picked for hers . . . but there was a clutter in the
locker and storage, a comb and brush with blond hair snarled
in it, a few sweaters, underwear, an old pair of boots, other
things—just left. And *cold* . . . the heat had been on maybe
since last night, had not penetrated the lockers. A woman's
cabin. Newer, cleaner than the rest of the ship, as if the ship
had gotten wear the cabin had not.

Pirates, Stevens had said; pirates had killed them all. If it
was one of those odd hours when he told the truth.

There was nothing left with a name on it, to know what
the woman had been, what name, what age—not rejuved: the
hair had been blond. Like Stevens' own.

Or whatever the name might have been.

And how did one man escape what happened to the others? That question worried her: why, if pirates had gotten the
others—he had stayed alive; or how long ago it had been,
that a ship could wear everywhere but these sealed cabins.
Questions and questions. The man was a puzzle. She stirred
in the bed, thought of sleepover nights, wondered whether
Stevens had a notion to go on with that on the ship as well,
in cabins never made for it.

Not now, she thought; not in this place. Not in a dead
woman's bed and in a ship full of deceptions. Not until it was
straight what she had brought her people into. She was

obliged to think straight, to keep all the options open. And keeping Stevens off his balance seemed a good idea.

Besides, it was business aboard—and no time for straightening out personal reckonings, no time for quarrels or any other thing but the ship under their hands.

The ship, dear God, the ship: she ached in every bone and had blisters on her hands, but she had sat a chair and had the controls in her hands—and whatever had gone on aboard, whoever the woman who had had this room and died aboard—whatever had happened here, there was that; and she had her cousins about her, who would have mortgaged their souls for an hour at *Dublin*'s boards and sold out all they had for this long chance. She could not go back, now, to waiting, on *Dublin*, for the rest of a useless life.

Hers. Her post. She had gotten that for the others as well, done more for them than they could have hoped for in their lives. And they were *hers*, in a sense more than kinship and ship-family. If she said walk outside the lock, they walked; if she said hands off, it was hands off and quiet; and that was a load on her shoulders—this Stevens, who figured to have a special spot with her. They might misread cues, her cousins, take chances with this man. No, no onboard sleepovers, no muddling up their heads with that, making allowances when maybe they should not make them. It was not dockside, when a Dubliner's yell could bring down a thousand cousins bent on mayhem. Different rules. Different hazards. She had not reckoned that way, until she had looked in the lockers. But somewhere not so far away, she reckoned, Curran slept in someone's abandoned bed and spent some worry on it. And the others—

She turned onto her stomach, fumbled after an unfamiliar console, punched in on comp.

Nothing. The room screen stayed dead.

She pushed com one, that should be the bridge. "Allison in number two cabin: I'm not getting comp."

A prolonged silence.

Everything unraveled, the presumed safety of being in Pell System, still in civilized places . . . the reckonings that there were probably sane explanations for things when all was said and done . . . she flung herself out of bed with her heart beating in panic, started snatching for her clothes.

A maniac, it might be; a lunatic who might have done harm to the lot of them. . . . She had no real knowledge

what this Stevens might be, or have done. A liar, a thief—
She looked about for any sort of weapon.

"Allison." Neill's voice came over com. "Got lunch ready."

"Neill?" Her heart settled to level. In the first reaction she
was ashamed of herself.

In the second she was thinking it was stupid not to have
brought her luggage into the cabin; she had a knife in that, a
utilitarian one, but something. She had never thought of
bringing weapons with her, but she did now, having seen
what she had seen . . . sleeping in a cabin that could become
a trap if someone at controls pushed the appropriate buttons.

"You coming?" Neill asked.

"Coming," she said.

It was better, finally, Sandor reckoned, with all of them at
once in the bridge sleeping area, with trays balanced on their
laps, a bottle of good wine passing about. It was the kind of
insane moment he had never imagined seeing aboard *Lucy*, a
thing like family, unaffordable food—Neill had pulled some
of the special stuff, and the wine had been chilling since loading; and it all hit his empty stomach and unstrung nerves
with soothing effect. He listened to Dubliner jokes and
laughed, saw laughter on Allison's face, and that was best of
all.

"Listen," he said to her afterward, catching up to her when
she was taking her baggage to her quarters—he met her at
the entry to the corridor, loaded with bundles. "Allison—I
want you to know, back then with the controls—I wasn't
thinking how it sounded. I'm sorry about that."

"You don't have to walk around my feelings."

"Can I help you with that?"

She fixed him with a quick, dark eye. "With ulterior mo-
tives? I don't sleepover during voyages."

He blinked, set hard aback, unsure how to take it—a moment's temper, or something else. "So, well," he said. "Not
over what I said . . . Allison, you're not mad about that."

"Matter of policy. I just don't think it's a good idea."

"It's hard, you know that."

"I don't think I'd feel comfortable sharing command and
bed. Not on ship. Sleepover's different."

"What, command? It's home. It's—"

"Maybe *Dublin* does things differently. Maybe it's another
way on this ship. But it's not another way that quickly. You

know, Stevens, I'll share a sleepover with an honest spacer and not care so much what name he goes by, but on ship, somehow the idea of sharing a cabin with a man whose name I don't know—"

"You handed me half a million credits not knowing—"

"I rate myself priceless, man. One of a kind. I don't go in any deal."

"I didn't say that."

"I'll bet you didn't."

"Allison, for God's sake, you twist everything up. You're good at that."

"Right. So you know you can't talk your way around me." She thrust past with the baggage. He caught a strap on her shoulder, peeled half the bundles away, and she glared back at him through a toss of hair. "Don't take so much on yourself, mister."

"Just the baggage."

"I don't need your help." She snatched at the straps he held and failed to get them back. "Just drop them in the corridor. I'll come back and get them."

"You can't take any help, can you?"

She walked off. "From the man who took a half million credits with never a thanks—" She stopped and looked back when he started after her with the bag, almost collided. "You choke on the words, do you, Stevens?"

"Thanks," he said. "That do it?"

"Just bring the bags." She turned about again, stalked one door farther and opened the compartment, tossed her belongings through the door and stood aside outside it, a wave of her hand indicating the way inside.

He tossed them after the first. "What about thanks?" he said.

"Thanks." She shut the door, still outside it.

"Look, you think you have to go through this to tell me no? I can take no. I understand you."

"What's the real name?" Quietly asked. Decently asked.

"Think it'd change your mind?"

"No. Not necessarily. But I think it says something about no trust."

"First name's Sandor."

A lift of both dark brows. "Not Ed, then."

"No."

"Just—no. Nothing further, eh?"

He shrugged. "You're right. It's not dockside, is it?" He looked into dark eyes the same that he had seen one night in a Viking bar, and he was as lost, as dammed up inside. "Can't break things up when they get tangled."

"Can't," she said. "So you understand it: I might sleepover with you when we get to Venture. I might sleepover with someone else instead. You follow that? I came. But if you reckon I came with the loan, figure again."

"I never," he said, "never figured that."

She nodded. "So we take this a little slower, a lot slower."

"So suppose I say I'd like to take it up again at Venture."

She stared at him a moment, and some of the tenseness went out of her shoulders. "All right," she said. "All right. I like that idea."

"Like?"

"I'm just not comfortable with it the other way."

"Might change your mind someday?"

"Ah. Don't push."

"I'm not pushing. I'm asking whether you might see it differently."

"The way you look at me, Stevens—"

"Sandor."

"—makes me wonder."

"I understand how you feel. About being on the ship. Maybe my talking like that, in front of the others back there—is a good example of what you're worried about. I didn't think how it went out. I know you know what you're doing. I just had my mind full . . . I've just got some things with the ship I haven't got straight yet. Things—never mind. I just have to get over the way I'm used to doing things. And dealing with the kind of crew I'm used to getting."

She tightened her mouth in a grimace that looked preparatory to saying something, exhaled then. It seemed to have slipped her. "All right. I understand that too. You mind fixing comp in my quarters while we're at it?"

His heart did a thump, attack from an unexpected direction. "I'll get it straightened out. Promise you. After jump."

"Security locks?"

"They seemed like a good thing when I had unlicensed crew aboard."

"Well, it's a matter of the comp keys, isn't it?"

It was not a conversation he wanted. Not at all. "Look, we

haven't got time for me to get them all down or for you to memorize them. We're heading up on our exit."

"Is there something I ought to know?"

"Maybe I worry a bit when I've got strangers aboard. Maybe that's a thing I've got like you've got attitudes—"

Her back went stiff. "Maybe you'd better make that clear."

"I don't mean like that. I'm dead serious. That's all I've got, those keys, between me and people I really don't know that well. And maybe that makes me nervous."

The offense at least faded. The wariness stayed. "Meaning you think we'd cut your throat."

"Meaning maybe I want to think about it."

"Oh, that's a little late. A little late. We're on this ship. And we're talking about safety. Our safety. If something goes wrong on my watch, I want those keys. None of this nonsense."

"Look, let's get through jump first. I'll get you a list then."

"Through jump, where we're committed. I don't consider the comp a negotiable item." She jabbed a thumb toward her cabin door. "I want my comp in there operative. I want any safety locks in this ship off. I want the whole system written down for all of us to memorize."

"We haven't got time for that. Listen to me. I'm taking *Lucy* through this jump; I don't want any question about that. I'll see how you handle her; and then maybe I'll feel safe about it. You look good. But I'm reckoning you never handled anything but sims in your life. And I'm sleeping on the bridge if I have to, to see no one makes a mistake. I'm sorry if that ruffles your pride. But even I haven't a good notion of what *Lucy* feels like loaded."

"*Don't* you?" Suspicion. A sudden, flat seizure of attention.

"I'll take the locks off when I know who I'm working with." He thrust his hands into his pockets, started away, to break it off. Instinct turned him about again, a peace offering. "So I'm a bastard. But *Lucy*'s not what you're used to, in a lot of senses. I haven't nursed her this far or got you out here to die with, no thanks. I'm asking you—I want you all on the bridge when we go into jump."

"All right," she said. A quiet all right. But there was still that reserve in her eyes. "You watch us. You see how it is. Sims, yes. And backup bridge. But you catch me in a mistake, you do that."

"I don't think I will," he said softly. "I don't expect it."

"Only you're careful, are you?"

"I'm careful."

They approached jump, a sleep later, a slow ticking of figures on the screen—a calm approach, an easy approach. Sandor checked everything twice, asked for data from supporting stations, because jumping loaded was a different kind of proposition. Full holds, an unfamiliar jump point—there were abundant reasons to be glad of additional hands on this one. "Got it set," he said to Allison, who sat number two. "Check those figures, will you?"

"Already doing that," Allison said. "Just a minute."

The figures flashed back to him.

"You're good," he said.

"Of course." That was the Dubliner. No sense of humility. "We all are. We going for it?"

"Going for it.—Count coming up. Any problems?—Five minutes, *mark*. Got our referent." He reached for the trank and inserted the needle. There was no provision on this one but a water bottle in the brace, for comfort's sake. No need. They would exit at a point named James's, and laze across it in honest merchanter fashion; and then on to Simon's Point, and to Venture.

The numbers ticked on.

"Message from Pell buoy," Neill said, "acknowledging our departure."

No reply necessary. It was automated. *Lucy* went on singing her unceasing identification, communicating with Pell's machinery.

"Mark," Sandor said, and hit the button. . . .

XII

... Down again, into a welter of input from the screens, trank-blurred. Sandor reached in slow motion and started to deal with it. Beside him, the others—and for a moment his mind refused to sort that fact in. There was the mass which had dragged *Lucy* in out of the Dark . . . they were at James's Point, Voyager-bound; and Ross's voice was silent.

"Got it," Allison was saying beside him, icy-cold and competent. "Just the way the charts gave it. . . ."

He was still not used to that, a stranger-voice that for a moment was desolation . . . but it was *her* voice, and there was backup on his right, all about him. "Going for dump," he said.

And then Curran's voice: "We're not alone here."

It threw him, set his heart pounding: his hand faltered on the way to vital controls. Velocity needed shedding, loaded as they were, tracking toward the mass that had snatched them. Things happened fast in pre-dump, too fast—

"Standing by dump," Allison said.

"That's *Norway*," Neill said then.

He hit the dump, kicked in the vanes, shedding what they carried in a flutter of sickening pulses. "She still with us?" he asked, meaning *Norway*. Sensor ghosts could linger, light-bound information on a ship which had left hours ago. No way to discern, maybe—but he wanted his crew's minds on it. Wanted them searching. Hard.

"Better set up the next jump in case," Allison said. "I don't trust this."

"Outrun that?" Sandor focused on the question through the trank haze. "You're dreaming, Reilly." They kicked off velocity again, a numbing pulse that scrambled wits a moment. He blinked and reached an unsteady hand toward comp, started lining the tracking up again.

"We're in," Allison said. "That's got us on velocity."

"Getting nothing more than ID transmission," Neill said.

"Got a solid image," Curran said. "They're *close*. That's confirmed, out there, range two minutes."

The image hit his screen, transferred unasked. "Should I contact them?" Neill asked. "I'm getting no com output."

"No." He blinked, the sweat running on his face, concentrated on the business in front of him—and that ship out there, right on them as a warship reckoned speed, silent, sullen—was Mazianni in all but name. He got a lock on the reference star, saw the figures come up congruent, fed them in and sent the information over to Allison's console.

"Got it clear," Allison said. "Still want me to take it, or do you want to hold it?"

He caught his breath, sent a desperate look over all the board in front of him. Vid showed them nothing but stars; other sensors showed the *G* well itself, the mass, the heat of an almost-star that was the nullpoint. And the pockmark that was *Norway*. A situation. A raw Dubliner recruit asking for the board, maybe not particularly anxious to have control at the moment. He shunted things over to the number two board. "She's yours." His voice was hoarse. He pretended nonchalance, let go the restraints, reached for the water bottle and drank. "Here."

Allison looked aside, a distracted flick of her eyes, took the bottle and drank a gulp, passed it back. He slipped it back into the brace and hauled his way out of the cushion.

Looked back again, toward the screens, with a tightness about his throat.

Norway. And Mallory was saying nothing. The presence did not surprise him. Somehow the foreboding silence did not either.

"Mainday shift," he said, "let alterday have it."

"Sir," Neill muttered, the first courtesy of that kind he had gotten out of them. Natural as breathing from a Dubliner on a bridge. Spit and polish, and he finally got it out of them. Neill stirred out of his place.

"Got another one," Deirdre said suddenly. "Got another ship out there."

Sandor crossed the deck to his chair in a stride and a half, flung himself into it.

"ID as Alliance ridership *Thor*," Deirdre said. "Coming out of occultation with the mass."

"One of Mallory's riders," Allison muttered.

"If they've got the riders deployed—" Neill said, back at his own post.

No one made any further surmises.

"Second signal," Deirdre said. "The ID is ridership *Odin.*"

"Deployed before we dropped in here," Sandor said.

"What do you know about it?" Curran asked.

"*Sir,*" Sandor said.

Curran turned his head. "From back at Pell, *sir*—did you expect this? What was it Mallory said?"

"That she's watching the nullpoint. I'm not at all surprised she's here. Or that she's not talking. What would you expect? A good morning?"

"Lord help us," Allison muttered. "And what kind of cargo have they handed us, that we get Mallory for a nursemaid?"

"I don't ask questions."

"Maybe we should have," Curran said. "Maybe we should get ourselves a couple of those canisters open."

"I'm reckoning you'd find chemicals and station goods," Sandor said. "I'd even bet it's Konstantin Company cargo, the same as we would have gotten. I don't think that's what Mallory's interested in at all. I think we're being prodded at."

"Because they're still breathing down your neck: that's what we've inherited—your own record with them. It's some kind of trap, something we've walked into—"

"You applied for Venture routing, Mr. Reilly. *Dublin* handed a marginer a half a million, stifled an inquiry, and headed us for Pell's most sensitive underside. A Unionsider. Put it together. Union and Alliance may be at peace, but Mallory's got old habits. Maybe you'd better think like a marginer, after all. Maybe you'd better start figuring angles, because they have them in offices, the same as dockside. And the powers that be on Unionside had them, when they got cooperative and wanted *Dublin* this side of the Line. But maybe you'd know that. Or maybe you should have sat down and figured it."

"If you've got it figured, then say it. Let the rest of us in on it."

"Not me. I *don't* know. But we're not making any noise we don't have to. We tiptoe through this point and get that cargo to—"

"Moving," Deirdre said. "*Thor's* moving on intercept."

Sandor dived for the board, a sweat broken out on his sides, sickly cold on his face. He stopped his hand short of

the controls, clenched it there in the reckoning that there was
nothing they could do. . . . No arms the equal of that; no
ability to run, loaded as they were.

(Ross? . . . Ross. . . . What's to do?)

"Contact them?" Allison asked.

"No."

"Stevens . . . Sandor . . . what precious else can we do?"

"We keep going on our own business. We let them escort
us through the point if that's what they have in mind. But we
don't open up to them. Let the contact be theirs."

She said nothing. Helm was still under her control. The
ship kept her course as she was, no variances.

"Message incoming," Neill said: "They say: Escort to outgoing range. They say: request exact time and range our departure from Pell."

"They're tracking us," Curran muttered.

"They repeat. They want acknowledgment."

"Acknowledge it," Sandor said. "Tell them we're figuring."
He sat down at comp, keyed through and downed the sound,
started calling up the information.

"Sir," Neill said. "Sir, I think you'd better talk to them.
They're insisting."

He snatched up the audio plug and thrust that into his ear,
adjusted the mike wand from the plug one-handed. "Feed it
through."

". . . accurate," he caught. "Lives ride . . . on absolute
accuracy, *Lucy*. Do you copy that?"

"Say again.—Neill, what's he talking about, lives?"

"To whom am I speaking?" the voice from the ridership
asked. "To Stevens?"

"This is Stevens, trying to do your calculations if you'll
blasted well give me time."

"Your ship will proceed to Voyager as scheduled. You'll
dock and discharge Voyager cargo. You have three days for
station call, to the hour. And you'll return to this jump point
on that precise schedule."

"Request information."

"No information. We're waiting for that departure data."

"Precise   time   local: 2/02:0600   mainday;   locator
8868:0057:0076.35, tracking on recommended referents, Pell
chart 05700."

"2/02:0600 precise?"

"You want our mass reckoning?" He was scared. It was a

track they were running, no question about it. He flung out
the question to let them know he knew.

"You carrying anything except our cargo, *Lucy*?"

"Nothing." The air from the vent touched sweat on his
face. "Look, I'll run that reckoning on my own comp and give
you our RET."

"Is 0600 accurate?"

"0600:34."

"We copy 0600:34. Your reckoning is not needed, *Lucy*."

"Look, if you want data—"

"No further questions, *Lucy*. We find that agreeing with
our estimate. Congratulations. Endit."

"We're in trouble," Allison said.

"They're accounting for our moves," he said. "Just figuring. I'd reckon Pell buoy scheduled us pretty well the way
they set it up." He shut down comp, back under lock. "So
they know now what our ETA is with the mass we're
hauling: every move we make from now on—"

"I don't like this."

"Every point shut down. Everything monitored. We make
a false move—and we're in trouble, all right." He thrust back
from controls. "Nothing's going to move on us here while
that's out there. Shut down to alterday. Mainday, go on rest."

"Look," Curran said, twisting in his cushion. "We're not
going through Pell System lanes anymore. We're not sitting
here to do autopilot, not with them breathing down our necks
and wanting answers."

"I'm here," he said, looking back. "I'm not leaving the
bridge: going to wash, that's all; and eat and get some sleep
right back there in the downside lounge. You call me if you
need anything."

"Instructions," Allison said sharply, stopping him a second
time. "Contingencies."

"There isn't any contingency. There isn't any blasted thing
to do, hear me? We've got three days minimum crossing this
point, and you let—" He saw her face, which had gone from
appeal to opaque, unclenched a sweating hand and made a
cancelling gesture. "They're one jump from Mazianni themselves, you know that? Let's just don't give them excuses.
We're a little ship, Reilly, and we don't mass much in any
sense. Accidents happen in the nullpoints. Now true a line
crosspoint and don't get fancy with it."

She gave him a long, thinking stare. "Right," she said, and turned back to business.

He walked, light-headed, back to the maintenance area shower, not to the cabins; *had* no cabin. The others had. He was conscious of that. And he had to sleep, and they chafed at the situation. He stripped, showered, alone there with the hiss of the water and the warmth and a cold knot in his gut that did not go away. Mazianni ships out there . . . and they had died out there, in the corridor, on the bridge, bodies fallen everywhere. Reillys sat and joked and moved about, but the silence was worse than before, deep as that in which *Lucy* moved now, with Mallory.

(Armored intruders, a name—a name on them, on the armor; but he could never focus on it, never get it clear in his mind; he had never talked about that with Ross; never wanted to know—until it was too late, and Ross never came back to the ship. . . .)

He had thought for a day on Pell that he was free, clear. But it was with them. It ran beside them, the nightmare that had been following *Lucy* for seventeen years.

They took it three and three, she and Curran, on a twelve-hour watch: three hours on and three off by turns, their own choice. Allison sat the number two chair on her offtime or padded quietly about the bridge examining this and that, while their military escort kept its position and maintained its silence.

From Sandor/Stevens, who had made his bed aft of the bridge in the indock lounge—not a sound, although she suspected that he wakened from time to time, a silent, furtive waking, as if he only grazed sleep and came out of it again. And from Neill and Deirdre, asleep in cabins four and five respectively, no stirring forth. Exhausted: none of them was used to this, and what kept Stevens going—

What kept Stevens going bothered her, at depth and at every glance back in his direction. Something wrenched at her gut—the memory of an attraction; the indefinable something that had made her crazy on Viking, that had gotten her linked with a no-Name nothing in the first place. Owner of his ship, he had said, in that bar; and maybe that had been enough, with enough to drink and a mood to take chances.

Not quite dead, that gut-feeling. And she had watched the man drawn thinner and thinner, from haggard to haunted—

not sleeping now, she was sure of it. Not able to sleep. That ship out there, that was one good cause. Or the cumulative effect of things.

And he was not about to trank out, no, not with the comp locked up and a warship on their necks; with two Reillys at the controls.

She and Curran talked, when they sat side by side at the main board, spoke in low tones the fans and the rotation could bury. They talked operations and equipment and how a man could have run a ship solo, what failsafes would have to be bypassed and how a man could talk his way past station law.

She reckoned all the while that they might be overheard. Quiet, she signed when Curran got too easy with the remarks. Curran rolled his eyes to the reflective screens and back again, reckoning what she reckoned. *No sleep, he signed back, the kind of language that had grown up over the years on *Dublin*, practiced by crew at work in noise, embellished by the inventive young and only half readable by outsiders. *Watching us.

*Yes.

*Crazy.

She shrugged. That was a maybe.

*Care? A touch at the heart, a swift touch at the head, sarcastically.

She made a tightening of her jaw, an implied gesture of her chin to the ship that paced them. *That. That concerns me.

*He keeps the comp keys.

*He's afraid.

*He's crazy.

She frowned. *Probable, she agreed.

*Do something.

There was no silence in sign. It translated as I won't. She turned a degree and looked Curran in the eyes.

This was her rival, this cousin of hers, the one that pushed, all the way, all the years. It was yang and yin, the both of them, that made alterday Third what it was, and carried Deirdre and Neill. Curran never stopped, never let up. She valued him for that, knew how to reckon him, how he wanted the number one seat, forever wanted it. It was one thing when there were twenty ahead of them—and another when they sat sharing a command. Watch it, she made her look say; and he understood. She read it in his eyes as easy as from a page.

Number two, she thought of him. And she caught herself thinking it with a stab of cold, that that was how it was. There was a man who had this ship, and there was a working unit of Reillys who knew each other's signals and had no need of explaining how it worked, who looked down familiar perspectives and knew what they were to each other and where all the lines were. Number two to her: it fell that way in seniority by two days, two days between her and Curran, between her and a man who would have been as good, at least in his own reckoning. Who could not have gotten them what she had gotten—

—not the same way, she could reckon him saying, raw with sarcasm.

But Curran never saw any way but straight ahead. Would never have blasted them out of their inertia. Would never have taken any chance but the one he was born with: dead stubborn, that was Curran. And it was his flaw. Possibly he knew it. It was why he was loyal: the same inability to swerve. It was a different loyalty from Deirdre's, which was a deepseated dislike of a number one's kind of decisions; or than Neill's, which was a tongue-tied silence: Neill's mind went wider than some, so it took him longer to put his ideas together—a good bridge officer, Neill, but nothing higher. She knew them. Knew what they were good for and how the whole worked, stronger than its parts. She looked down from where she sat and their reflexes all went toward each other and toward her in a sequencing so smooth no one thought about it.

She was number one to them. To Curran she had to be. To justify his taking orders and not giving them, she had to be. And the others—it all broke apart without herself and Curran at their perpetual one-two give and take. Curran was jealous of Stevens, she realized that all in a stroke, a jealousy that had nothing to do with sex; with a pairing, yes; with a function like right hand and left. For her to form another kind of linkup, taking another man in a different way, in which an almost-brother could not intervene, in which he had no place—

What was Curran then? she thought—too proud to settle to Deirdre and Neill's partnership, and cast out of hers in favor of a stranger met in a sleepover. He had to go on respecting her judgment: that was part of his rationale. But that left him. That flatly left him.

She cast a second and sidelong look at her cousin, settling deeper into the cushion, folding her arms. "I'll think of something," she said.

"Going to eat?" he asked after a moment.

She looked at the elapsed time. 1101. She nodded, got out of the seat and walked off toward the galley.

A cold sandwich, a cold drink from storage . . . mealtime, as they reckoned time aboard, from the time of their arrival at the nullpoint. There was no need to force a realtime schedule on tired bodies, no need to reckon realtime at all except in communications, and they were getting no more of that. They had become introverted in their passage, disconnected from other timescales. And there was, when all the movement and human noise was absent—a silence that made her eat her sandwich pacing the small floor space of the galley; that sent her eye to the vacant white plastic tables and benches of the galley mess, and her mind to spacing out the number that could have sat at the tables—

Thirty. About thirty. Double that for mainday and alterday shifts, a ship's crew of about sixty above infancy. And the vacant cabins and the silences. . . .

She had expected a lot of 1 G storage on the ship, a lot of the ring given over to cargo. Customs would expect that. It was a question how far customs would break with courtesies and search the cabins: more likely, they contented themselves with the holds and did a tight check of the flow of goods on and off. A perfect setup for a smuggler, nested in a ship like this, with a good story about pirates and lost family.

But a woman had lived in her cabin before her. Another of Stevens' women, might be . . . but there were the other cabins, all lived in like the first several—they assumed. She had clambered in and out of the barren, dark-metal core storage, entered all the holds they used in dock . . . but the ring beyond the downside area and the cabins and the galley she had not seen. None of them had. They were still visitors on the ship they crewed.

She finished the sandwich, tossed the drink container into the waste storage, and the sound of the chute closing was loud.

1136. There was time enough, in her free hour, to walk

round the rim. To come up on Curran from the other corridor that let out onto the bridge.

She left the galley area, rejoined the central corridor that passed through that, walked past other doors, all cabins, by the numbers of them. She tried a door, found it unlocked. The interior was dark and bitter cold. Power-save. A cabin, with the corner of an unmade bed showing in the light from the door. Rumpled sheets. She logged that oddity in her mind, closed the door and walked on, to an intersecting corridor. She entered it, found another bank of cabins behind the first, a dark corridor of doors and intervals. The desolation afflicted her nerves. She walked back to the main corridor, kept going, the deck ahead of her horizoning down as she traveled.

A section seal was in function: she came on it as a blank wall coming down off the ceiling and finally making an obstacle of itself. Maybe four seals—around the ring. Four places at which the remaining sections could be kept pressurized, if something went wrong. It sealed off the docking-topside zone, the loft.

She stopped, facing that barrier, her heart beating faster and faster—looked at the pressure gauge beside the seal manual control, and it was up.

The loft . . . was the safety-hole of the young on every ship she knew of. Farthest from the airlock lifts; farthest from the bridge, farthest from accesses and exits. And sealed off. It might open. It might; but a section seal was for respecting: gauges could be fatally wrong, for everyone on the ship.

And no one was ass enough to keep hard vacuum in the ring, behind a closed door.

She hesitated one way and the other. Caution won. She reckoned the time must be getting toward 1200—no time and no place to be late. She turned about again—faced Stevens.

"*Hang* you, coming up on a body—"

"It's cold in there," he said. He was barefoot, in his robe, his hair in disarray.

"What's there?" she asked. Her heart had sped, refused to settle. "Cargo space?"

"Used to be the loft. Sealed now. I'll turn the heating on in my watch. I didn't think of it. Never needed to go there."

"You give me the comp and I'll fix it."

He blinked. She wished suddenly she had not said that,

here, her back to the section seal, halfway round the ring from Curran. "I'll fix it," he said. "I'll do it now if you like."

"You're supposed to be off. You have to follow me around?"

Another slow blink. "Got up to get a snack. Thought you were in the galley."

"I'm supposed to be on watch." She walked toward him, past him, and he fell in with her, walked beside her down the corridor into the galley. She stopped there and he stopped and stood. "Thought you were going to get something."

He nodded, went over to dry storage and rummaged out a packet, tore it with his teeth and got a glass. His hands shook in pouring it in, in filling it from the instant heat tap.

"Lord," Allison muttered, "your stomach. You shouldn't drink that stuff when you've got a choice."

"I like it." He grimaced and drank at it, swallowed as if he were fighting nausea.

"You're wiped out, Stevens."

"I'm all right." His eyes had a bruised look, his color sallow. He took another drink and forced that down. "Just need to get something on my stomach."

"You watching us, Stevens? You don't want us loose unwatched? I don't think you've been sleeping at all. How long are you going to keep that up?"

He drank another swallow. "I told you how it's going to be." He turned, threw the rest of the brown stuff in the glass into the disposal and put the glass in the washer. " 'Night, Reilly. Your noon, my midnight."

"Why don't you go get in a real bed, Stevens, a nice cabin, turn out the lights, settle down and get some sleep?"

He shrugged. Walked off.

1158. She was due. She walked behind him, watched his barefoot, unsteady progress down the corridor, walked into the bridge behind him and stood there watching him find his couch in the lounge again. He lay down there on his side, pulled the blankets about him, up to his chin, stiff and miserable looking.

The gut-feeling was back, seeing the disintegration, a man coming apart, biological months compressed into days—hell on a solo voyage while Reillys sipped Cyteen brandy.

She looked at Curran, whose eyes sent something across the bridge—impatience, she thought. She was late. Curran would have seen Stevens leave; she imagined his fretting.

"Your turn," she said, coming to dislodge him from the number one seat. "Any action?"

"Nothing. Everything as was."

She settled into the cushion. Curran lingered, tapped her arm and, shielded by the cushion back, made the handsign for question.

*Negative problem, she signed back. And then a quick touch at Curran's hand before he could draw away. *We two talk, she signed further. *Our night.

*Understood. A moment more he lingered, knowing then that something was on her mind. She gave a jerk of her head toward the galleyward corridor. *Out, she meant; and he went.

Watch to watch: it was the tail of her second, 1442, when Neill came wandering out of the cabins corridor, shaved and combed and fresh-looking. Deirdre followed, pale and sober, looked silently at Stevens sleeping there. *All right? The up-lifted thumb. It was a question.

Allison nodded, and they padded back again, to the little personal time they had in their schedules. She had the ship on auto, their escort running placidly beside them. She watched Curran at his meddling with the comp console, quiet figuring and notetaking. There was not a chance he could crack it. Not a chance.

A bell went off, loud and sudden, down the corridors the way Neill and Deirdre had gone. She looked up, a sudden clenching of her heart, at the blink of a red light on the lifesupport board. The bell and the light stopped. The section seal had opened, closed again. "Deirdre," Curran was saying into com. "Neill. Report."

A weight hit Allison's cushion, Stevens leaning there. "Section seal's opened," she said. "Are they all right, Stevens?"

"No danger, none."

She believed it when Neill's voice came through. "Sorry. We seem to have tripped something."

Exploring the ship. Trying to do the logical thing, going around the rim. "You all right?" Curran asked.

"Just frosted. Nothing more. Section three's frozen down, you copy that."

"You got it shut?"

"Shut tight."

"Here," Stevens said hoarsely, tapped her arm. "Vacate. I'll get the section up to normal. Sorry about that."

"Sure," she said. She slid clear of the cushion and he slid in.

"Just go one," he said. "I'll take care of it, do a little housekeeping. Take a break, you and Curran. We don't need to keep rigid schedules. God knows she's run without it."

Curran might have gone on sitting, obstinate; she gathered him up with a quiet, meaningful glance, a slide of the eyes in the direction Neill and Deirdre had gone. "All right," he said, and came with her, walked out of the bridge and down the corridor.

And stopped when she did, taking his arm, around the curve by the galley.

*He might hear, Curran signed to her. Pointed to the com system.

She knew that. She cast a look about, looking for pickups, found none closer than ten feet. "Listen," she said, "I want you to keep it quiet with him. Friendly. I don't know what the score is here."

"What's he running around there, with a sector frozen down? Contraband, you reckon?"

"I don't know.—Curran, have you tried the doors on the cabins—the other cabins? Something terrible happened on this ship. I don't know when and I don't know what. Hit by the Mazianni, he says; but this—The loft is frozen; the cabins left—you know how they were left . . . there's a slept-in bed around there, frozen down."

"I tell you this," Curran said in the faintest of whispers, "I don't sleep well—in that cabin. Maybe he's worried for himself—about us doing to him what occurs to him to do to us. I don't like it, Allie. Most of all I don't like that comp being locked up. That's dangerous. And you know why he got us out of there . . . not to look over his shoulder while he works, that's what. I wouldn't put it past him, spying on us. Or murder, if it came to it."

"No," she said, a shake of her head. "I don't think that. I never have."

"You ever been wrong, Allie?"

"Not in this."

He frowned, a look up from under his brows. "Maybe the record's still good. And maybe we go on like this and we have a run-in with the military—what's he going to do, Allie? Which way is he going to jump? I don't like it."

"He's strung out. I know it. I know it's not right."

"Allie—" He reached out, touched her shoulder, cousin for the moment and not number two. "Man and woman—he thinks one way with you and maybe he thinks he can get around you; but you let me talk it out with him and I'll straighten it out. And I'll get those comp keys. No question of it."

"I don't want that."

"You don't want it, I don't want it. But we're in trouble, if you haven't noticed. That man's off the brink and he's going farther. I propose we have it out with him . . . we. Me. No chaff with me. He knows that. You just stay low, stay out of it, go to your cabin and we'll put the fear in him."

"No."

"You think of something that makes as good sense? You going to ask him and he'll come over? I'll figure you tried that."

She bit at her lip, looked up the corridor, where Neill and Deirdre came down the horizon. "Sorry," Neill said again; and Deirdre: "Who's minding the ship?"

"He is.—What was it, around there?"

"Loft," Deirdre said. She clenched her arms about her. "A mess—things ripped loose—panels askew—didn't see all of it, just from the section door. Dark in there.—Allie. . . ."

"I know," she said. "I figured what was in there." She thrust her hands into her pockets, started back.

"Where are you going?" Curran asked.

"To my cabin." She looked back, straight at Curran, straight in the eyes. "I'm off. It's your shift. Maybe you'd better get back to the bridge. I'll be there—a while."

XIII

Lucy had gotten along, running stable under auto: Sandor shut down comp and stared a moment at scan, numb, the dread of the warship diminished now. It was not going to jump with them: had no capacity to do that. Mallory herself was sitting still, watching—he could not imagine that much patience among the things they told of Mallory. He did not believe it: she was waiting for something, but it had nothing to do with him. He began to hope that she just wanted them out of her way.

And if it was other Mazianni she was hunting—if she expected other traffic—

He got up, looked once and bleakly at the couch he had quit. There was a little time left in main-night. But the effort to sleep was a struggle hardly worth it, lying there awake for most of the time, to sleep a few minutes and wake again. He had done that all the night. Nervousness. And no chance of tranking out. Not as things were.

He headed for the shower, trusting the autopilot—a scandal to the Dubliners: he imagined that. They wore themselves out sitting watch and he walked off and left it. There were things that wanted doing—scrubbing and swabbing all over the ship, work less interesting to them, he was sure: but he began to think in the long term, a fleeting mode of thought that flickered through his reasonings and went out again. There was the loft—

They had never done anything about the loft, he and Ross and Mitri: no need of the space—*Lucy* was full of empty space; and walking there—they just avoided it. Put it on extreme powersave. The cold kept curious crew out. When he was alone on the ship he had never gone past the galley. It was dead up there . . . until the Reillys started opening doors and violating seals. Opening up areas of himself in the process, like a surgery. He gathered his courage about it, the

149

hour being morning: a man was in trouble who went to bed with panic and got up with it untransformed. He tried to look at it from other sides, think around the situation if not through it.

A little time, that was what he needed, to break the Reillys in and get himself used to them.

But the comp—

(Ross . . . they wouldn't have given out that money for no reason. No one's that rich, that they can spill half a million because a few of their people take a fancy to sign off—half a million for a parting-present. . . .

(People don't throw money away like that. People aren't like that.

(Ross . . . I know what they want. I loved her, Ross, and I didn't see; I was afraid—Pell would have taken the ship— and what could I do? But they think I've sold her; and maybe I have. What do I do, Ross?)

The warm water of the shower hit his body, relaxed the muscles: he turned up the cold on purpose, shocked himself awake. But when he had gotten out he had a case of the shivers, uncommonly violent . . . too little food, he reasoned; schedule upset. He reckoned on getting some of the concentrates: that was a way of eating without tasting it, getting some carbohydrates into his body and getting the shakes out.

They had to make jump tomorrow maindawn. He had to get himself strung back together. Mallory was not going to take excuses out there. Mallory wanted schedules and schedules she got.

He dressed, shaved, dried his hair and went out into the corridor, back to the bridge.

Curran was sitting against a counter—Neill and Deirdre with him. "I'm for breakfast," Sandor said. "I think we could leave her all right, just—"

"Want to talk to you," Curran said. "Captain."

He drew a deep breath, standing next to the scan console— leaned against it, too tired for this, but he nodded. "What?"

"We want to ask you for the keys. There's a question of safety. We've all talked about it. We really have quite a bit of concern about it."

"I've discussed that problem. With Allison. I think we agree on it."

"No. You don't agree. And we're asking you."

"I'll take up the matter with her."

"Are you sure there's no chance of our reasoning with you?"

"I told you."

"I think you'd better think again."

"There are laws, Mr. Reilly. And they're on my side in this." He started away from the counter, to break it off. The others moved, cutting off his retreat—his eye picked Deirdre, the one he could go over—but there was no running. He turned about and looked at Curran. "You want to settle this the hard way? Let's clear the fragile area and talk about it."

"Why don't we?" Curran got off his counteredge and waved them all back, a retreat into the lounge area among the couches, but Sandor went for the corridor, toward the cabins, a slow retreat that drew all of them in that direction.

Allison was in her cabin. He was sure of that, the way he measured his own frame and Curran's and knew who was going to win this one, especially if Curran got help. He reached for the door switch, and Curran caught him up and knocked his hand aside.

He landed one, a knee to the groin and a solid smash to the neck that knocked Curran double—a knee to the face, and Curran hit the wall as he spun about to see to Neill.

A blow at his legs staggered him and Neill and Deirdre moved all at once as Curran tackled him from behind and weighed him down.

He twisted, struck where he had a moment's leverage, over and over again—almost flung himself up, but a wrench at his hair jerked him hard onto his back and they had him pinned. "Out of it," Neill ordered someone. "Out." He kept up the struggle, blind and wild, hunting any leverage, anything. "Look out."

A blow smashed across his jaw, for a moment absorbing all his wit, a deep black moment without organization: he knew they had his arms pinned, and his coordination was gone.

"Look at me," a male voice was saying. A shake at his hair, a hand slapping his face and steadying it. "You want to use sense, Stevens? What about the keys?"

There was blood in his mouth. He figured they would hit him again. He heaved to get a hand loose.

A second blow.

"Stop it." Neill's voice. "Curran, stop it."

Again the hand shook at his face. He was blind for the

moment, everything lost in dark. "You want to think it over, Stevens?"

He tried to move. The blood was shut off from his right hand; the left had life in it. He heaved on that side, but the lighter weight on that arm was still enough. "Curran." That was Deirdre. "Curran, he's out—stop it."

A silence. His eyes began to clear. He stared into Curran's bloody face, Neill and Deirdre's bodies in the corner of his eyes, holding onto his arms. "You shouldn't have hit him like that," Neill said. "Curran, stop, you hear me, or I'll let him loose."

Curran let go of his face. Stared down at him.

"He's not going to give us anything," Deirdre said. "We've got trouble, Curran. Neill's right."

"He'll give it to us."

"Curran, no."

"What do you want, let him up, let him back at controls where he can do what we can't undo? No. No way. You're right, we've got trouble."

Sandor gave a heave, sensing a loosening of Deirdre's arms. It failed; the hold enveloped his arm, yielding, but holding. "Get Allison," he said, having difficulty talking. And then he recalled it was her door they were outside. She might have heard it; and stayed out of it. The realization muddled through him in the same tangled way as other impressions, painful and distant. "What do we do?" Neill asked. "For God's sake what do we do?"

"I think maybe we'd better get Allison," Deirdre said.

"No," Curran said. "*No.*" He took hold again of Sandor's bruised jaw. "You hear me. You hear me. You're thinking how to get rid of us, maybe; not the law—that's not your way, is it? Thinking of having an accident—like maybe others have had on this ship. We'll find you a comfortable spot; and we've got all the time we like. But we're coming to an agreement one way or the other. We're having a look at the records. At comp. At every nook and cranny of this ship. And maybe if we don't like what we find, we just call Mallory out there and turn you over to the military. You can yell foul all you like: you think that'll make a difference if we swear to the contrary? Your word against ours—and what's yours worth without ours to back it? They'd chew you up and swallow you down—you think not?

He started shivering, not from fear, from shock: he was

numb, otherwise, except for a small quick area of shame. They picked him up off the floor and had to hold him up for the moment; he got his feet under him, did nothing when Curran grabbed his arm and pushed him into the wall. Then he hit, once and proper.

Curran hit the wall and came back off it. "No," Neill yelled, and got in the way of it. And suddenly Allison was there, the door open, and everything stopped where it was.

No shock. Nothing of the kind. Sandor stared at her, a reproach.

"Sorry," Curran said in a low voice. "Things seem to have gotten out of hand."

"I see that," she said.

"I don't think he's willing to talk about it."

"Are you?" she asked.

"No," Sandor said. His throat hurt. He said nothing else, watched Allison shake her head and glance elsewhere, at nothing in particular.

"How do we settle this?"

She was talking to him. "Forget it," he said past the obstruction in his throat. "It was an idea that won't work. We go on and forget it. I've got no percentage in carrying a grudge."

"I don't think it works that way," Curran said.

"No," she said, "I don't either."

"There's cabins," Curran said.

"Lord—"

"It's done. I figure a little time to think about it—Allie, we don't sleep with him loose."

"You can't lock them," she said. "Without the keys."

"I'd laugh," Sandor said, "but what comes next? Cutting my throat? Think that one through: you kill me and you've got no keys at all. We'll go right on out of system."

"No one's talking about that."

"I'll lay bets you've thought about it.—No, I'll go upsection. Close a seal. An alarm will ring if I leave it. You have to have everything laid out for you? You're inept, you Dubliners. Ought to take you several days to work yourselves up to the next step."

He walked off from them, toward the section two cabins, reckoning all the while that they would stop him and devise something less comfortable. There was silence behind him.

He passed the section seal, pressed the button.
The seal shot home.

Allison sat down on the armrest of the number two cushion and looked at her cousins—at Curran, who sat on the
arm of number one, blotting at a cut lip. Neill and Deirdre
rested against the central console slumped down and very
quiet. "How?" she asked.

Curran shrugged—looked her in the eyes. "It just got out
of hand."

"When?"

Curran ducked his head. He was bloodstained, sweating,
his right eye moused at the cheekbone. "He swung," he said,
looking up again. "Caught me. He won't bluff." It was possibly the worst moment of Curran's life, being wrong in
something he had argued. Her own gut was tied in a knot.

And after that, silence, all of the faces turned toward her,
where the decisions should have come from in the first place.
She leaned her arms on her knees, adding it up, all the wrong
moves, and the first was abdicating. It made her sick thinking
of it. All the good reasons, all the rationale collapsed. It was
not only an ugly way to have gone, for good reasons—the
game had not worked, and now it was real: Stevens understood it for real—or knew that they knew it had to be. "It's
stupid," she objected, slammed her fist into her hand. She
looked up at faces that had no better answer. "No ideas?"

Silence.

"We could get him off this ship," Curran said in a subdued
voice. "We could ask the military to intervene. Say there was
an argument."

"You reckon to do that?"

"We're talking about our lives. Allie, don't mistake him
like I did: he backed up on the docks, but he's been running
hired crew and he's survived; there's those cabins. And the
loft."

"It was depressurized," Deirdre said. "Maybe he got holed
in some tangle; but little ships don't survive that kind of
thing. The other answer is some access panel going out; and
you can blow it from main board, can't you?"

"So what do we do? We've got twenty-four hours to get
those comp keys out of him or to get him back at controls, or
we go sliding right past our jump point and out of the system. And he knows it."

Silence.

"Allie," Curran said, "he's a marginer. At best he's a liar and a thief. He's lied his way from one end of civilization to the other. He's conned customs and police who know better. At the worst—at the worst—"

"You think he's conned me?"

"I think he was desperate and we gave him a line. But he's keeping the keys in his hands and maybe he's had other crew aboard who never made it off. We don't know that. We can't let him loose."

"You got another idea? Calling the military—that still doesn't give us the keys. They'd have to haul us down; or we lose the ship. Might as well apply to leave the ship ourselves. Hand it back to him. Go back to Pell, beached. In a year, maybe we can explain it all to the Old Man. And go back to *Dublin* and go on explaining it. You think of that?"

"What do we do, then?"

"He's got no food in that section," Deirdre said. "There's that. There're things he needs."

Allison drew a long breath, short of air. So they were around to that, the logical direction of things. "So maybe we come up with something more to the point than that. That's what he was saying, you know that? He knows what kind of a mess we're in. We can't rely on him at controls—how much do you think you can rely on comp keys he might give us if we put the pressure on? He's out-thought us. He's not going to bluff."

Silence.

She rested her hands on her knees and stood up. "All right. It's in my watch. So I'll talk to him. I'm going up there."

"Allie—"

"Al-li-son." She frowned at Curran. "You stay by com and monitor the situation. Only one way he's going to trust us halfway—a way to patch up things, at least; make a gesture, make him think we think we've straightened it out. God help us." She headed for the corridor, looked back at a trio of solemn faces. "If you have to come after me, come quick."

"If he lays a hand on you," Curran said, "I'll break it a finger at a time."

"Don't take chances. If it gets to that, settle it, and call the military." She walked on, raw terror gathered in her stomach. Her knees had a distressing tendency to shake.

There was no more chance of trusting him. Only a chance

to make him think they did. He was, she reckoned, too smart to kill her even if it crossed his mind: he would take any chance they gave him, come back to them, bide his time.

She hoped to get them to Venture Station alive: that was what it came to now. Asd if they were lucky, there might be a strong military authority there.

He sat in the corridor—no other place in section two that was heated: he had the heat started up in number 15, and if the sensors worked, the valve that shut the water down in 15 would open and restore the plumbing. He never depended on *Lucy*'s plumbing. At the moment he was beyond caring; he was pragmatic enough to reckon priorities would change when thirst set in.

And in an attempt at pragmatism he made himself as comfortable as he could on the floor, nursed bruised ribs and wrenched joints and a stiff neck, trying to find a position on the hard tiles that hurt as little as possible. The teeth ached; the inside of his mouth was cut and swollen: there was a great deal to take his mind off more general troubles, but generally he was numb, the way the area of a heavy blow went numb. And he reckoned that would start hurting too, when the shock of betrayal had passed. In the meantime he could sleep: if he could find a spot that did not ache, he could sleep.

The alarm went off—the door down the curve opened from their side, jolting his heart. He scrambled up—staggered into the wall and straightened.

Allison by herself. The door closed again; the alarm stopped. He stared at her and the numb spot gained feeling and focus, an ache that settled everywhere. "So, well," he said, "got around to figuring how it is?"

"Look, I'm here. You want to talk or do you want me to let be?"

"I won't give it to you."

She walked closer, the length of the corridor between them. Stopped near arm's length. "I won't pass it to Curran. I'm sorry.—Listen to me. I reckoned maybe we were too close for reason. I just figured maybe Curran could get the sleep-over out of it; maybe—Hang it, Stevens, you're strung out on no sleep and you're risking our lives on it. Not just mine. Theirs; and I got them into it. You don't trust them. Maybe not me. But I figured if you and Curran could sort it out—

maybe it would all work. That maybe if you got it straight with them, if all the heat blew out of it—"

"Misfigured, did you?"

"Don't be light with me. Say what you think."

"All I want—" His throat spasmed. He thrust his hands into his pockets and disguised a second breath with that. "I don't give you the time of day, Reilly. Let alone the comp keys. Now we can go on like this. And maybe you'll think of other clever ways to get at it. But you loaned me money; you didn't buy me out. You figure—what? To trump up something to get me between you and the police at Venture? And then to offer me another deal? Sorry. I've got that figured out. Because if they get me, Reilly, you're stuck on a ship you can't even get out of dock. Embarrassing. Might raise questions about your title to her. Might cost you a long time to get that straightened out, long-distance to Pell and wherever *Dublin* might be. Not to mention—if they send me in for restruct—I'll spill what happened here, all in the little pieces of my mind. And there goes the Reilly Name. So refigure, Reilly. Nothing you do that way's going to work."

"You're crazy, you know that?"

"You know, I really took precautions. I signed on drunks and docksiders and insystemers, and I got through with all of them. I figured a big ship like *Dublin* might try to doubledeal me, but you're pirates, Reilly—I never figured that. Mallory's out there hunting Mazianni and here's a ship full of them."

Her face flushed. He had that satisfaction. "You don't take that seriously, do you?"

"I don't see a difference."

"Stevens—"

"Sandor. The name's Sandor."

"I'm sorry for what happened. I told you why; I told you—Look, Curran thought you'd bluff. That was his thinking. Now he knows better. So do all of us. You want to come back to the bridge and sort this out?"

He ran that through his mind several ways, and none of it eased the ache. Stood there, obstinate, only to make it harder.

"Stevens—what's it take?"

"Worried, are you? We're not even near the jump point. And what when we're across it? A replay? I only go for this once, Reilly. The next time you lay a hand on me it's war. You'll get me. Sure you will. I've got to sleep, after all. But let's just lay it on the table. You may not be able to haul it out of me. And then what? Then what, Reilly?"

"It's crazy to talk like that."

"How much do you want this ship?"

"A lot. But not that way. I want us working with each other. I want our hands clean and all of us in one piece, not killed because you're still running a loaded ship like a margin cargo—you're blind crazy, Stevens. Sandor. You've got too many enemies in your own head."

"It doesn't work. You take it on my terms. That's all you've got. Up the ante, and that's still all you've got."

"All right," she said after a moment, stood there with a look in her eyes that seemed halfway earnest. She nodded toward the section seal. "Let's go."

He nodded, walked along with her. "They're listening," he said in a low voice. "Aren't they?"

She looked at him, a sudden, disturbed glance. They reached the section seal and she stopped and reached for the button. He was quicker, his hand covering it. He looked her in the eyes, that close, and the closeness murdered reason for the instant. The scent of her and the warmth and the remembrance of Viking and Pell—

"You could have had it all," he said. "You know that."

"You never trusted us. Not from the start."

"I was right, wasn't I?"

She was silent a moment. "Maybe not."

The quiet denial shot around the flank of his defenses. He turned his head, pressed the button.

The siren went. The door shot open. He was facing Curran and Neill. He was somehow not surprised.

"He's coming back," Allison said. She closed the door again. The siren stopped. "We've got it settled."

The faces in front of him did not believe it. He reacquired his own doubts, nerved himself with the insolence of a thousand encounters with docksiders. Offered his hand.

Curran took it, a small shudder of hesitation in the move, a grip that spared bruised knuckles—but Curran's hand was in no better condition; Neill's next—Neill's earnest expression had a peculiar distress.

"Sorry," Neill said.

He meant it, Sandor reckoned. One of them meant it. And knew it was all a sham. He felt a pang of sympathy for Neill, which was insane: Neill would be with the rest of them, and he never doubted it.

"Deirdre's on watch, is she?"

"Yes."

"I'm going to have my breakfast and wash up. And I'll rest after that . . . find myself a cabin and rest a few hours. You'll wake me if something comes up."

He walked on—away from them. Stopped in the galley and opened the freezer, pulled out a decent breakfast, pointedly keeping his back to the rest of them as they passed.

It was a quiet supper, hers with Curran. Curran was eating carefully, around a sore mouth, and not in a mood for idle conversation. Neither was she. "You think he'll go along with it all the way to Venture?" Curran asked once. "Maybe," she said. "I think he's had the angles figured for years. We just walked into it."

And a time later: "You know," Curran said, "the whole agreement's a lie. Look at me, Allie. Don't take on a face like that. He's a liar, an actor—he knows right where to take hold and twist. I knew that from the start. If you hadn't stepped in when you did—"

"*What* would you have done? I'd like to have known what you would have done."

"I'd have beaten a straight answer out of him. He says not. But that's part of the act. He's harder than I thought, but I'd have peeled the nonsense away and gotten right where he lives, Allie, don't think not. Wouldn't have killed him; not near. And it might have settled this. You had to come out the door—"

"It didn't go your way the first time. How much would it take? How many hours?" Her stomach turned. She pushed the food around on her plate, made herself spear a bite and swallow. "You heard what he said. We've got him working now. Another set-to—"

"You go on *believing* what he says—"

"What if it is the truth? What if it's the truth all along?"

"And what if it's not? What then, Allie?"

"Don't call me that. I don't like it."

"Don't redirect. You know what the stakes are. We're talking about trouble here. You sit the number one; you've got to have the say in it. But you're thinking below the belt."

"That's your assumption."

"Don't tell me a male number one wouldn't have gotten us in this tangle."

"Ah. There we are. What if it were a woman and it were you calling the shots? Dare I guess? You'd take it all, wouldn't you? You think you would. But would you sleep sound in that company? No. You think it through. I'm not sleeping with him. And he even asked."

"Maybe you should have."

She was reaching for the cup. She slammed it down, spilling it. "You need your attitudes reworked, Mr. Reilly. You really do. Maybe we really need to figure the logic that carries all that. Let's discuss your sleepovers, Mr. Reilly—or don't they have any bearing on your fitness to command?"

His face went red. For a moment he said nothing at all. Then his eyes hooded and he leaned back. "Hoosh, what a tongue on ye, Allie. Do you really want the details? I'll give you all you like."

She smiled, a move of the lips, not the rest of her face. "Doubtless you would. No doubt at all. You had your try; and he knocked you flat, didn't he? So while we're discussing my personal involvement here, suppose we add that to the count: is it just possible you have something personal at stake?"

"All of that's aside. The question's not what we see; it's what Stevens is . . . and where we are. And what we do about it."

"And I'm telling you it didn't work."

"You stopped it. It's ugly; it's an ugly thing; I don't like it; but it would have settled it and your way hasn't got us anywhere but back behind start. Way behind."

She thought that over, and it was true. "Where did we ever get off doing something like this? Where did we ever learn to think about things like this?"

"It's not us. It's the company you came up with."

"Suppose he told the truth. Suppose that for a minute."

"I don't suppose it. You're back where you were, falling for a good act. And you think every customs agent and banker who ever believed him didn't think he looked sincere? Sincere's his stock in trade, him with that fair, blue-eyed innocence."

She took a napkin, blotted the spilled coffee, wiped the bottom of the cup and took a drink, and a second.

"So we go on," Curran said. "Next jump—and him running it."

"What would you do?"

"No more than I had to."

She shook her head. Got up and cleaned the plate and tossed the cup, put things in the washer.

"Alli-son. I'm not willing to risk my life on your maybe."

She looked back at him. "You're my number two. Isn't that your job?"

"If there's reason—"

"My reason is a judgment call. And I'm making it."

"On what percentage? It gets us into another spot like this one. On that understanding—just so we agree where we're going—it's my job. Right."

She walked over and squeezed his shoulder, walked past and out of the galley.

XIV

"That's five minutes to range limit," Allison said. "Transmitting advisement to our escort."

"Got it," Sandor murmured back, busy at final adjustments. The reports from the other stations came in, routine and indicating all stable. It had an especially valuable feel, the familiar cushion, the rhythm of operations, his hands on the controls again, as if nothing had happened. Wild thoughts came to him, like stringing the next two jumps, seeing whether his Dubliner companions had the stomach for that—he imagined screams of terror and shouts of rage; and maybe they could not haul the velocity down—would become a missile traveling out into the Deep beyond any control, too much mass for her own systems and exponentially doomed. . . . Or even minutely fouling up the schedule they had given to the military that still ran beside them. Being hauled down by Alliance military—that would give the Dubliners something to worry about . . . if it was worth falling into the hands of the military himself. He still preferred his Dubliners to either fate. Allison and Curran and Deirdre and Neill—Allison. Allison. It hurt, knowing what she had wanted; what, subconsciously, he had seen—that for her it was *Lucy* herself. She wanted what he wanted, the way he wanted—and the loneliness in her was filled without him. She had *family*. He had known. It was his solitude that gave him strange ideas. It was listening to stationer tapes and forgetting what family was, and where right and wrong was.

Forgetting Ross and Mitri and all the voyagers in the dark. Forgetting what *Lucy* contained . . . as if Dubliners could forget their own ways.

He had had time in the hours shut in his cabin—in the cabin that had been Papa Lou's, amid the remnant of things that he and Ross and Mitri had not sealed away under the plates, taking everything that might have identified the Kreja name to customs—he had had time to reckon what had happened. He might have hated them. He reckoned that. But it was too tangled for hate. It was survival, and maybe it had started out as something better than that.

He understood Allison, he reckoned: generous sometimes, and where it touched her Name, hard enough to cut glass. She would not have come to him in worthlessness, the way he would not have left *Lucy* and gone to her penniless; she came with her crewmates about her, her wealth, her substance in the account of things. And he could not blame her for that.

Even—he had reckoned, with more painful slowness—there was worth in Curran Reilly, if he could only discover what it was. He believed that because Allison believed it, and what Allison valued must be worth something. He took that on faith. There was worth in all of them.

But he meant to break Curran Reilly's arm at next opportunity.

And meanwhile he had come out of his cabin, nodded a pleasant good day, sat down at controls and proceeded with jump prep as matter of factly as if he were only coming on watch.

"Set it and retire?" he had asked of Allison, as blandly innocent a face as he knew how to wear, his customs-agent manner. "Or shall I take her through?"

"You'll take her," Allison had to say. There was no safe alternative, things being as they were with comp. And Curran's face, a twist of his head and a look in his direction, had had the look of a man with a difficult mouthful going down.

No word to him yet of warnings. Maybe they felt threats superfluous. They were. Data came to him on schedule, to screens, to his ear, quiet voices and businesslike.

"Two minutes to mark."

"All stable."

"M/D to screen three. All on mark."

"Scan to four. *Norway*'s moving."

His heart did a turn. The image came up on screen four. Mallory was underway—had been, for some lightbound time.

"Message incoming," Neill said. "Acknowledge?"

"Put it through," he said . . . *he* said, and not Allison. The realization that the moment was thrown in his lap and not routed to Allison shocked him. But they had to: the military would expect him. "That's a tight transmission," Neill said. "Same mode reply . . . We're receiving you, *Odin*."

"This is *Odin* command," the answer came. "Captain Mallory sends her compliments and advises you there are hazards in the Hinder Star zones. Wish you luck, *Lucy*."

That was polite. The tone surprised him. He punched in his own mike. "This is Stevens of *Lucy*: do we expect escort at our next point?"

A silence. "Location of Alliance ships is restricted information. Exercise due caution in contacts."

"Understood, *Odin* command." On the number four screen, *Norway* was in decided motion, gathering speed with the distinctive dopplered flickers of a military ship on scan.

"*Odin*'s just braked," Curran said. "Losing them on vid."

"Up on scan," Deirdre said, and that was so: the image was there, the gap between them widening.

"Twenty-four seconds to mark," Allison said. "Jump point minus fifteen minutes twenty seconds."

He checked the belts, the presence of the trank on the counter. His eyes kept going back to that ominous and now closer presence coming up on them. *Norway* could lie off and make nothing of their days of passage when she woke up and decided to move. He tried to ignore that monumental fact, bristling with weapons, bearing down by increments scan was only guessing. He went about his private preparations as his crew had begun to do: settling in, being sure of comfort and safety for the jump to come.

"Minus ten minutes," Allison murmured. "Hang, what's Mallory up to?"

"She won't crowd us," Sandor said. "She's not crazy, whatever else."

He put the trank in. Began to glaze over. . . . His concern for everything diminished. He stared at the scan image for an instant, hyper and fascinated, recalled the necessity to track on other things and focused his mind down the tunnel it required. "Take her through," he said to Allison—caught the roll of a dark eye in his direction . . . suspicion; question— "Take her," he said again, as if nothing else had happened, as if it were only the next step in checking out his novice crew. Allison's face acquired that panic the situation deserved, one's first time handling jump. He shunted control to her board and she diverted her attention back where it had to be. "Eight minutes," he said, reminding her. He was crazy: he knew so. The trank had blurred all the past, created a kind of warmth in which he was safe with them simply because they had no alternatives. Relinquishing things this way, he was in command of all of them . . . and Allison Reilly had failed another prediction. He sensed her anger at him; and Curran's hate; and the perplexity of the rest—smiled a trank-dulled smile as they flashed toward their departure—

"Five minutes," he said, on mark. Allison gave him another look, as if to judge his sanity, diverted her attention back to the board.

The seconds ticked off. His Dubliners, he thought. Possibly they would begin it all again where they were going. Maybe they would do more than they had already done. In one part of his soul he was cold afraid. But he was always afraid. He was used to that. He knew how to adjust to things he was afraid of, which was to grin and bluff—and he had that faculty back again.

"Minus forty-five seconds."

"All stable," Curran said.

"We're going," Allison said, and that was that: she had uncapped the switches.

(Ross . . . it's not me this time. But she knows what she's doing. In most things. Let's go, then. The first time—without my help. She's good, Ross . . . they all are. And I don't know where we go from here. They don't know either. I'm sure of that. And I think they're scared of what I'll make them be. . . .)

The vanes cycled in, *Lucy* tracking on the star that gave them bearings, and they went—

—in again, a pulse *down* that made itself felt all along the nerves . . .

And no need to move, no need: Allison was there, giving orders, doing everything that ought to be done. "Dump," she ordered: comp, on silent, was blinking alarm. Sandor performed the operation, neat pulses which slipped them in and out of here and now, loaded as they were, shedding velocity into the interface, while the dark mass lent them its gravitation, pockmark in spacetime sufficient to hold them . . . friendly, dangerous point of mass. . . .

They made it in, making more speed than they had used at the last point . . . Allison's choice. "Will she handle it?" she asked on that account.

"Ought to," Sandor said. "In a hurry, Reilly?"

No answer.

"It's lonely here," Curran said. "Not a stir anywhere."

"Lonelier than the average," Allison said. "Didn't they say they were monitoring all the points?"

No answer from any quarter. Sandor took the water bottle from beside the console, took a drink and set it back again. He unbelted.

"Going back to my quarters," he said. "Good luck with her, Reilly."

"Alterday watch to controls," Allison said. "Change off at one hour."

Maybe there was something she wanted to say. Maybe—he thought, in a moment of hope—she had come to her senses. But there was nothing but fatigue in her face when she had gotten up from controls. Fatigue and a flushed exhilaration he understood. So she had gotten the ship through: that was something to her. He had forgotten the peculiar terror of a novice; had taken *Lucy* into jump for the first time when he was fourteen. Then he had been scared. And many a time since then.

He walked to his quarters without looking back at her and Curran and the others, solitary . . . back to the museum that was his cabin, and to the silence. He closed the door, keyed in on comp with the volume very low.

"Hello, Sandy," it said. That was all he wanted to hear. "How are you?"

"Fine," he said back to the voice. "Still alive, Ross."

"What do you need, Sandy?"

He cut the comp off, on again. "Hello, Sandy. How are you?"

He cut it off a second time, because while they could not access the room channels from the bridge without the keys, someone would see the activity. He stood there treasuring the sound, empty as it was. He could get one of the instruction sequences going, and have the voice for hours—he missed that. But they would grow alarmed. His quarantine gave him this much of Ross back; in that much he treasured his solitude.

He showered, wrapped himself in his robe, went out to the galley—found Allison and Curran, still dressed, standing waiting for the oven he wanted to use. He stopped, set himself against the wall, a casual leaning, hands in pockets of the robe, a studious attention to the deck tiles.

A clatter of doors and trays then. He looked toward them,

reckoning that they were through. Watched them pour coffee and arrange trays for the rest of them. "Here," Allison said to him, "want one?"

He passed an eye over them: four trays. "I'll do my own, thanks. It's all right."

"Galley's yours."

He nodded, went to the freezer, pulled an ordinary breakfast. His hands were shaking: they always did that if he was late getting food after a jump. "Did the jump real well," he said to Allison, peace offering while she was gathering up the trays.

Small courtesies had to be examined. She looked up, two of the trays in her hand while Curran went out with the other two. Nodded then, deciding to be pleased. "Better," she said, "when I can do all of it."

She had to throw that in. He nodded after the same fashion, not without the flash of a thought through his mind, that it was several days through the nullpoint and that they might have something in mind. "You'll be all right," he said, offering that too.

She went her way. He cooked his breakfast, shivering and spilling things until he had gotten a spoonful of sugar into his stomach and followed the nauseating spoonful with a chaser of hot coffee. That helped. The tremors were at least less frequent. The coffee began to warm his stomach—real coffee. He had gotten used to the taste of it, after the substitutes.

The oven went off. He retrieved his breakfast, sat down, sole possessor of the galley and the table. It was a curious kind of truce. They retreated from *him*, as if they found his presence accusatory. And he went on owning his ship, in a solitude the greater for having a ship full of company.

When? he kept wondering. And: what next? They could go on forever in this war. He kept things courteous, which was safest for himself; and they knew that, and played the game, suspecting everything he did.

He wandered back to the bridge when he was done. He had that much concern for the ship's whereabouts. The Dubliners sat on the benches at the rear, having the last of their coffee—a little looser than they had been, a little more like Krejas had run the ship, because it was safe enough to sit back there with *Lucy* on auto. Not spit and polish enough for some captains; not regulation enough: there was a marginal hazard, enough to say that one chance out of a million could kill them all before they could react—like ambush. Unacceptable risk for *Dublin Again*, carrying a thousand lives; with ample personnel for trading shifts—but here it was only reasonable. Four Dubliner faces looked up at him, perhaps disconcerted to be caught at such a dereliction. He nodded to them, went to the scan board—heard a stir behind him, knew someone was afoot.

Nothing. Nothing out there. Only the point of mass, a lonely gas giant radiating away its last remnant of heat, a star that failed . . . a collection of planetoid/moons that were on the charts and dead ahead as they bore, headed toward the nadir pole of the system. Nothing for vid to pick up without careful searching: the emissions of the gas giant came through the dish. But no sign of anything living. No ship. That was nothing unusual at any nullpoint. But Mallory had made a point of saying that the points were watched.

He straightened and looked at the Dubliners—Curran and Allison on their feet, the others still seated, no less watching him. "Got our course plotted outside the ring," he said quietly, "missing everything on the charts. Old charts. You might keep that in mind. In case."

"You might come across with the keys," Curran said.

He shrugged. Walked the way he had come, ignoring all that passed among them.

"*Stevens*," Curran's voice pursued him.

He looked back with his best innocence. No one moved. "Thirty-six hours twenty-two minutes to mark," he said quietly. "What do you think you'll find where we're going? A station Pell's size? Civilization? I'd be surprised. Do you want to start this over—try it my way this time?"

"No," Allison said after a moment. "Partners. That's the way it works."

"Might. Might, Reilly."

"If we go at it your way."

"This isn't *Dublin*. You don't get your way. You signed onto my ship and my way is the way she runs. Majority vote wasn't in the papers. Cooperative wasn't. My way's *it*. That's the way it works. You sit down and figure out who's on the wrong side of the law."

He walked off and left them then, went back to his own quarters—entertained for a little while the forlorn hope that they might in fact think about that, and come to terms. But he had not hoped much, and when no one came, he curled up and courted sleep.

A suited figure tumbled through his vision, and that was himself and that was Mitri. He opened his eyes again, to drive that one away; but it rode his mind, that image that came back to him every time he thought of solitude. He shivered, recalling a boy's gut-deep fear, and cowardice.

("Ross," he had called, sick and shaking. "Ross, he's dead, he's dead; get back in here. I can't handle the ship, Ross—I can't take her alone. Please come back—Ross. . . .")

The feeling was back in his gut, as vivid as it had been; the sweating cowardice; the terror—He swore miserably to himself, knowing this particular dream, that when it latched onto his mind for the night he would go on dreaming it until *Lucy*'s skin seemed too thin to insulate him from the ghosts.

He propped himself on his elbows in the dark, supported his head on his hands. . . . finally got up in the dark and turned up the light, hunting pen and paper.

He wrote it down, the central key to comp, and put it in the drawer under the mirror, afraid of having it there—but after that he could turn out the lights and go back to bed.

Mitri gave him peace then.

He slept the night through; and waked, and fended his way past Deirdre and Neill at breakfast. In all, there was a quiet over all the ship, less of threat than of anger. And a great deal of the day he came and sat on the bridge, simply took a post and sat it—because it was safer that way, for the ship, for them. He took his blanket and his pillow that night and slept there, so that there was that much less distance between himself and controls if something went wrong.

"Give it up," Allison asked of him, on her watch.

He shook his head. Did not even argue the point.

And Neill came to him, when they were minus eight hours from mark: "It was a mistake, what we did. We know that. Look, Curran never meant to get into that; he made a mistake and he won't admit it, but he knows it, and he wishes it hadn't gone the way it did. He just didn't expect you'd go for him; and we—we just tried to stop someone from getting hurt."

"To stop Curran from getting hurt." He had not lost his sense of humor entirely; the approach touched it. He went serious again and flicked a gesture at the Dubliner's sleeve. "You still wear the *Dublin* patch."

That set Neill off balance. "I don't see any reason to take it off."

And that was a decent answer too.

"I'm here," Sandor said, "within call. Same way I've run this ship all along. You're safe. I'm taking care of your hides."

They left him alone after that, excepting now and again a remark. And he lay down and went to sleep a time, until they reached minus two from mark and he had jump to set.

His crew had showed up, quiet, businesslike. "So we go for civilization," he said. And with a glance at Allison, at Curran: "A little liberty ought to do good for all of us. Sort it out on the docks."

He imagined relief in their faces, on what account he was not sure. Only they all needed the time.

And he was glad enough to quit this place, dark and isolated as the well-traveled nullpoints of Unionside had never been isolated.

He took his place at the number one board, began working through comp on silent . . . They might have stood over him, put it to a contest; they declined that.

Perhaps after the station liberty, he told himself, perhaps then he could get his bearings, mend what was broken, find a way to make his peace with them. A ship run amiss could become a small place indeed. They wanted different air and the noise of other living humans but themselves.

They were that close to safety; and if they could get into it, head home with a success to their account—then they were proved, and the record was clear; and everything might be clean again.

Then there was hope for them.

XV

. . . Venture system: a star with a gas giant companion and a clutter of debris belting it and the star. And a small, currently invisible station that had been the last waystop for Sol going outward. FTL had shut it down; Pell's World, Downbelow . . . had undercut Sol prices for biostuffs, closer, faster. A rush for new worlds had run past it, the Company Wars had cut it off for half a century—But there was a pulse now, a thin, thready pulse of activity.

No buoy to assign them routing: they had been warned of that. Sandor dumped down to a sedate velocity closer to system plane than a loaded ship should—but there was no traffic.

"Lonely as a nullpoint," Allison muttered, beside him. "If we didn't have station signal—"

"Never expected much here," Sandor said. "It's old, after all. Real old."

"Com's silent," Neill said. "Just noise."

"Makes me nervous," Curran muttered. "No traffic, no buoy, no lanes—can't run a station without lanes. They're going to get somebody colliding out here, running in the dark."

"I'm going after a sandwich," Sandor said. "I'm coming back to controls with it."

"You stay put," Allison said. "Neill, see to it for all of us. Anything. Make it fast."

Neill slid out. Functions shunted: com and cargo to Deirdre, scan one and two to Curran; Allison kept to her sorting of images that got to number one screens, his filter on data that could come too fast and from confusing directions. Nothing was coming now . . . only the distant voice of station.

"We're coming up on their reply window," Curran said.

"Ready on that," Deirdre said.

Neill came back, bearing an armful of sandwiches and

sealed drink containers. Sandor opened his, wolfed down half
of it, swallowed down the fruit juice and capped it. The
silence from station went on. No one said anything about it.
No one said anything.

"Picking up something," Curran said suddenly. "Lord, it's
military. It's moving like it."

The image was at Sandor's screen instantly. "Mallory," he
surmised.

"Negative on that," Neill said. "I don't get any *Norway*
ID. I don't get any ID at all."

"Wonderful," Allison muttered.

"Size. Get size on it." Sandor started lining up jump, reckoned their nearness to system center. "Stand by: we're turning over."

"You'll get us killed. Whatever it is, we can't outrace it."

"Get me a calculation on that." He sent them into an axis
roll, cut in the engines as drink containers went sailing, with
a collection of plastic wrap, half a sandwich and an uniden-
tified tape cassette. "Cargo stable," Deirdre reported, and he
reached up through the drag that tended to pull his arm
aside, kept on with the calculations.

"We can't do it," Allison said. "We won't clear it, reckoning they'll fire. I've got the calculations for you—"

No word of contact: nothing. He flicked glances at the
scan image and Curran's current position estimate . . . saw
number three screen pick up Allison's figures on plot. The in-
tersection point flashed, before the jump range.

"You hear me?" Allison asked sharply. "Stevens, we can't
make it. They're going to overtake."

"They still don't have an ID pulse," Neill said. "I don't get
anything."

"They're going to overtake."

"What do you expect us to do?" Sandor stopped the jump
calculation while they hurtled on their way. His body was
pressed back into the cushion, his pulse hammering in his
ears, drowning other sounds.

"Haul down," Allison shouted at him. "Lord, haul down
before they blow us. What do you think you're doing?"

His mind was blank, raw panic. Instinct said away; common sense and calculations said it was not going to work.
And excluding that—

"Stevens!"

"*Cut it*," Curran shouted at him. "Stevens, you'll kill us all; we can't win it."

He looked at the Dubliners, a difficult turning of his neck. "Suit up. Hear? I'll cut back. Allison, Dierdre, Neill, get below, suit up and hurry about it. Curran, I want you. The two of us—get that Dublin patch off. *Move*, hang you all."

He cut the power back—buying them time and losing some. The Dubliners moved, all of them, nothing questioning, not with a warship accelerating in pursuit. They scattered and ran, crazily against the remaining acceleration. The lift worked, behind him: only Curran stayed, zealously ripping at the patch.

"What's the score?" Curran asked. "Set up an ambush for them aboard?"

"No. We're the only crew, you and I. You signed on at Pell, got thrown off *Dublin*." He reached to the board, put cabins two, four, and five on powersave. "Get up there and strip down their cabins; shove everything into yours. Move it, man."

Curran's face was blanched. He nodded then, scrambled for the corridor, staggering among the consoles.

The gap was narrowing. No hail, even yet; no need of any. The ship chasing them knew; and they knew; and that was all that was needed. It all went in silence. The other posts were shut down, all functions to the main board now.

"We're suiting," Allison's voice came to him over com out of breath. "I'm suited. Now what?"

"Got all kinds of service shafts down there. Pick one. Snug in and stay there—whatever happens. If they loot us and leave us, fine. If they take us off the ship—you stay put."

"No way. No way, that."

"You hear me. You get into a hole and wait it out. I know what I'm talking about and I know what I'm doing."

"I'm not hiding in any—"

"*Shut up, Reilly*. Two of us is the maximum risk on this and I picked my risk . . . two of us of Curran's type and mine—looks like smugglers. You want to get Deirdre and Neill killed, you just come ahead up here. You got the hard part down there, I know, but for God's sake do it and don't louse it up. Please, Reilly. Think it through. That ship's a Mazianni carrier. They have maybe three thousand troops on that thing. Do what I tell you and make the others do it. We got a chance. They don't hang around after a hit. Maybe you can do something; maybe there're people left at Venture. Maybe other ships coming in here—If nothing else, they may leave.—And Reilly—you listening to me?"

"I'm hearing you."

"Comp access code's in my cabin. Top drawer."

"Hang you, Stevens."

"Sandor. It's Sandor Kreja."

Silence from the other side. He could hear her breathing, soft panting as with some kind of exertion.

"You'll be taking water with you," he said. "You don't use that suit oxygen unless you have to. You might have to last a day or so in there. Now shut that com down and keep that flock of yours quiet, hear?"

"Got you."

He cut the acceleration entirely. The stress cut out; and with equal suddenness his contact with Allison went out. He felt cold, worked his hands to bring the circulation back to them.

He had it planned now, all of it, calm and reasoned. He looked up as Curran came back, out of breath and disheveled. "Just talked to Allison," Sandor said. "They're going into the service shafts and staying put. I gave her the comp code. You keep your mouth shut and swallow that temper; we're going to get boarded and we've got no choices. You're my number two, you don't know anything, we've got a military cargo and we've run together since Viking. We're running contraband gold and we'd run anything else that paid."

Curran nodded, no arrogance at all, but a plain sober look that well enough reckoned what they were doing. . . . So here's the good in the man, Sandor said to himself, in the strange quiet of the moment. He's got sense.

He turned a look to the screens. The com light was flashing.

"Belt in," he said to Curran. "They're coming on."

There was the muted noise and shock of lockto. Allison lay still in the light *G* of their concealment, in absolute dark, felt Deirdre move slightly, a touch against her suit, and Neill was back there behind Deirdre. Her fingers rested on the butt of one of the ship's three guns—they had gotten that from the locker . . . taken two and left one, in the reckoning that any boarders might suspect a completely empty weapons locker. Likewise the suits: two were left hanging. They must have

done something about the cabins topside, she reckoned; they
must have.

A second crash that resounded close at hand: and that was
the lock working. Allison shivered, an adrenalin flutter that
made her leg jerk; Deirdre could feel it, likely, which sent a
rush of shame after it. It would not stop. She wanted to do
something; and on the other hand she was cowardly, glad to
be where she was.

And Curran and Stevens up there—Sandor. *Kreja.* She
chased the name through her mind, and it meant nothing to
her, nothing she had known. Curran and Sandor. They
thought they were going to die. Both of them. And she had
followed orders because she was blank of ideas, out of her
depth. Like hiding in her cabin while her unit tried to settle
things with the man who had title to the ship. Like not knowing answers, and taking too much advice. She had a new per-
spective on herself, hiding, shivering in the dark while she
threw a cousin and a man she had slept over with to the
Mazianni, men who would keep their mouths shut and protect them down here—

Not for the ship, not for the several million lousy credit
ship, but for what a ship was, and the lives it still contained,
down here in the dark.

Another sound, eventually, the passage of someone through
the corridors, not far away, sound carried clear enough into
the pressurized service shafts, into her amplified pickup. They
could come out behind the invaders, maybe cut them down
with their pathetic two handguns if surprise was on their
side—

But a thousand troops to follow—what could they do but
get themselves hauled down by the survivors?

She added it up, the logic of it, a third and fourth time,
and every time Stevens/Sandor came out right. He knew ex-
actly what he was doing. And had always known that she did
not. She lay there, breathing the biting cold air that passed
through her suit's filters, with a discomfort she did not dare
stir about to relieve, and added up the sum of Allison Reilly,
which was mostly minuses—No substance at all, no guts; and
it was no moment to try to prove something. Too late for
proofs. She had to lie here and take orders and do something
right. Grow up, she told herself. Think. And save everything
you can.

They were topside now, the invaders. Suddenly she began

thinking with peculiar clarity—what they would have done, leaving some behind to secure the passage between the ship, some to guard the lift. Going out there would mean a fire-fight and three dead Dubliners.

That did no good. She started thinking down other tracks. Like saving *Lucy,* which was for starters on a debt, and hoping that the most epic liar she had ever met could con the Mazianni themselves.

He had a fine survival sense, did Stevens/Kreja. Supposing the Mazianni left him and Curran in one piece—

Supposing that, they might need help. Fast.

Her foot started going to sleep. The numbness spread up her leg, afflicted the arm she was lying on. Holding her head up was impossible, and she let it down against the surface of the shaft, found a way to accommodate her neck by resting her temple just so against the helmet padding. Small discomforts added up, absorbed her attention with insignificant torments. The air that came through the filters was cold enough to sting her nose, her face, her eyes when she had them open. The numbness elsewhere might be the cold. She could lose a foot that way, if the heating failed somewhere and that was the deep cold that had sent that leg numb.

She kept her eyes shut and waited, let the numbness spread as long as she dared, felt Deirdre move, perhaps because Neill had moved, and took the chance to shift to the other side.

No communication from the other two. Wait, she had told them. And they still waited, not using the lights, saving all the power they could.

Then came the sound of the lift working, and her heart pounded afresh. Whatever was done up there was done: they were leaving. Or someone was. She heard the tread of heavy boots in the corridor, the working of the lock.

If they were alone up there, if they were able—there were the suit phones. Sandor and Curran would try to contact them—

Then they started to move, a hard kick that dislodged all of them, converted the shaft in which they were lying into a downward chute.

Neill stopped them: a sudden pileup of suited bodies against the bulkhead seal a short drop down, Neill on the bottom and herself and Deirdre in a compressing tangle of limbs, weighed down harder and harder until there was no chance to straighten out a bent back or a twisted limb. The gun was still in her hand: she had that. But her head was bent back in the helmet that was jammed against something, and it was hard to breathe against the weight.

They'll break the cargo loose, she thought, ridiculous concern: they were in tow, boosted along in grapple by a monster warship, and it could get worse. Maybe four G; a thing like that might pull an easy ten. Maybe more, with its internal compensations. Her mind filled with inanities, and all the while she felt for hands—Deirdre's caught hers and squeezed; she knew Deirdre's light grip; and Neill—she could not tell which limbs were his or whether he was unconscious on the bottom of the heap—O God, get a suit ripped in this cold and he was in trouble. She had picked their spot in the shaft with an eye to reorientation, but she had not reckoned on any such startup; had never in her life felt the like. Her pulse pounded in cramped extremities. A weight sat on her chest. It went on, and she grew patient in it, trying to reconcile herself to long misery—

Then it stopped as abruptly as it had begun and *Lucy's* own rotation returned orientation to the shaft wall. She crawled over onto a side, chanced the suit light. Deirdre's went on, underlighting a disheveled face; and then Neill's, a face to match Deirdre's. She gave them the Steady sign.

*Station, Deirdre said.

*Affirmative, she answered. There was no other sane answer. *They have the station.

*Question, Neill said. *Question. Get out of here.

*Stay. She made the sign abrupt and final, doused her light. The other lights went out.

Two hours, the MET suit clock informed her, a red digital glow when she punched it. Two hours ten minutes forty-five seconds point six.

They might make the station in a few hours more. Might be boarded and searched and stripped of cargo. They might hijack the ship itself. She imagined hiding until they were weak with hunger, with never a chance to get at food, and then to have the ship start out from station again, with a Mazianni crew aboard, and themselves trapped.

Or short of that, a search turning up cabins full of recent clothing, unlike the rest of *Lucy's* oddments. Clothing with shamrock patches. And the Mazianni would know what they had—a key to a prize richer than Mazianni had ever ambushed.

They knew too much.

The armored troops moved about the bridge, looking over this and that, and the one unarmored officer sat the number one post, doing nothing, meddling with a great deal. Sandor was aware of him, past the ceramics and plastics bulk of the trooper who held a rifle in his direction and Curran's; he sat where they had set him, on a couch aftmost in the downside lounge, and waited, while troopers got up into the core, and visited the holds. And all the while he kept thinking about the acceleration that had for a time pressed them all against the bulkhead, and how service shafts running fore and aft could become pits that could break bone. Allison had thought of that; surely she had taken some kind of precaution. The sweat beaded on his temples and ran, one trail and another, betraying the calm he tried to keep. *Australia*, the stencilled letters said on the armor of the man/woman who stood nearest: and a number, meaningless to him. The trooper had no face, only reflective plastic that cast back his own diminished image, a blond man with his back against the wall; Curran's reflection behind him, with another trooper's back—both of them under the gun. *Australia* meant Tom Edger; meant Mazian's second in command, of no gentle reputation. And he kept seeing the bridge as it had been in that first boarding—felt the ghost of the pain in the scar in his side; and the dead about him—He had let them board, *he* had, when all that he knew was against it. He understood that day finally, in a way he had never understood. He sat paralyzed, and trying to think, and his mind kept cycling back and back . . . staring down the rifle barrel that was aimed at his face.

No shots fired yet. No damage taken. They were limpeted to the belly of a monster, frame to frame; and he had never appreciated the power in the giant carriers until he felt it slam a loaded freighter's mass along with its own into a multiple *G* acceleration. They could not have outrun it . . . had gained most of the time they had had simply in the delicate maneuvers that brought airlocks into synch. And maybe the Mazianni had been as patient as they had been because he had cooperated.

Thinking like that led to false security. He had a rifle

muzzle in front of his face to deny it. He had time to notice intimate detail in the equipment, and still did not know if it had been this ship or *Norway* or still another that had caught *Lucy/Le Cygne* before. He had a sense of betrayal . . . outrage. Venture Station was doing nothing to stop what had happened: the station belonged to the Mazianni, was in their hands. A vast horror sat under the cracks in that logic, the suspicion that there were things even Alliance might not know, when they made an ex-Mazianni like Mallory the chief of their defense.

A military cargo, Mallory had said. A delivery to Venture, where *Australia* waited. Supplies—for allies? The thought occurred to him that a power like Alliance, which consisted of one world and one station—besides the Hinder Stars and the merchanters themselves—could be threatened by a power the size of the Mazianni . . . a handful of carriers that now came and went like ghosts through the nullpoints, struck and vanished. The Mazianni could *take* Pell.

Especially if Mallory had rethought her options and decided to go the other way.

A handful of independent merchanters, he reckoned, were not going to be allowed to go their way. There was no hope of that at all. And possibly the Mazianni had a use for a merchanter ship that was scheduled to return to Pell.

The focus of his gaze flicked between the gun and the Mazianni who worked over the controls. And when the man turned the seat and got up, he had a panicked notice what the question was.

The man moved up beside the trooper . . . for a moment the gun moved aside and came on target again. "I need the comp opened up," the officer said. "You want to give it to me easy?"

"No," Sandor said quietly. And something settled into place like an old habit. He took a deeper breath, found his mind working again. "I trade. Maybe run a little contraband here and there. I've dealt the far side of the law before this. And before I trade my best deal off, I'll talk to Edger himself."

"You know, I wouldn't recommend that."

"I'm not stupid. I don't plan to die over a cargo. I figure we're going to offload it at Venture. Figure maybe you've got that sewed up tight. Fine. You want the cargo—fine. I'm not anybody's hero. Neither is my partner. I'll talk to Edger and

I'm minded to deal, you can figure that. Might work out
something."

The Mazianni studied him a long moment—a seam-faced
pale man, the intruder onto *Lucy*, of indefinite age. He
nodded slowly, with eyes just as dead. Sandor let it sink in,
numb in his expectation that it was all prelude to a pounce
... realized then to his own astonishment that the deal was
taken. "We'll go with that," the Mazianni said, and walked
back to controls.

Sandor looked up at the trooper's faceplate—not for sight
of that, but for a look at Curran without turning about; the
Dubliner sat still, not a muscle moved. His own heart was
beating double-time, a temptation to self-congratulation tem-
pered by a calculation that the other side had an angle. Not
stupid either, the Mazianni. Suddenly he reckoned that
Mazianni and marginers must have similar reflexes, similar
senses—living on the fringes of civilization, off the fat of others. It was like the unrolling of a chart laid out plain and
clear; no enigmatic monsters out of his childhood—they were
quite, quite like himself, out for profit and trade and unpar-
ticular how it came. Always the best advantage, the smart
move—and the smart move at the moment was not taking
apart the man with the comp key, the man with a ship that
had Alliance papers and clearance to dock at Pell.

He knew how to play it then. What he had to trade. But it
was not a question now of a scam, minor wounds on a vast
corporation. He was not unimportant any more. And he earnestly wanted his obscurity back.

(Ross . . . got a problem, Ross. You got a tape that covers
this one? I might save my crew. Curran . . . and Allison . . .
Where's right? Do we play it for the ship or for some station
and people we don't know; and how does anybody else figure
in it when it's our precious delicate selves in Mazianni hands?
. . .) His mind drew pictures and he shoved them out again,
preferring the gun in front of him to the images his mind
could conjure.

He settled his mind, trusted himself to ingenuity. He was
thinking again, and his blood was moving—like sex, this
necessity to figure. No preconceptions, but a fair idea what
the opposition would be after . . . a knowledge of all the
angles.

He was still figuring when the ship dumped velocity—an
interface dump that shocked his mind numb with the unex-

pectedness of it. Military maneuver, a brush with jumpspace with such suddenness he found a tremor in his muscles—Curran swore softly, almost the first word Curran had spoken. Sandor looked that way—met the Dubliner's eyes that for once showed fright. No gesture between them: nothing—Curran was too smart for it. He had picked well, he thought, another matter of instinct. There was no soft center to Curran Reilly. What made them enemies made the Dubliner a good wall at his back. Not a flicker, beyond that startlement.

A shock then that rang through the hull—and Sandor glanced instinctively in its direction, his heart lurching: but they had ungrappled, nothing worse. They were loose, and *Lucy* was under her own helm, with a stranger at the controls.

They were headed in to dock. He felt the small shifts of stress and focused his eyes beyond his guard, where he could see the glimmer of screens without making out the detail.

They were headed for a reckoning of one kind and the other. He felt his own nerves twitch in response to this and that move the ship made under foreign hands—felt a ridiculous anxiety that they might come in rough, as if a scrape was the worst they had to worry over.

It was rough, a jolting into dock that sent a shudder through his soul. He swore, for the guard to hear, but not for the man who had done it, whose good will he wanted, if it could be had.

XVI

The silence had gone on for a long time . . . since dock. Rotation was stopped. The ship had all the attendant sounds of coming and going for a while—

And then nothing. Nothing for a very long while. Allison fretted, ate and drank in the long dark hours because she had reached the point of fatigue, and she had to, not because her stomach had any appetite for it.

Neither Deirdre nor Neill offered suggestions—not since the first, when they felt the breakaway from the grapple and knew that they were going in on their own.

Now there were machinery sounds missing, like the noise of unloading. That took comp, to open the holds and run the internal machinery . . . and that meant that the Mazianni had not gotten the keys—in some sense or another. Bravo, she tried to think; but the other chance occurred to her too, that they were dead up there. And the silence continued, from the part of the ship they could hear.

She could make a fatal mistake, she reckoned, foul it all up—either by sitting too long or by rushing ahead when she ought to sit still and wait—and take their losses and hope—

For what? she thought. Sandor had never reckoned on being hauled into station, docked and occupied at leisure. There was no percentage in waiting for Mazianni to get what they wanted and move a crew in. She conceived a black picture, herself and her crew surviving in the crawlways, waiting a chance when some Mazianni crew should try to take *Lucy* out—and launching an attack. But they would be debilitated by hunger and inactivity, at disadvantage, underarmed—the Mazianni could crew *Lucy* with a dozen, and tilt the odds impossibly against them.

She turned on her suit light. *Going up, she signed to the others, making out only blank faceplates casting back her light in the darkness. But the blank heads nodded after a moment, and Neill patted her ankle with a clumsy glove. They were willing.

She moved ahead in the shaft, reckoning that somewhere toward the bow had to be a crawlspace leading to main level: they were downside as they had docked, because they were under the bridge/lounge area, and she recollected the geography of main level, went on the best estimate she had reasoned out over the hours, where the access shaft might be. It was slow-motion movement, carrying the weight of the suits and slithering forward, trying not to hit metal against metal—She kept the light on, and turned and signed *quiet to the others—needless caution. They knew. A slip, the banging of a plastic clip or metal coupling against the metal of the shaft might set any occupation wondering.

She had to stop from time to time—stopped when she had found what she had hunted for, staring up into the access shaft—disgusted with herself because she was out of breath and doubting she could make the climb in one G.

She had to, that was all. Could not send Neill up there to get killed because he was strongest. She had to be ready to use the gun and use it right; and none of them had ever fired a gun except in light-sensor games.

She sucked in a breath and started, a slow upward climb, taking the same cautions. The weight of the pack dragged at her arms, threatened to tear her hands from the rungs, bruising bones in her fingers even through the gloves. She took it on her legs as much as possible, a dozen rungs, a few more; and reached a hatch beside the ladder in the shaft. She hooked an elbow around the rungs, almost disjointed by the weight, got the gun from its holster and hooked the edge of that hand into the unlock lever of the access panel. It hung, took another shove that tore muscles all the way to the groin, gave with a crash her pickup magnified.

The door swung out: a coveralled man had stood up from the number one seat, whirling in an adrenalin-stretched instant. She fired, a panic shot—watched in cold disbelief as the man folded and fell. She thrust her leg over and through the access threshold, at the corner of the maintenance corridor, stumbled out and fell skidding to one knee as terror, the deck slope, and the weight of the suit combined to take her feet out from under her. She came up with the gun trained wide on the bridge—but there was no one, only the one man, who was not moving.

No sign of Curran or Sandor. Nothing. They were gone.

Taken somewhere, she thought, struggling to her feet as Deirdre and Neill followed her. She staggered across the deck and stopped, hanging on the arm of the number one cushion, the gun trained downward at a corpse in blue coveralls. She swallowed her nausea and fired again for good measure, greatly relieved that the body prone on the floor failed to react. Then she shoved off from the command pit and circled the area through the other consoles, staggering from the weight and sucking too-warm air through a sore throat. She fumbled the oxygen on, felt for the corridor wall, her vision limited by the helmet, got the door open to Sandor's cabin and used the still-burning suit light to find her way in the dark of it. She cast about for the drawer he had named, pulled open the toiletries drawer under the mirror and rummaged among the dried-up remnants of some previous tenant—a man, that one—shoved jars and tubes aside, found it, a slip of paper that her gloved hands could not unfold. She ripped a glove off, found a number.

Good luck, he had written along with it. *If you've got this, one of two things has happened. In either case, take care of her.*

She blinked, caught by an impulse of guilt . . . remembered what she was about, then, and what was at stake, and headed out of the cabin—past Neill in the doorway. She went for the bridge, staggering and leaning back in the downward pitch of the deck. Neill followed her, as reckless and reeling.

Deirdre had gotten her helmet off, and set it on the console and dragged the body out of the way. Allison jerked the other glove off, fought with the helmet catches and lifted it off. The backpack weighed on her—she started to shed that, and abandoned the thought in her anxiety to get at comp.

She bent over the keyboard and keyed the number in.

"Hello, Sandy," a voice said, nearly stopping her heart. A menu of functions and code numbers leapt to the screen in front of her. *"How are you?"*

She picked the security function, keyed it through. A list of accesses came to the screen with x's and o's.

"Sandy, is there some problem? I can instruct in security procedures if you ask me. In any case, secure the bridge; this is always your last retreat. Stay calm. Always keep food and water on the bridge in case. Keep a gun by you and power down the rest of the sectors if it comes to that."

"Lord," Neill muttered. "What's it *doing?*"

"It's right," she decided suddenly, looking about her. "We put the locks on. He's gone; and Curran is; and they've got them out there somewhere. We've got to be sure there's no one left in the holds." The computer went on in its monologue, unstoppable. She keyed the doors closed, one and the other, and took comp back to its listing.

"What can I do for you?" it asked.

And waited. She stared at the boards, panting under the weight she carried. A wild idea occurred to her, that they might all go out onto the docks and try whether some resistance might be left on Venture Station: if they could join up with stationers trying to fight off this intrusion—

No, she thought, it was too remote a chance. Too likely to end in a shooting: there were probably Mazianni guards right outside.

And the Mazianni would expect to change guards on the ship at some reasonable interval.

She kept running through the listings, finance, and plumbing and navigation. Customs, one said; and Law; and Banks; and Exchange; and In Case, one said. She pushed that one.

"Sandy," the voice said gently, *"if you're into this one, the worst has happened, I guess; and of course I don't know where or who—but I love you, Sandy—I'll say that first. And there are several things you can do. I'll lay them out for you—"*

She stopped it with a push of the key, collapsed into the cushion under the weight of the pack, under the weight of shock. Sandy. Sandor. It was indisputable title—to *Lucy* and what it held.

"That was some*body*," Deirdre said. "Lord, Allie—what kind of rig is this?"

She started shedding her pack, struggling out of her suit. "I don't know. But it's *his*. Sandor's. And whoever it was thought things through."

"They've got him and Curran," Neill said. "If we knew where—"

"Wrong odds," she said. She freed her upper body, stood up and shed the rest of it. Panting, she settled back again and looked up at them. At both of them. "I'll tell you how it is. We hold onto the ship; and if they try to take it we get ourselves some of them. That's it."

They nodded, helmetless both. She loved them, she thought

suddenly. Everything had come apart. She had just killed
someone . . . had gotten herself and her crewmates into a
situation without exit, a dead end in all senses. Sandor and
Curran gone—taken off the ship—lost. . . . Everything had
gone foul, everything from the moment she had planned to
have her way in the world, and her two cousins stood there,
able to have added it all up, and gave her a simple consent.
The way Curran had done. And Sandor, for whatever tangled
reasons.

Her throat swelled, making it painful to swallow. Her mind
started working. "I'm betting they're still alive," she said,
"Curran and Sandor—or the Mazianni would have gone at
the ship with a cutter. They still reckon to get the ship intact."

She reached and punched in on com, scanning through it,
trying to pick up Mazianni transmissions, but there was nothing readable. Only the station pulse continued. . . . false in-
dication of life. She turned on vid as it bore—and it
produced a desolate image of a primitive torus, vacant
except for the vast bulk of a carrier berthed near them,
and another object that might be yet another freighter docked
farther on, indistinct in the dark and the curve of the station.

"Got ourselves a target if we wanted to take it," Neill said.
"Even a creature that size—has a sensitive spot about the
docking probe."

"Might," she agreed. "Wonder what the guns are worth."
She went for the comp listing, called it up. The voice began,
talking in simple terms, advising against starting anything.

"Shut up," she told it softly.

It kept on, relentless, and got then to what the guns were
worth, which was not much.

But there was that chance, she reckoned; and then she got
to reckoning what the bristles were on the frame of the monster next to them . . . and what that broadside would leave of
them and a good section of Venture Station.

"*Don't try to fight*," the young-man's-voice of the computer
pleaded with them. "*Use your head. Don't get into situations
without choices.*"

It was late advice.

XVII

"I told you," Sandor said, "I've got no inclination to heroics. You want to deal, I'll deal."

It was a tight gathering, that in the cold dockside office—a dozen Mazianni, mostly officers, in a dingy, aged facility, heated by a portable unit, with some of the lights burned out—a desk cluttered with printouts. And burn-scars on the walls, that spoke of violence here at some point. There was no sign of the former occupants, nothing. He stood across the desk from Edger himself, and Curran was somewhere behind him, back among the guns that kept the odds in this meeting to Edger's liking.

"What have you got to deal with?" Edger asked him.

"Look, I don't want any trouble. You keep your hands off my ship and off my crewman."

"Might have need of personnel," Edger said.

"No. No deal at all on that. Look, you want cargoes—I'm not particular. You feed me goods and I'll shift them where you like. You want some of your own people to go along, fine." There was a chair a trooper had his foot in. Sandor gestured at it, looking at Edger. "You mind? Captain to captain, as it were—" Edger made a careless, not quite amused gesture and he captured the chair from the trooper, dragged it over and sat down, leaned on the desk and jabbed a finger onto it amid the papers. "Do I figure right, you've got your sights on Pell? Maybe Mallory's playing your game out there; maybe you're going to pull it off."

"Mallory."

He sat back a fraction, playing it with a scant flicker; but the hate in Edger's eyes was mortal—So, he thought, having tried that perimeter. Play it without principles. All the way. "Her cargo aboard," he said. "She hauled me in before undock, said she was watching. And she's out there. Overjumped us. Just watching. That's what I know. I'm not partic-

187

ular. You want Mallory's cargo, welcome to it. And if you want trade done somewhere across the Line I'm willing—but not Pell. Not and answer questions back there."

Edger was a mass murderer. So was Mallory. But there was a febrile fixation to Edger's stare that tightened the hairs on his nape. No dockside justice ever promised Edger's kind of dealing.

"Suppose we discuss it with your man back there," Edger said.

"Discuss what?"

"Mallory."

"*I'll* discuss Mallory. I've got no percentage in it."

"Where is *Norway*?"

"Last time I saw her she was off by James's Point."

"Doing what?"

"Waiting for something. She's working with Union. That's the rumor. They've got all the nullpoints sewed up and Union's working with her. So they say."

Edger was silent a moment. Shifted his eyes to his lieutenant and back again. "What cargo?"

"I don't know what cargo. I didn't want Mallory on my neck. I didn't break any seals."

"Junk, Captain Stevens. *Junk*. We looked. Recycling goods." Edger's voice rose and fell again; and Sandor's mind went to one momentary blank.

"She set me up," he exclaimed. "That bastard bitch set me up. She *knew* what was here and sent me into it."

No reaction from Edger: nothing. The eyes stayed fixed on him, feverish and still, and the noise of his protest fell into that silence and died.

"Look, I don't know anything. I swear to you, I'm a marginer with legal troubles; and Mallory offered me hazard rate for a haul—offered me a way out, and a profit, and she set me up. She bloody well set me up."

"I'm touched, Stevens."

"It's the *truth*."

"It's a setup, Stevens, you're right in that much.—Hagler, take a detail and persuade Stevens he's hired; get that ship working."

"Hired for what?"

"Don't press your luck, Stevens. You may survive this voyage . . . if you learn."

A hand descended on his shoulder. He got up, without protest, calculating wildly—to get back aboard again, get sealed in there with a crew and take care of them. . . . Allison and her cousins would be there; and there was suddenly a way out—

Everyone was moving, the gathering adjourning elsewhere with some dispatch. They were pulling out, he reckoned suddenly. They could not afford to sit at rest if they suspected Mallory was on the loose. A warship out of jump, not dumping its velocity—he did the calculations mentally, fogged in the terror of them, let himself be taken by the arm and steered for the door, a gun prodding him in the back. A ship like *Norway* could be down their throats scant minutes behind its lightspeed bow wave of ID and interference . . . could blow them out of this fragile, antique shell of a station.

There never had been a major settlement here, he surmised. It was a setup, all of it, all the leaks of routes and trade—and he had not betrayed Mallory: Mallory had primed him with everything she wanted spread to her enemies. Canisters of *junk* for a cargo—

He looked about him as they went out onto the open dock, so chill that breath hung frosted in the air and cold lanced to the bone. They herded him right, the jab of a rifle barrel, all of them headed out . . . and he looked back, saw them taking Curran off in the other direction.

"Curran!" he yelled. "Hold it! Blast you, my crewman goes with me—"

Curran stopped, looked toward him. Sandor staggered in the sudden jerk at his arm, the jab of a rifle barrel into his ribs—

Kept turning, and hit an armored trooper a blow in the throat that threw the trooper down and sent a pain through his hand. He dived for the gun, hit the floor and rolled in a patter of shots that popped off the decking. The fire hit, an explosion that paralyzed his arm. He kept rolling, for the cover of the irregular wall, the gun abandoned in panic.

"Move it," someone yelled. "Get him."

A second shot exploded into his side, and after that was the cold pressure of the deck plates against his face and a stunned realization that he had just been hit. He heard voices shouting, heard someone order a boarding—

"Give up the freighter," he heard called. "You just shot the bastard and it's no good. Come on."

He was bleeding. He had trouble breathing. He lay still until the sounds were done, and that was the best that he knew how to do.

Then he lifted his head and saw Curran lying face down on the plates a distance away.

He got that far, an inching progress across the ice cold plates, terrified of being spotted moving. The wounds were throbbing, the left arm refused to move, but he thought that he could have gotten up. And Curran—

Curran was breathing. He put his hand on Curran's back, snagged his collar and tried to pull him, but it tore his side. Curran stirred then, a feeble movement. "Come on," Sandor said. "Out of the open: come on—let's try for the ship."

Curran struggled for his feet, collapsed back to one knee; and blood erupted from the burn in his shoulder. Sandor made the same try, discovered he could get his legs under him, offered a hand to Curran and steadied him getting up. "Get to cover," he breathed, looking out at all that vacant dock, foreign machinery more than a century outdated, a dark pit of an access. That was *Australia* back there, two berths down, dark and blank to the outside; and *Lucy* was in the other direction . . . *Lucy*—

They made it twenty meters along the wall; and then the cold and the tremors got to them both. Sandor hung onto the wall, eased down it finally, supporting Curran and both of them leaning together. "Rest a minute," he said.

"They'll blow the station," Curran predicted. "Hard vacuum.—Come on, man. Come on." It was Curran hauling him up this time; and they walked as far as they could, but it was a long, long distance to *Lucy*'s berth.

Curran went down finally, out of strength; and he was. He held onto the blood-soaked Dubliner, both of them tucked up in the cover of a machinery niche, and stared at what neither one of them could reach.

Seals crashed. *Australia* was loose, preparing for encounter. Sandor went stiff, and Curran did, anticipating the rush of decompression that might take them; but the station stayed whole.

Then a second crash of seals.

"Allison," Sandor said, and Curran took in his breath.

Lucy had prepared herself to break loose.

Someone with the comp keys was at controls.

* * *

"They're wanting an answer," Neill said from com—turned a sweating face in Allison's direction.

"No," Allison said.

"Allie—those are *guns* out there."

"They know comp's locked and their man might not answer. *No,* don't do it."

"They're moving," Deirdre said.

Vid came to her screen, a view of a monster warship, the twin of *Norway,* a baleful glow of running lights illuminating the angular dark surfaces of the frame. Cylinder blinkers began their slow movement as the carrier established rotation.

"They've broken communication," Neill said, and Allison said nothing, waiting, watching, hoping that the behemoth that passed near them would reckon their man's silence a communications lockup. And that they would not, in passing, blow them and the station at once.

"Movement our starboard," Deirdre said, and that image came too: another ship had been around the rim, and it was putting out. "Freighter type," Deirdre said.

"One of theirs," Allison surmised.

There was a silence for a moment. "Get down there," she said then, "and get those port seals complete. We'd better be ready to move."

"Both of us?" Deirdre asked.

"Go."

All the functions came to her board; her cousins scrambled for the lift back in the lounge that would take them down to the frame. They had to get the seals complete or blow the dock and damage themselves, with no dockside assistance in their undocking.

And meanwhile the warship glided past them, while they played dead and helpless.

That was a panic move, that. The Mazianni had picked up something on scan: she dared not activate her own, sat taking in only what passive sensors could gather . . . no output, no visible movement on the exterior, except the minuscule angling of the cameras that she reckoned they would miss.

A force left on the docks might have spotted that closure of seals; it might have been better to have done nothing. Might have—

She could be paralyzed in might haves. She had two of her own out there—on that ship; on the station—no way of finding that out. It hurt. And there was no remedy to that either.

She cleared it out of her mind for the moment, focused finally, functioning as she had not been functioning since somewhere back on Viking. So things were lost; lives were lost. She had several more to think of, and the captain of that ship out there was her senior in more than years and firepower. No match at all: the only chance was to go unnoticed, to prepare the ship to ride out the destruction of the station as a bit of flotsam, if it happened.

If that warship scented something out there, something sudden enough to draw it out, *something* was loose in Venture System.

Mallory, it might be. She fervently hoped so.

The red telltales winked to green, indicating the ports sealed. Deirdre and Neill had gotten them secure. In a moment she heard the working of the lift.

Com beeped. She listened. It was the characteristic spit and fade of distant transmission, numerical signal, an arriving ship for sure. She punched it through to comp, flurried through an unfamiliar set of commands.

Working, the young-man's-voice said, familiar sound by now, soothing. The answer came up. *Finity's End.* Alliance merchanter, headed into ambush. She reached toward the com, and vid suddenly lost the movement of the Mazianni warship—a surge of power that for a moment wiped out reception. They moved—Lord, they moved, with eye-tricking suddenness . . . and her own people were headed across the deck toward her from the lift with no idea what was in progress. If she had the nerve she would put in com, give out a warning—and get them all killed.

"Neihart's *Finity* just arrived," she said. "Headed into it."

Two bodies hit the cushions and started snatching functions to their own boards, without comment.

Warn them or not? There was a chance of making a score on the Mazianni if they lay low: of breaking things loose at their own moment, if they could pick it. Their guns were nothing. A pathetic nothing; and *Finity* had far better than they had—that was a guessable certainty.

"Got another one," Neill said; and then: "Allie: it's. *Dublin.*"

The blood went from her face to her feet.

"We've got to warn them," Deirdre said.

"No. We sit tight."

"Allie. . . ."

"We sit tight. We've got the Mazianni base. We give *Dublin* a chance if we can. But we don't tip it premature."

"What, premature? They're headed into a trap."

"No," she said. Desperately. Just no. She had worked it out, all of it, the range they needed. The odds of the troops. Suddenly the balance was tilted. Near two thousand Dubliners; the Neiharts of *Finity* might number nearly as many—a Name on the Alliance side, armed and not for trifling.

"They're not dumping," Deirdre said. "The way that's coming in they haven't dumped. Permission to use scan."

"*Do it.*"

The freighters were coming in at all gathered velocity—they *knew*, they knew what they were running into. Allison sat still, clenched her hands together in front of her lips. Scan developed in front of her, a scrambled best estimate of the Mazianni position and that of the merchanters revising itself second by second as Deirdre fought sense out of it.

"We're moving," she said, and committed them, a release of the grapples and a firing of the undocking jets. *Lucy* backed off and angled, and she cut mains in, listening to the quiet voice of the ghost in *Lucy*'s comp assure her she was doing it right.

"We go for them?" Neill asked, an optimistic assessment of their speed and their firepower.

"Ought to get there eventually," she said. "Mark they don't run us down. Just keep our targets straight." She asked comp for armaments, keying in that function.

"*Sandy,*" comp objected, "*are you sure of this?*"

She keyed the affirmative and uncapped the switches. A distressing red color dyed her hand from the ready light. It was a clumsy system . . . a computer/scan synch that was decent at low velocities, fit for nullpoint arguments, but nothing else.

"*Got another one,*" Neill said. And: "*Lord, it's Mallory!*"

Her hand shook above the fire buttons. She looked at scan, a flick of the eye that was in *Norway*'s terms several planetary diameters duration. The garble sorted itself out in com; and then she saw the angle on scan.

She fired, a flat pressure of her hand, at what she reckoned for the Mazianni's backside, a minuscule sting at a giant with two giant freighters coming on at the Mazianni and its companion, and a carrier of its own class in its wake. Other blips developed; riderships were deployed.

And then something was coming at the pattern broadside: "*Union* ship," she heard reported into her ear . . . and suddenly everything broke up, sensors out, a wail of alarm through *Lucy*'s systems.

It passed. She still had her hand on controls. "*Hello, Sandy,*" comp said pleasantly, sorting itself into sense again. Scan had not. They had ships dislocated from last estimated position. The ID signals started coming in again.

"That's *Dublin,*" Neill said, "and *Finity. Norway* and her riders. *Liberty.* That was a Union ship that just passed us. . . ."

"Outbound," Deirdre exclaimed. "Lord, they're running, the Mazianni are taking out of there . . . and that Mazianni freighter's *blown.* . . ."

She sat still, with the adrenalin surge still going hot and cold through her limbs and an alarming tendency to shake.

"Do we contact?" Neill asked. "Allie, it's *Dublin* out there."

"Put me through," she said; and when she heard the steady calm of *Dublin*'s Com One, she still felt no elation. "*Dublin* Com, this is *Lucy.* We've got two missing, request help in boarding the station and searching."

"We copy, *Lucy.*" Not—who is this? Not—hello, Allison Reilly. Ship to ship and all business. "Do you need assistance aboard?"

"Negative. All safe aboard."

"This is *Norway* com," another voice broke in. "Ridership *Odin* will establish dock; nonmilitary personnel will stay at distance. Repeat—"

She had cut the engines. She rolled *Lucy* into an axis turn and cut them in again, defying the military order. Let them enforce it. Let *Norway* put a shot toward them in front of witnesses, after all else *Norway* had done. She heard objection, ignored it.

"*Dublin,* this is *Lucy.* Request explanation this setup."

"Abort that chatter," *Norway* said.

"Hang you, *Norway*—"

A ridership passed them, cutting off communication for the moment—faster than they could possibly move. *Norway* had followed. *Lucy* clawed her slow way against her own momentum, and there was a silence over *Lucy's* bridge, no sense of triumph at all.

She had won. And found her size in the universe, that she counted for nothing.

Even from *Dublin* there was no answer.

"They've got them," the report came in via *Norway* com, even while *Lucy* was easing her way into a troop assisted dock. And in a little time more: "They're in sorry shape. We're making a transfer to our own medical facilities."

"How bad?" Allison asked. "*Norway*, *Lucy* requests information."

"When available. Request you don't tie up this station. *Norway* has other operations."

She choked on that, concentrated her attention on the approaching dock, listened to Deirdre giving range.

Norway sat in dock; the Union carrier *Liberty* was in system somewhere, poised to take care of trouble if the Mazianni had a thought of coming in again. *Dublin* and *Finity* moved in with uncommon agility.

"They can't be hauling," Deirdre said. "They came down too fast."

"Copy that," Allison said, and paid attention to business, smothering the anger and the outrage that boiled up through her thinking. No merchanter ran empty except to make speed; so *Dublin* itself had been cooperating with *Norway* and Union forces. *Norway* had beaten them out of Pell; and somehow in the cross-ups of realtime they had leapfrogged each other, themselves and *Norway* and *Dublin* with Neihart's *Finity*. *Norway* had *known* the score here: that much had penetrated her reckonings; and if *Dublin* had come in empty, it was to make time and gain maneuverability. She had no idea what *Dublin* could do empty: no one could reckon it, because *Dublin* had never done the like.

For a lost set of Dubliners? She doubted that.

The cone loomed ahead. "*Docking coming up, Sandy*," comp said. She paid attention to that only, full concentration . . . the first time she had handled docking, and not under the circumstances she had envisioned—antiquated facilities, a primitive hookup with none of the automations standard with more modern ports.

She touched in with the faintest of nudges, exact match

. . . felt no triumph in that, having acquired larger difficulties.

"My compliments to the Old Man," she said to Neill, "and I'll be talking with him at the earliest. On the dock."

Neill's eyes flickered with shock in that glance at her. Then they went opaque and he nodded. "Right."

She shut down.

"*Dublin*'s coming in," Deirdre said. "*Finity*'s getting into synch."

She unbelted. "I'll be seeing about a talk with the Old Man. I think we were *used*, cousins. I don't know how far, but I don't like it."

"Yes, *ma'am*," Deirdre said.

She got up, thought about going out there as she was, sweaty, disheveled. "We'll be delivering that body to *Norway*," she said. "Or venting it without ceremony. Advise them."

"Got that," Neill said.

Her cabin was marginally in reach with the cylinder in downside lock. She made it, opened the door on chaos, hit by a wave of icy air. The cabin was piled with bundles lying where maneuvers and *G* had thrown them, not only hers, but everyone else's—clothes jammed everywhere, personal items strewn about. She waded through debris to reach her locker, found it stripped of her clothes and jammed with breakables.

She saw them in her mind, Curran and Sandor both, taking precautions while they were in the process of being boarded, fouling up the evidence of other occupancy, as if this had been a storage room. And they had kept to that story, as witness their survival. All riding on two men's silence.

She hung there holding to the frame of the door, still a moment. Then she worked her way back out again, down the pitch of the corridor to the bridge.

"*Dublin* requests you come aboard," Neill said.

"All right," she said mildly, quietly. "At my convenience. —I'm headed for *Norway*."

"They won't let you in."

"Maybe not. Shut down and come with me."

"Right," Deirdre said, and both of them shut down on the moment and got up.

Down the lift to the lock: *Norway* troops were standing guard on the dock when they had gone out into the bitter cold, three battered merchanters in sweat-stained coveralls.

There was a thin scattering of movement beside that, a noise of loudspeakers and public address, advising stationers in hiding to come to dockside or to call for assistance. Men and women as haggard as themselves, in work clothes—came out to stand in lines the military had set up, to go to desks and offer papers and identifications—

"Poor bastards," Neill muttered. "No good time for them, in all of this."

She thought about it, the situation of stationers with Mazianni in charge. They were very few, even so. A maintenance crew—there were no children in evidence, and there would have been, if it had been a station in full operation. All young; all the same look to them.—"You," an armored trooper shouted at them. "ID's."

Allison stopped, Deirdre and Neill on either side of her— "Allison Reilly," she said, and the rifle aimed at them went back into rest. "Papers," the trooper said, and she presented them.

"We've got two of ours in *Norway* medical section," she said. "I'm headed there."

The trooper handed the papers back, faceless in his armor. "Got the *Lucy* crew here," he said to someone else. "Requesting boarding."

And a moment later—a nod to that unheard voice. . . . "One of you is clear to board. Officer on duty will guide you."

"Thanks," Allison said. She glanced at Neill and Deirdre, silent communication, then parted company with them, walked the farther distance up the docks to the access of *Norway.*

Another trooper, another challenge, another presentation of papers. She walked the ramp into the dark metal interior without illusions that Mallory had any interest in talking to her after what they had done.

She was an inconsequence, with her trooper escort, in the corridor traffic, came virtually unremarked to the doorway of the medical section. An outbound medic shoved into her in his haste and she flattened herself against the doorway, gathering her outrage and fright. A second brush with traffic, a medic on his way in—"Where's the *Lucy* personnel?" she asked, but the man brushed past. "Hang you—" She thrust her way into a smallish area and a medic made a wall of himself.

"Captain's request," the trooper escorting her said. "Condition of the *Lucy* personnel. This is next of kin."

The medic focused on her as if no one until now had seen her. "Transfused and resting. No lasting damage." They might have been machinery. The medic waved them for the door. "Got station casualties incoming. Out."

She went, blind for the moment, was shaking in the knees by the time she walked *Norway*'s ramp down to the dockside and headed herself toward *Dublin*. The troopers stayed. She went alone across the docks, with more of anger than she could hold inside.

Megan met her at the lock—had been standing there . . . no knowing how long. She looked at her mother a moment without feeling anything, a simple analysis of a familiar face, a recognition of the heredity that bound her irrevocably to *Dublin*. Her mother held out her arms; she reacted to that and embraced her, turned her face aside. "You all right?" Megan asked when they stood at arm's length.

"You set us up."

Megan shook her head. "We knew *Norway* had. We shed it all . . . we knew where *Finity* was bound and we put out with them. Part of the operation. They gave you false cargo; mass, but *nothing*. And you hewed the line and played it honest but it wouldn't have made a difference. Mallory gave you what she *wanted* noised about. And sent you in here primed with everything you were supposed to spill. If you were boarded, if they searched—they'd know you were a setup. But all you could tell them was what Mallory wanted told."

The rage lost its direction, lost all its logic. She was left staring at Megan with very little left in reserve. "We were boarded. Didn't Deirdre and Neill say? But we got them off."

"Curran and Stevens—"

'They're all right. Everything's fine." She fought a breath down and put a hand on Megan's shoulder. "Come on. Deirdre and Neill aboard?"

"With the Old Man."

"Right," she said, and walked with her mother to the lift, through *Dublin*'s halls, past the staring, silent faces of cousins and her own sister—"Connie," she said, and took her sister's hand, embraced her briefly—Connie was more pregnant than before, a merchanter's baby, pregnancy stretched into more than nine months of realtime, a life already longer and thinner than stationers' lives, to watch stationers age while it grew up slowly, with a merchanter's ambitions.

She let her sister go, walked on with Megan into the lift, and topside—down the corridor that led to the bridge. She was qualified there, she realized suddenly: might have worn the collar stripe . . . posted crew to a *Dublin* associate; and it failed to matter. She walked onto the bridge where Michael Reilly sat his chair, where Deirdre and Neill stood as bedraggled as herself and answered for themselves to the authority of *Dublin*. Ma'am was there; and Geoff; and operations crew, busy at *Dublin* running.

"Allison," the Old Man said. Rose and offered his hand. She took it, slump-shouldered and leaden in the moment, her sweat-limp hair hanging about her face as theirs did, her crew, her companions, both of them. "You all right?"

"All right, sir."

"There wasn't a way to warn you. Just to back you up. You understand that."

"I understand it, sir. Megan said."

"Small ship," the Old Man said. "And expendable. That's the way they reckoned it." He gestured toward the bench near his chair. She folded her hands behind her, locked her aching knees.

"Won't stay long," she said.

"You don't have to have it that way." The Reilly sat down. "You can turn your post over to Second Helm . . . take a leave. You're due that."

She sucked at her lips. "No, sir. My crew can speak for themselves. But I'll stay by *Lucy*."

"Same, sir," Deirdre said, and there was a like murmur from Neill.

"They owe us," she said. "They promised us hazard rate for what we're hauling, and I'm going to Mallory to collect it."

The Reilly nodded. Maybe he approved. She took it for dismissal, collected her crew.

"You can use *Dublin* facilities," the Old Man said. "During dock. We'll help you with any sorting out you need to do."

She looked back. "Courtesy or on charge?"

"Courtesy," the Old Man said. "No charge on it."

She walked out, officer of a small ship, a poor relation come to call. Doubliners lined the corridor, stared at her and her companions, and there was something different. She did not bother to reason what it was, or why cousins stared at them without speaking, with that bewilderment in their eyes. She was only tired, with more on her mind than gave her time for politenesses.

XVIII

Dublin was in port: he had heard that much, when they took Curran out and left him behind, among the station wounded. He lay and thought about that, putting constructions together in his mind, none of which made particular sense, only that somewhere, as usual lately, he had been conned.

So there was a reason *Dublin* had handed out a paper half million; and *Norway* had landed on the case of a petty skimmer with customs problems. He had pursued his fate till it caught him, that was what.

Allison. All of *Lucy*'s crew was safe. They had told him that too, and he was glad, whatever else had happened. He had no personal feeling about it—or did, but he had no real expectation that Allison would come down into the depths of *Norway* to see him. He made a fantasy of such a meeting; but she failed to come, and that fit with reality, so he enjoyed the fantasy and finally stopped hoping.

He was, before they took out the station casualties, a kind of hero—at least to the few men next to him, who had gotten him confused with the captains of ships like *Dublin* and *Finity's End* and, he had heard, even the Union ship *Liberty*, who had done the liberating of their station. Mostly *Norway*. Mostly the tough, seasoned troops of the Alliance carrier had invaded the halls and routed out what pockets of Mazianni remained holding stationer hostages. The same troops had found him holding Curran, trying to keep him from bleeding to death, which was how he had spent the battle for Venture Station, crouched down in a small spot and confused about who was fighting whom. The gratitude embarrassed him, but it was better than admitting what he really was, and fighting a silent war across the space between cots, so he took it with appropriate modesty.

It was someone to talk to, until they moved the stationers out.

"When do I get out?" he asked, hoping that he was going to.

"Tomorrow," the medic promised him, whether or not that came from official sources.

He was not in the habit of believing official promises, and he was trying to sleep the next morning after breakfast when the medic came to ask him if he could walk out or if he had to have a litter.

"Walk," he decided.

"Got friends waiting for you."

"Crew?"

"So I understand."

He took the packet the medic tossed down, his own shaving kit. A change of clothes. So they had come. He was heartened in spite of himself, reckoned that somehow it had turned up convenient in *Dublin*'s books.

It got him out of *Norway*. That much. He shaved with the medic's help—no easy trick with one arm immobilized. Got dressed.—"Here," the medic said, stuffing a paper into his pocket. "That's the course of treatment. You follow it. Hear me?"

He nodded, only half interested. A trooper showed up on call to take him out. "Thanks," he told the medic, who accepted that with a dour attention; and he left with the trooper. "Got to walk slow," he told the woman, who adjusted her pace to suit.

It was not a far walk—not as far as it might have been on something *Norway*'s size. He came down the lift and out the lock, taking it as slowly as reasonable, only half light-headed.

And they were there, Allison, Deirdre, Neill; and Curran, at the foot of the ramp. He went down and met offered hands, took Curran's. "You all right?" he asked Curran.

"Right enough," Curran said, embraced him carefully with a hand on his sound shoulder. Looked at him with that kind of gratitude the stationer had had, which he took in the same understanding.

"Allison," he said then, and took *her* hand—a forlorn pain went through him, a flicker of the dark eyes. "Well, you did it right, Reilly, top to bottom. Must have."

"I should have come after you," she said. "I didn't know you were on the dock."

"Then how could you? No way. It worked, didn't it?"

"Got us all in one piece."

"I'm usually right." He touched Deirdre's arm and took Neill's hand, looked back at Allison and saw a trooper beckon.

"Captain's waiting," the trooper said, waved a hand toward the dockside offices.

"Mallory," Allison said.

He nodded. His heart had turned over. He started that way—at least it was not far across the dock; the same office, the place of recent memory. He felt numb in the cold, and no little disoriented.

"*Dublin*'s in on the conference," Allison said. "The Old Man; our legal counsel—you've got that behind you."

"Good to know," he said.

"You don't believe it."

"Of course I believe it. You say so."

She gave him one of those looks as they went into the office, into a gathering thick with military in blue and merchanters in silver and white.

Repeat scene: only it was Mallory behind the desk, and Talley close by her . . . one of the breed exchanged for another.

"Captain," she said, a courteous nod.

He paid her one in return. He looked further about him, noted the patches: *Dublin*'s shamrock on the silver, and on the white, the arrogant black sphere of *Finity's End*, a Name so old they had no insignia at all: and rejuv-silvered hair other than Mallory's, a gathering of senior officers in which one Sandor Kreja would have been a small interest—give or take a bogus cargo and half a million credits.

"Wanted to straighten a matter out with you," she said. "—Need a chair, Captain?"

"No." An automatic no, half-regretted; but no one else was seated but Mallory . . . he refused to be the center of things along with her; but he was: he reckoned that.

"Any time you change your mind," she said, "feel free. It's really not fair to call you in like this, but *Norway*'s prone to sudden departures. And I'm sure others don't want to log too much dock time.—Are you sure about the chair, Captain?"

He nodded. A small trickle of sweat started down the side of his face. Small talk was not Mallory's style. He disliked it, them, this whole gathering.

"You played it straight," she said. "I rather hoped you might, Captain. But I was a little surprised by it."

"You were a little *late*." He recovered his sense of balance, pulse rate getting up again. "You took our arrival rate. You cut it pretty long on our side."

She shrugged, passing off the wounds, the deaths on station. "You bettered your rate by a few hours . . . didn't you?"

He thought back then, through the fog of realtime—the haste they had used through the second jump, Allison in command and mutiny on the bridge. The anger went out of him. "Maybe we did," he said.

"We were on time, absolutely.—But you managed well enough.—Tell me. . . did you tell them where to find me?"

"I reckoned you meant me to. You don't set much store by heroes, do you?"

Mallory laughed. It surprised him, that quick, cold humor. "Land on your feet, do you? No, I didn't expect it."

"So I spilled all I knew and invented some. But I'll trust you're going to stand by our agreement."

"On what, Captain?"

"Hazard rate. On military cargo."

She thought a moment, wondering, he thought.

"I didn't breach the seals," he said, "but they did. And they knew I was a plant. That wasn't comfortable."

"No, I daresay not." She turned over some papers on her desk. "Vouchers for the pay you're due. No dock charge at Venture, under the circumstances. Let's treat it as lifesupport freight."

Mallory had, he thought, a certain sense of humor. He was going to get out of this. He was insanely tempted to like Mallory, in sheer gratitude. "Captain," he said. *Thanks* stuck in his throat.

"That's an interesting rig, your ship." She failed to let go of the papers and he let go of them in a sudden chill, cursing his momentary trust. "Everything under lock—papers of clouded origin—backing from one of Union's major Names. You know there was a time, Captain, I wondered about *Dublin* itself . . . keeping your company."

"We don't take that," a *Dublin* officer said.

"Oh, I'm assured otherwise. Our allies from across the Line vouch for you. But you have odd associates.—Tell me, Captain Reilly—what motive to lend to a marginer . . . on that scale?"

"Private business."

"I don't doubt." She offered the papers a second time. Sandor took them, his fingers gone cold. He wanted to sit down. The room proved hot/cold and confused with sound. "Your papers, Captain—are altered. Do you know that?"

He blinked . . . felt the edge of the desk with his fingertips, tried to summon up his wits. "That's not so."

"And you run gold under the plates."

"Private store. My own property. I expect it to be there when I board."

Mallory considered him slowly. "Of course it is."

"If you ran that thorough a search on Pell—"

"We wondered."

"That's under *Dublin* finance," Allison said from behind him. "The papers say that too. We're good for any debts."

He looked around slowly at the Dubliners—at Curran's sweating pale face, and Allison's flushed one, Deirdre and Neill unfocused behind them. The rest of the room blurred. They had it, he reckoned. The keys and the excuse. He made a small shrug and looked around again at Mallory. "That's the way the papers are set up."

"I know that too. As long as *Dublin* stands good for it."

"No question," the Reilly said.

He tucked the voucher into his pocket, finding about all the strength he had gathered deserting him. He could make it back to *Lucy*, he reckoned, if he got that far. He wanted that, just to get home, however long it lasted.

"You want to let me see the aforesaid papers, Captain?"

He felt in his pocket, of the jacket draped about his shoulder on the left, fumbled the packet out and gave it into Mallory's hands.

"They *are* faked," she said, riffling through them. "Pell caught that. Paper analysis didn't match. Good job, though. They're going to go over to disc on this kind of thing: it's going to put a lot of paper-traders out of business. Some merchanters howl at the prospect; but then some have reason, don't they? You really ought to get that title straightened up."

She offered them back. He took them, blind to anything else.

"That ought to be all," she said. "*Dublin* vouches for you.

And Union, to be sure, vouches for *Dublin*. So we don't ask any more questions."

"Can I go?"

She nodded, dark eyes full of surmises. He kept his face neutral, turned about and walked out, in the company of Allison and her crew, unasked. Allison put herself in front of him and he stopped outside, dizzy and none too steady on his feet. "Get it clear," she said. "*Dublin*'s with us. They won't *do* anything. You can clear the Name up, go by your own, you understand that? You can get the papers cleared."

"Maybe I don't want to."

"For what?—Who is it that recorded the comp messages? It's you he talks to, isn't it? Who was he?"

He looked at the decking, across the dock, at the scant foot traffic, at the overhead where lonely lights gave the dock what illumination it had.

"You want to talk about it?" Curran asked.

"Not particularly."

"Brother?" Allison asked.

He shrugged. "Might have been."

"He set it up," Allison said, "for somebody who really didn't know how to run a ship. To teach everything there was. It must have taken him a long time to do that. I figure he must have thought a lot about your being able to take care of yourself."

"None of your business."

"We're not welcome there, are we?"

He thought a moment about that one. "You coming back?" he asked, looking at her. "Or do they send me a new set of Dubliners for the run back?"

"We're coming back," she said. "You know we know how to work comp. Do everything. We're pretty good."

It was about the humblest he was likely to get out of Allison Reilly, and it set him off his balance again. "I know you're pretty good," he said, shrugged it off. Looked up, then, at her and the others, one face and the other.

"Excuse me," he said, and walked back into the office and others' business. Aides moved: rifles swung fractionally in the hands of guards. Mallory's face had an uncommon degree of wariness. "It's Kreja," he said, feeling the presence of Allison and the others close at his back. He took his papers from his pocket, another tiny movement of the rifles which had not quite given up their focus. "*Le Cygne* and Kreja. Maybe I ought to get the papers straightened out."

Mallory looked up at him curiously. "*Is* it? And how do you come by that Name? It's a long time out of circulation."

He wondered in that moment—decided in the negative. Mallory's puzzlement seemed for once other than a mockery. "I was born with it," he said. "I'd like it back."

Mallory settled back in her chair, a hand on her desk. "Not a difficult matter. Pan-Paris, was it? That was a time ago."

Breath failed him. "Would you know what happened?"

"I *heard* what happened."

He believed that. Mallory was trustable—in some degree. He believed that much.

"Give me the papers," she said. And when he laid them on the desk she simply took them and wrote in longhand. "*Le Cygne*. Name of owner?"

"Sandor Kreja."

The pen flourished and stopped. She handed the papers back. The corrections were there. *S. Mallory* was written below: *amended by her authority.*

"Kreja."

A hand was offered him from his right. One of the Reillys—*the* Reilly: he had heard him answer. He took the hand, suffered the friendly pressure, escaped then past the door in his own company.

"That's straight," he said. He pocketed the papers, along with the voucher, walked a fragile course toward *Lucy/Le Cygne*'s dock, with his Dubliners about him. "Going to have to go out on the hull when we get time. Do a name change."

"Not much chance of getting cargo here," Allison said. "But hazard rate ought to cover it both ways."

"Game for another run?"

"They're keeping military watch on the whole line for the time being. So the rumor runs."

"Nice to pick up rumors. I'm not sure I believe all of them."

"I figure they'll hold by this one."

They reached the access. It was about the limit of his strength and Curran's, who was out of breath as he was going up the ramp—a young Dubliner plastered himself against the wall of the lock as they came in with a quick "Sir—Ma'am" and Sandor gave the boy a dazed and misgiving stare as his own Dubliners pulled him past. "I didn't clear any boarders," he said, finding more of them by the lift. "Hang it, Reilly—"

"Borrowed help," Allison said. The corridor was clean. The inside of the lift car was clean, spit and polish. "Young Dubliners wanted some exercise."

The lift let them out in the lounge/bridge area. Scrubbed decks, polished panels, every smudge and smear and tarnish cleared away. It looked new again, except for the tape patches on the upholstery. "You cleaning her up to take possession?" he asked outright.

"No," Allison said.

"Can't touch anything without fingerprinting it."

"That's fine. It's old habits."

He looked back at them standing there, reckoned how the place would feel without them. Nodded then. "Looks like she used to," he admitted, and turned back and walked onto the bridge.

She went out, *Le Cygne* did, with empty holds, moving lightly as she could in that condition.

Comp talked to them, commending them that they had got it right. *"Jump coming up, Sandy. Find your referent."*

"Got it," Allison said from number two post, talking back to comp and to him, and the numbers came up on the screen.

The checks came in from the others, routine matters.

They headed for Pell, for station cargo this time, and reckoned *Dublin* would pass them on the way. There was a bet on, inside *Le Cygne,* about elapsed-time and drinks when they got there. He reckoned to win it, knowing his ship.

But it was all one account, anyway.